The Ecstasy of Freedom

First Copy
Leonard Hague

The Ecstasy of Freedom

BOOK I

Leonard Hogue

2005

The Ecstasy of Freedom

The author was born in the state of Mississippi more years ago than he would like to remember; not as the son of a large plantation owner or even a small one, but the son of a sharecropper who owed the property owner; landlord if you wish; half of his crop of cotton, corn and sorghum each year; and almost his soul. He helped his father and older two brothers in the fields from the age of six.

His father was almost under bondage to the property owner as Jasper was in the story. He was not allowed to do outside work but with every opportunity he sneaked and plowed from daylight until dark for other people, furnishing the team, feeding them and receiving fifty cents per day.

The family moved to California during the great depression of the nineteen thirties where for years the family moved up and down the state working to barely survive and everyone in the family harvested everything from apricots to peaches to grapes to cotton and many other crops, and yes, to prunes; so the author was literally a "California prune picker."

The author has at sometime in his career, if that it was, done almost everything that he has taught Jasper to do in the three books; The Ecstasy of Freedom books one, two and three.

At the ripe old age of sixteen the author was foreman on a ranch that raised apricots, almonds, peaches, walnuts, hay and various row crops as well as hogs, chickens and horses and the author was raising hogs to sell. The rancher along with the author did their own blacksmith work. The rancher had a large freight wagon as well as a buggy, a surrey and a spring wagon that he entered in fairs; along with "Babe and Beauty" that are featured in book one, and other huge Percheron horses and mares, some of which the author had a hand in training.

At seventeen during world war two he worked as a welder in a shipyard and while he was not busy at his own profession he learned to use acetylene torches, and how to use a chipping gun.

At eighteen the author, along with his grandfather had a small cattle and horse ranch; he broke a few horses for other people as well as for himself and shod his own horse. He also trapped for furs to sell; at the same time the author was driving a commercial truck until the draft board interfered. "You're in the army now," they said.

After service he owned and operated a commercial truck and trailer, tried farming part time, worked in two sawmills, even tried panning and using a sluice box for gold, worked as a deputy constable, owned and operated a lapidary shop and was a builder for the past forty plus years.

The highlight of his life was when he was a minister and presbyter for the southern half of Alaska. He voluntarily took on the job of organizing and working on churches.

When asked how may states he has been in he say fifty-one; the fifty first is the one in which he spends most of his time; "state of confusion."

He says that at eighty, one foot may not be in the grave but both feet are slipping.

If you like book one you'll love the rest of the story of The Ecstasy of Freedom which is in three segments; book one, book two and book three all of which should be published simultaneously or closely following each other.

All of my work is original and I have not intentionally copied or otherwise used any material from another author.

As you may already know, in book one, Jasper, a runaway slave from a Mississippi plantation goes across the river on a raft. His whole goal in life is getting an education. He rescues an Indian brave, stays with the tribe and becomes an adopted Indian brave. He falls in love with the chief's daughter, Early Flower and plans to stay and marry her.

In book two he changes his mind and goes across the country as guide and scout with a wagon train to California as he studies with a schoolteacher and falls in love with her daughter. He has many adventures and learns many things along the way.

In book three he gets shanghaied on a ship and goes around the horn to Boston. Through an ingenious method he escapes and goes back by way of the tribe's winter camp to see Early Flower then returns to California.

Throughout books two and three he learns many things about cattle, trapping sawmilling, panning gold, building and other things and narrowly escapes many perils.

In the three books I have learned Jasper many of the traits that I have learned in my eighty years.

If you would like another book for a friend or would like to reserve books two or three or both; or learn about three other completely different and original books in progress please email me at ljhogue@hotmail.com or hogueleonard_80@yahoo.com and I will make a special effort to reply to each one received.

I would also appreciate any comments, good or bad, sent to my email addresses.

Many thanks to my late wife Ruby for her support and encouragement when I was onto other endeavors and had left my writing go for many years. Even when we were traveling full time around the country she never interfered with my writing endeavors. I had my computer mounted in a closet in the trailer and later in the motor home and could have put much more effort to writing. The fault for not continuing my endeavors to publish my works lies completely on my shoulders.

CHAPTER I

Jasper was afraid; not afraid as some people would be afraid, but terrified. He was in a dense forest trying to sleep when animals began making noises that seemed to be on all sides of him. They seemed to be tearing at the soil or otherwise making a scratching sound as he had seen and heard a bull do on more than one occasion. It was so dark that he could see nothing and all he had to protect himself with was a knife, so he clutched it tightly in his right hand and waited for the attack to occur.

The only times that he had spent the entire night in the woods had been with Mr. Brisley's son George and they had always been almost within sight of the Big House. He was so afraid that he was cringing in the old clothes that he had brought to use for a bed, placing them over him so that when the attack came he would have some protection while he tried to use the knife.

He knew that a knife would be poor protection as dark as it was, but he had honed it until it was sharp enough to cut paper but that didn't alleviate his fears in the least because slashing at something blindly with the clothes interfering may have rendered his knife useless. When morning finally came he looked around and discovered that during the night a skunk or a number of skunks had been tearing at the old rotten logs all around his bed, near his head, looking for bugs and small grubs or termites.

He could have felt embarrassed at himself for being so afraid, but he was not because the only thing that he knew about where he had spent the night before was what people had told him. They had said that there were panthers, wolves, coyotes and even some bears there. After all he was in strange country and even in a different state.

He had crossed the river on a raft the day before and when it had gotten so dark that he could no longer see, he had merely crawled into a small dense thicket, taken the old rags out of his tote sack and tried to sleep, which soon became impossible.

Jasper was a tall boy, and fairly heavy for his age, and very strong. He had been doing the work of a man and been treated like a man for years, but at seventeen he could still be considered a boy.

Jasper had been thinking about leaving home for a long time! Not just home as most people know home, but the only home that he had known since he could remember; and he had a memory like an elephant. He could remember everything that had happened since he had been a small boy, and the first few years of his life had been very pleasant.

Then things had begun changing for him and the last few years of his life had become almost unbearable. Since Mr. Brisley's son George had been in charge he had become completely unreasonable.

He had thought about leaving since he had been told as a small child that he belonged to Mr. Brisley and would forever have to do what him or his son George told him to do. He was supposed to have no mind of his own as most people have, but was to be like a pawn in a game of life to be used at the will of his owner; to be moved and thrown around at will. But he definitely had a mind of his own even at a young age and wanted something out of life except being told what to do all of his life.

But he knew that he could not leave at his age and as he

grew older he had more or less resigned himself to doing the best he could to please them and trying the best that he could to get along with them. He had decided that he would just do his work and be as inconspicuous as possible.

Then Mr. Brisley's son George had whipped him. Not just a whipping as some of the other slaves had been whipped, but because he would not beg and plead with him to stop, he had been whipped with a blacksnake whip until he was a bloody mess from his shoulders all the way down his back.

That's when he began thinking more seriously about leaving. But how would he ever accomplish such a feat? He knew that the minute he was missed that he would be branded as a runaway and would be hunted like an animal until he was caught and returned to be beaten again.

Then the memory of his former life on the plantation vividly came to him and overall it was a pleasant memory. Except for a few times when he had been frustrated about one thing or another, his earlier life had been a happy one.

As he trudged along behind the plow pulled by two old mules he was reminiscing about his life many years before.

He remembered a particularly typical fall day along the Mississippi River near the city of Greenville where he had spent his entire life, on the plantation of Mr. Brisley, as had all of the other slaves except his mother and grandmother. The weather was hot and humid, as was the case that time of the year. That is if a thunderstorm didn't pass through. This happened quite often during the summer and fall months.

It was cotton picking time when the majority of all able bodied persons on the plantation, men and women alike, spent the full day every day, pulling a cotton sack behind them. Even the little kids were there, the very small ones waiting at the ends of the rows for their fathers and mothers to pick out to the end of the row where they waited. The ones a little older were walking along the long rows picking a little cotton here and there and leaving it in little piles for their parents to pick up when they reached that point or putting it in their parent's sacks. The ones a little older than those were ahead of their parents putting cotton in a burlap bag dragged behind them by a rope tied around their shoulders.

Everyone, that is, except Jasper's mother who worked in Mr. Brisley's house all day every day; and of course Jasper, who was too young to go to the fields alone. Of course he could have gone with his grandmother each day, but his mother had convinced Mr. Brisley that she needed him to watch his little brother. He didn't realize how lucky he was that he could stay with her while she did the housework.

Of course not everyone was picking cotton; some were gathering corn, cutting and hauling hay for the livestock or doing other chores that needed to be done every day, but picking cotton was the priority job at that time. The cotton needed to be picked and out of the fields before the rainy season hit with a vengeance.

Jasper's father usually stayed with the wagon, him being very strong, carrying the full sacks up the ladder and dumping the cotton in the wagon. It wasn't unusual for a full sack to weigh one hundred pounds or more.

Jasper remembered lying on his back under the big trees, only a short distance from the Big House. He didn't dare go very far into the woods because his mother had told him to stay close around so he could hear her call in case his little brother should awaken, then he could come in and play with him while she was doing the housework. He was lying on his back, not moving so as not to disturb the wildlife, which was nearly always in the woods near the house. He was looking around for the birds that he could hear in the tall trees that were on all sides of him. He was lying flat in that particular spot partly because it was very hot and he was in the shade and partly because he knew that birds usually came to the black walnut trees that grew in profusion around the house.

He imagined that he could hit one of the birds with the arrow that he already had notched in the bow that he held in his left hand.

There were some but they were in the very top of a tree. Why should they be in the top of a black walnut tree? There were bees and moths near the bottom for them to catch and he could not imagine them being so high. Near the bottom there was also a large web that still held a few caterpillars they could catch. He must be very still and wait for one to come down closer. Watching and waiting, that's what he was doing; watching and patiently waiting.

As he was listening to the crickets and the tree frog that had started croaking, since he had been up since George had left with Mr. Brisley early that morning, his eyelids were getting heavier each moment. The sun woke him in time to see the birds start coming lower. One bird came down to one of the lower branches and he aimed the arrow directly toward it, taking his time and pulling the arrow as far as he dared without breaking the bow. He had gotten in a hurry a few times and had broken bows, so he had developed in himself a calm, patient, determined attitude. Calmness not often noted in a boy of his age and certainly not the patience that he was exhibiting.

That patience and determination he would carry with him throughout his lifetime. Patience and determination that would prove beneficial when he planned activities such as he was doing at that moment as well as any other endeavors that he undertook. For him that was a real undertaking and he would put all of his concentration and effort into getting that bird, although he had never hit a bird with an arrow he was determined to give it his best shot.

That was not an isolated incident. He needed that patience and determination because he had to entertain himself most of the time since he was usually alone during the day while his little brother was asleep. When his brother was awake he was usually confined to the house, watching him and keeping him out of things. But even then he was virtually alone while he was playing because his brother could not play the games that he preferred. And he could not go outside and play; he could barely walk.

Oh! He could take him outside once in a while all right, but he had to promise his mother that he would not leave the yard with him. He definitely couldn't take him near the river or into the woods and those were his favorite places.

He had cut that bow from a live black walnut limb so it would not break as easily as the ones George and he had cut from green or dry cottonwood limbs. He had sometimes pulled a cottonwood bow as far as he thought was safe and just as he was ready to fire, he would hear, crack; there went another bow.

He had gone into the blacksmith shop where they kept the cowhide and talked the blacksmith into cutting him some long thin strips of rawhide so he could make that bow. Wouldn't George be surprised? George never gave him credit for doing anything. That's when he learned that leather would stretch. But it was still better than the small strings they had been using,

He was not an ordinary boy, as boys go. Although he didn't know it at the time, he was a boy born in bondage; in bondage to the owner of the largest plantation along that side of the Mississippi River; there were no plantations along the river to compare with it, north, south or within fifty miles to the east. Of course he had no way at that time of knowing what was on the West Side of the Big River as he and all of the other people there called the Mississippi River.

He was a slave!

But at that time he had no idea that he was a slave.

His mother, not wanting to hurt him by informing him so early in life, had protected him to the point that he knew nothing of his heritage or his ancestry except knowing her and his father. Oh, he knew his grandmother, because she lived with them, but he had heard his grandfather only casually mentioned in conversations.

He was well built for strength, but he had not yet filled out and developed his weight and muscles to any significant degree, but he was very fast for his age, faster than any boy was of his age on the plantation. And most of the older boys could not compete with him in a foot race.

If only George was there! He was older and maybe he could hit one of the birds! No, he couldn't. Although George was older, when they were shooting arrows, even though Jasper couldn't shoot as far he could beat George at hitting a target nine times out of ten.

George was a husky boy, a little short for his age, but very strong. "Big and strong," the slaves always said. "He'll be big and strong like his father." He also had brown hair and blue eyes; hair like his father had before it began graying, which Jasper thought was too long, combed down the back of his head. Except for being younger and shorter, he could have passed for his father. He always wore the same type of blue or striped overalls and red or blue plaid shirts like his father wore around the plantation.

The men working on Mr. Brisley's plantation wore the same type of overalls because they were so useful with all of the pockets, but their shirts were made from any material available, sometimes even cloth from sugar sacks.

But the slaves on the neighboring plantations were not so lucky. They wore any kind of clothing available whether or not they fit them. The women wore sugar sack dresses as a general rule but Mr. Brisley let them have cloth to make calico dresses for Sunday if he let them go to the little local church or if some of the neighbors came for the day. He seemed to be the only plantation owner around that wanted their slaves to look presentable when they were seen by neighbors.

The children wore anything that was available including clothes made from sugar sacks and cut downs from clothes half worn out by their older brothers and sisters.

Jasper loved to explore the woods especially near the river but he knew how far he could explore alone, but he had one advantage when George was there. Unlike his mother who watched him like a hawk watches a chicken when he is circling overhead, Mr. Brisley seemed to care little about where George and he went when they were around home as long as they were home in time for supper. After supper they could go into the woods again as long as they were home by dark or shortly thereafter.

Jasper could hardly remember when he began following George into the woods; at least since he was three years old. George would lose interest in any activity fast and Jasper would have to encourage him, "Come on George," he would say. "Are you chicken to go farther into the woods? Let's see what is by the river." That would usually anger George to the point that he would go with Jasper.

Where was George? Mr. Brisley should be home with him before dark, but he hadn't seen hide nor hair of the team. He knew that he could hear the team and wagon before they were near the barn and he was getting anxious for them to get home. He had been playing there most of the day, patiently waiting.

Mr. Brisley had gone into town to deliver a big load of cotton and to pick up supplies early that morning and had taken his son George with him. Jasper was always lonely and disappointed when they left because he could never go with them. He always had to stay there and play with his little brother.

I had better try for that bird before it gets tired of sitting there and flies away.

Missed again!

Then he heard the sound. Unless he was mistaken it was the far down the river chug, chug sound of a steam engine on a boat coming up the river. Very few of the new steamers came by there and he was trying to resist the temptation to go to the river and watch it pass. After all, his little brother had been asleep for only a short time and he was sure that he would have time to go to the river and watch it pass and then be back before his brother awoke and his mother came outside looking for him.

The best way to get a young boy to do something is to tell him that he can't do it especially a boy like Jasper; a boy with his intelligence; a boy with his natural curiosity; a boy with his cunning and energy; a boy with nothing to do all day while he is alone.

Usually he was definitely alone; everyone at the plantation except his mother and his little brother and sometimes the blacksmith, who was also the foreman, had their work cut out for them; planned well in advance by Mr. Brisley and dictated to them by his foreman. They were always doing some of the chores that were required of them on a daily basis.

No matter; whether or not the other boys were busy, they couldn't play with Jasper. None of them were allowed near the Big House at any time unless they came with their fathers to do some task, such as working in the garden, fixing something that was broken or tending the many flowers that grew all around the front of the house. But he wasn't allowed to go from the area alone, especially to the river. But it would take the boat only a few minutes to pass and it sounded like it was on his side of the river, near the bank. Surely he would be back before his mother even missed him.

He stood there spellbound watching the boat come alongside him. It was a small boat, especially for a steamer and Jasper could see the people on board. He waved vigorously to them and they waved back. How exciting it was to watch, but how much more exciting it would be if he was on the boat with them. Why didn't they ever come closer to his side of the river so he could see them up close? If only they would come closer so he could see the people better he would imagine that he was on the boat with them as it chugged up the river, at least until it was out of sight around the bend ahead.

When the boat was passing where he was he began running as fast as he could alongside the river almost keeping up with it up the bank until it passed a point of land that projected into the river; a little peninsula with no trees; only grass. Suddenly, since he was out further than he should have been the overhanging bank broke off, dropping him in water over his head. He struggled until he was on the bank; and since he had gone to the river without permission he knew that he would be in trouble with his mother if he went back to the house soaked to the skin.

Even though he was wet and cold he couldn't resist standing there and watching two canoes going down the river near the bank along the far side. He couldn't see them very well, them being in the shade and the sun being in his eyes, but he assured himself that they were Indians. Who else would be going down the river in a canoe? He was intrigued with Indians after hearing the men talk about them and after being told so many times that he looked like one. How he would like to see some of them come down his side so he could see them up close so he could see for himself what they looked like. Then he could see for himself if he should be proud that he looked like them.

One of these days he would have a canoe like those and he would go across the river; then he could see for himself what they looked like instead of having to rely on what other people said and maybe he could have an Indian friend. Maybe he could talk George into asking Mr. Brisley for a canoe; he got George almost everything he asked for. No need! If George had a canoe he wouldn't go across the river anyway; he would be afraid to leave the bank in it. Jasper couldn't even talk him into going out into the river on the raft they had built. He would get mad when Jasper would call him a 'fraidy cat, thinking that it would get him to go farther but he still refused so Jasper had to be content with pushing it along the bank while George and he were on the river together.

Jasper needed a place inside to dry his clothes and he could hear the blacksmith working with steel on the anvil, so he decided that the best thing he could do was to go there until his clothes were dry.

"How did you get soaked like that?" the blacksmith asked him when he entered.

Jasper was sure that he knew what had happened and he was afraid that he would tell his mother, so he chose to ask a question instead of answering.

"I'm cold and I don't want to go to the house wet, may I stand by the forge until I'm dry?"

"Sure you can, but you must have gone to the river alone again."

"You won't tell my mother, will you, please?"

When he returned his mother was outside with his brother looking for him.

"Where have you been? I have been having so much trouble keeping you out of the woods alone; I thought that you had gone there again. You were told to stay around the house," his mother said.

"I was at the blacksmith shop."

"You know that Mr. Brisley would be mad if he came home and found you bothering the blacksmith. I need you to watch your little brother."

"Aw! Gee! Do I have to? I want to be out here when Mr. Brisley brings George home. He wants me to go into the woods with him. Besides I wasn't bothering the blacksmith, I was only standing by the forge, watching him."

"Oh! All right! Come in until they get here, then I'll watch your brother."

When Jasper was inside watching his brother he couldn't practice writing his name and numbers because his brother would bother him, so most of the time while he wasn't keeping his brother out of something, he would play by himself or stand by the window looking out at the woods, or watching the road, waiting for George to come home from town or from school. How he would like to be out in the woods watching the wild-life. At least he could be outside watching for Mr. Brisley so he would be ready when he brought George home.

When there were no birds or animals around he would sometimes practice writing his name and numbers or practice writing the alphabet on the ground with a stick while he was in the edge of the woods waiting for George; he wanted to be better at everything than George was.

Jasper's mother was a tall woman, taller than most of the slave women; and strong. Mr. Brisley had often said that she was as strong as most of the men and that she never seemed to tire. She was also lighter complexioned than any of the other women;

and any of the men, for that matter. Her complexion was almost as light as Jasper's.

Her hair was not jet black like most of the others, but had a slight but noticeable red tint to it, and her eyes were a very dark blue instead of the dark brown or black of the others. The main thing that identified her as a slave was her hair, which she always kept clean so that it literally shined in the sunlight was always worn like the others; in tight little short curls all over her head.

Her husband could not read or write. Neither could her mother, who lived with them, or any of the other slaves. Therefore she could be called the real matriarch of the family; and of the whole plantation, for that matter. Most of the other slaves asked her advice when they had a problem or were sick, or even when they had a problem with their children.

No one on the plantation really had anything to do except what he or she was told to do by Mr. Brisley or his foreman. It could be said that their minds was not their own because they had very little thinking to do on their own behalf. Mr. Brisley did all of their thinking and planning for them. Jasper's mother kept an account of all birthdays and ages of the younger ones. The older ones she kept the ages of as well as she could by getting dates from the elder slaves. None of the other slaves were able to do that so if they forgot their ages or birthdays they had to ask her. They said that they kept ages by guess and by golly.

Although she had to work all day every day at the Big House, with her mother's help she did the housework and cooking for her family; sometimes they didn't have supper until well after dark.

"I hear the wagon coming. Can I go outside now, please mommy, can I?" Jasper pleaded as he pranced around, looking out through the window.

"Go ahead. Your brother will be asleep again soon anyway and I already have Mr. Brisley's supper ready."

She tried to be lenient with Jasper because she well understood his situation because she had been in about the same situation almost all of her life. At the other plantation her mother, even though she had a husband, spent most of her time at the main house in a little room and took care of the family and while she was very young she had been almost confined there; then after they were bought by Mr. Brisley, before she married, her mother and her had been confined to the little room out back. They hardly co-mingled with the other slaves except when the Brisley's had one of their Sunday get-togethers and parties.

When the wagon stopped George bounded off the seat and they immediately disappeared into the woods where they would be until they were called to supper or until it was dark.

"Don't you two go too far because I want you here by dark," they heard Mr. Brisley yell as they went into the woods.

He didn't have to worry about them being back by dark because even though Jasper would stay in the woods as long as possible, George was not about to stay very deep in the woods after dark. He was so scared of the dark that when the sunlight left the woods, so did George.

Mr. Brisley was a tall man; and heavy; and strong, or had been before he became ill and began losing weight and looking weak. He was a man in his late fifties with slightly graying hair and not a trace of a beard or mustache. He had blue eyes and hair that had been brown and thick until the gray had invaded what was left.

Except when he needed to go to another town for business, even though he wore the same type of overalls that the other men wore, he always wore store bought flannel shirts.

His family had not always been farmers and slave owners. His grandfather had come over the Atlantic alone, as a young man from England, and married an Indian woman near the East

Coast. Then they cane nearly half way across the country on horseback. They had come down the river from Saint Louis in a canoe and by chance had come ashore at the plantation that the Brisley's had then owned for three generations, and asked for a job.

The owner had been a young man who had inherited the plantation from his grandfather, his father being deceased, and knew nothing about farming or controlling slaves. Mr. Brisley's grandfather, having been a builder in his native England, also had no experience with farming or with slaves. But he had been in charge of men since he had been very young and he was offered the job of overseer, He immediately became popular with the slaves because he was more understanding than the young owner was.

The young owner was not interested in farming, so after a short time he sold the plantation to Mr. Brisley's grandfather. He had been so anxious to get rid of the farm that when he and Mr. Brisley's grandfather agreed on a price, he sold it to him on a long term contract.

His grandfather had started with three strikes against him. He had a mortgage to pay off; he was a foreigner in a strange land and the other farmers called him a squaw man. It was a full generation before the Brisley's had completely outlived the stigma. And probably would not have then except for the determination of Mr. Brisley's father. He was determined to make the Brisley name a household word in the county.

He began by building the Big House as it later became known as, and clearing all of the land that he could, with the help and resources at his disposal, and becoming the largest farmer in the county. Then he began cultivating friendships with all of the other plantation owners by having large parties at the Big House as everyone had already begun calling it. When some of the other plantation owners saw how much more work his slaves accomplished, compared to theirs, they began asking his advice on how to get their slaves to work harder. Word traveled fast and he soon became very popular, known and respected throughout the county.

The next day Mr. Brisley went to the neighboring plantation, taking George with him and leaving Jasper alone again with nothing to do.

"I want you to go with me and learn something about business. This time come inside with me and listen to what we say. Don't play with his daughter like you did the last time," he heard Mr. Brisley say as they were leaving.

"But Pa, I never get a chance to play with her except at recess time at school."

"This meeting will be more important."

How Jasper would like to go with them. He would be more than happy to stay in the house or anywhere that Mr. Brisley said if only he could go. He had never been off the plantation except to the little church next to it and he could see the beginning of Mr. Brisley's fields from there.

While they were gone Jasper was questioning his mother as he almost constantly did while they were alone.

"Mommy, why does Mr. Brisley say that I could pass as an Indian?"

"Maybe because you have even a lighter skin than mine and because you are so tall for your age. I have seen a few Indians going along the river in their canoes and they were as light as you are, and tall.

"Do you think that I could pass as an Indian?"

"I reckon you could."

Jasper was very tall as a seven year old, and quite large for his age, weighing nearly as much as George. He was also very bright for his age. He had his mother's complexion and hair color as well as her dark blue eyes. His hair was somewhat lighter than anyone else's hair on the plantation, even his mother's. He wasn't dressed nearly as well as George, having only clothes that his mother had made for him. He didn't even have overalls to wear like George and the men who worked in the fields had.

His mother had made his clothes too large for him so he could wear them more than one year before he outgrew them, and he had to go barefoot. How he would like to have bib overalls and lace up shoes like George had; overalls that fit him. George always looked so nice in his bib overalls and store bought shirts.

When he had a chance to look in Mr. Brisley's mirror he would size himself up and wonder what he would look like in clothes like the ones that George wore. And why did Mr. Brisley say that he looked like an Indian? He could see that he had almost the same light complexion as George, but his mother was a little darker than he was. His grandmother was almost black and his father and little brother were almost as black as the coal that the blacksmith used for the forge.

Maybe someday my mother will explain it to me, but when I ask she always says that I am too young, he thought as he pondered the mystery of why he could pass as an Indian.

He was always asking anyone that he would be with questions as long as he or she would listen and answer him. Some of the men, and women as well, would get tired of his questions and say, "go on boy and play," or "didn't you know that curiosity killed the cat?" But Mr. Brisley would try answering most of the questions that he would ask, as thoroughly as he would answer George's questions. But George was never as curious and seldom asked questions as Jasper did. When his mother had time between her chores at the Big House she would answer question and teach him how to make letters and numbers. He had learned the alphabet and could count to a hundred and could write his name, but he wanted to learn to read and write like George was learning to do. He had learned to read and write a few words but he thought that if he had a few books he could learn some words himself. If Mr. Brisley would let him have only one book to take with him he could learn to read it. His mother could get books but she would let him look at one only occasionally when Mr. Brisley and George were gone. Then she would watch every move he made while he had a book.

He was lonesome all day while George was in school because he had the whole day to spend around the house with nothing to do except to watch and play with his little brother and he could not keep up with Jasper.

"Mommy, why can't I go to school like George?" he once asked his mother.

"You are too young to understand now but you will never be allowed to go to school."

"Could you go to school when you were little?"

"No, I wanted to go but I never had a chance."

"Then how did you learn so you could teach me my letters and how to count?"

"I have been doing all of the cooking, cleaning and washing for the Brisley's since I was a little girl. I stayed in the little room out back and took care of his sick wife before she died. His wife had been helping him with his books, so when she became ill he began teaching me so I could help him. During the winter when there was no work to do in the fields, he spent almost full time teaching me. Now he's trying to teach George, but he seems to have no interest in learning. He has his hands full just keeping George in school and getting him to do his homework."

"Then why don't you teach me to keep books?"

"Although you're too young now to understand, that's what I'm teaching you now. First you need to learn your numbers much better and learn to read more than a few words."

"I've been trying to get you to teach me to read better, but most of the time you only teach me my numbers and how to count."

"If I had time I could teach you to read much better and teach you about business, but first remember that Mr. Brisley owns much more than this plantation, so you should listen while we are talking about the books when you have a chance, then when you are older you can take care of a business."

"I have been listening and trying to learn, but George never wants to learn anything. He never even wants to go to school and I can hardly ever get him to teach me what he learns in school anymore. If I could go to school I would never want to stay home. Why can't I go in George's place when he wants to stay home?"

"You want to go so bad I would like to send you, but they wouldn't let you in the school house."

"Why wouldn't they let me in?"

She would like to explain to him that he was a slave and only white folks could go to school, but she wanted to wait until he was older. She would also like to explain that the plantation owners didn't want their slaves to learn to read and write because they would be much more independent and harder to control. But she thought that he would be much harder to teach if he had such negative thought on his mind. She wanted to wait on that also so she merely said; "You are entirely too young to understand now."

"When George is in school and I have to watch my brother I have nothing to do. Why can't I have a book to carry with me and look at while he is in school? You hardly ever let me try reading a book."

"You know that you can't go into Mr. Brisley's study."

"But George can have books."

"He will let George have only certain books unless he reads them in his study."

"George doesn't want any books. All he wants to do is play. If I just had one book that I could keep with me I'm sure that I could learn to read it."

"Hush up child; you know that you can't have books unless I'm right with you, so go and practice writing your name and numbers."

George was three years older than Jasper and since his mother had died when he had been only a baby, he had been taken care of completely by Jasper's mother. Jasper could not remember not coming to Mr. Brisley's house to stay all day every day and after his brother was born she would bring both of them to the Big House early every morning. She would cook Mr. Brisley's breakfast; then take care of George; getting him ready for school or whatever he was doing that day. Then she would do the cleaning, washing and cooking as well as helping Mr. Brisley with his books, then go home in the evening. Jasper was too young to understand how hard and how long his mother worked. She still had the work at her own house to do before bedtime.

She had always taken him with her so when he was old enough he would play with George. George would sometimes refuse to play with him saying that he was just a baby, but when Mr. Brisley would hear him he would tell him to not mistreat Jasper. It didn't seem to do any good because George had always been very stubborn.

Jasper remembered when George began learning to read. At first he was excited and proud that he could go to school and when he came home he would show Jasper what he had learned that day. Jasper was too young to learn very much, but George always acted so smart that he wanted to do anything that George could do, so he was trying to remember everything that George told him.

Then George lost interest in school, but he had gotten Jasper interested and he wanted to learn everything. But Jasper couldn't learn much from George in the evenings because all George wanted to do was play. When he came home, after very reluctantly doing his homework he would bolt out of the house and head for the woods, with jasper right behind him.

"Why don't you want to go to school," Jasper asked George one day. "If I could go I would never want to stay home. I would learn everything that I could."

"Do you realize that it must be five miles to that school house? I have to ride that old bay horse, which is the roughest riding horse that we have. He is the only one that is no good hooked to a wagon or anything that requires two horses because he will not work with another horse, so I'm stuck with him. But I guess I'm lucky because some of the kids have to ride mules and they are slower than horses and much more stubborn."

"I would like to go to school if I had to walk. I'm sure that I could learn a lot more if I was in school."

"You would get tired of that old teacher telling you what to do all day. When we get there she has us younger ones to read while the older ones do arithmetic. Then we practice our numbers while the older ones learn spelling. Then we can go outside for a few minute for what she calls recess, and then we go back inside and learn writing. Then we go outside to eat our biscuit and jelly. The last time we go inside we learn geography before we come home."

"Geography, what is that?"

"Why do you ask so many questions? You know that you

can't go to school. You are only a little kid and you can't learn the things that I'm studying."

"I could too! I can learn anything that you can. You just tell me everything that you learn everyday and I'll remember."

"I just started learning about other states. The teacher calls this the great land, and she said that you could ride a horse in almost any direction for weeks before you reached an ocean."

"I don't know what an ocean is but I would like to see one someday. If I could go where there was an ocean, I wouldn't care if I never came back to where I can't even go to school. Mr. Brisley won't even let me go with you and him to town."

"You know that you are too young to go with us to town. You will get in real trouble one of these days if you don't stop talking about such things."

Jasper remembered that ever since he had been very young Mr. Brisley had taken George to town with him every time he went when he was out of school. He knew that George had been going since he was his age, or even younger than he was and he couldn't understand why he couldn't go with them, because he could play with George at the Big House. When they were both there they played together almost constantly and were treated like brothers by Mr. Brisley.

One day when Mr. Brisley came out to where they were playing to get George for the trip to town, Jasper asked, "Mr. Brisley, why can't I go to town with you and George?"

"You are too young to understand why I can't take you. You have to stay home with your mother and little brother."

"Just because you play with me while we're here, you are not my brother and I don't want you going to town with me," George angrily said.

"I don't want to hear you talk that way again, George, Jasper going to town with us would be my decision."

Every time that George would go to town with Mr. Brisley Jasper would try to be brave and not cry, but he would pout and wonder why he couldn't go.

"Mr. Brisley won't let me go to town with them. Why can't I go with them sometimes?" Jasper asked his mother. "When they leave I have no one to play with."

"You are too young to understand now, but when you are older you will understand. He may not think that it would look right if he took you and didn't take some of the other boys. And he wouldn't have time to watch you while he took care of business. Besides he has been ill a lot lately and may not feel like watching you all day."

"But he takes George."

"Yes, but George is his son."

"When he's here he treats me like his son."

"You are too young to understand why he treats you that way, but he would have no place to put you while he was taking care of business."

"If I could go I would sit on the wagon seat all day if I had to. I want to see what town looks like. George thinks he's so smart because he can go to town and I can't. He sometimes brags about going to town and he makes me mad; so mad that if he wasn't so much stronger than me I would hit him as hard as I could."

"Maybe when George is in school again he will take you sometimes. Maybe I can put a bug in his ear."

A bug in his ear, Jasper thought, If I had known that I would have done it a long time ago.

"You don't mean a real bug do you?"

"No, silly, I meant that I would talk to him about it some-time."

"Why does Mr. Brisley talk to me while we're here but when we're outside with the other kids he doesn't even notice me?"

"You are entirely too young to understand now."

CHAPTER 2

School had started for the winter and even though most of the plantation owners kept their boys home to help see that the crops were harvested and taken care of before they started attending school, George had none of those responsibilities. In fact he had no responsibilities at all and played most of the time. He didn't even saddle his own horse in the morning; leaving that chore to one of the workers that would do it while they were harnessing the horses and mules for the day.

Very early one morning after George had left for school Mr. Brisley came to where Jasper was standing while he sadly looked toward the curve in the road that George had gone around on his way to school, wishing that he could go with him.

"I'm taking a load of cotton to town. Would you like to ride along with me?"

"Would I; I've been hoping every day that you would ask me. I'll go and ask my mother."

"I have already talked to her so get your coat and tell your mother goodbye."

"I wish I had some shoes to wear like George has." Jasper said as he pranced around. He wanted to race to the house but the wagon was already loaded, the team was hitched up and ready to go at any minute and he wondered if Mr. Brisley would leave without him while he was finding his mother to tell her goodbye. He knew that when the team was hitched up and ready that Mr. Brisley usually left immediately.

"Don't get so excited. I won't leave without you and I'll see that you have shoes when we get to town."

Jasper ran into the house and when he didn't see his mother he was running from room to room until he found her and said goodbye. Then he was running from room to room looking for his coat. It had been warm and he hadn't worn it for the last few days, so he didn't remember where he had left it. His mother found it for him and he was out of the door in seconds.

Jasper had always liked Mr. Brisley, but that made him feel especially fond of him and he was so anxious to go that he could hardly wait to get on the wagon. He knew that he could climb up the wheel and get on the seat because he had done it so many times before pretending that he was going to town, and pretending that he was Mr. Brisley and was driving the team himself, so before Mr. Brisley climbed up he was on the seat and ready to go.

Mr. Brisley was known far and wide for his horses. The working stock used in the fields was ordinary horses and mules, but the ones that he reserved for his own use were the largest blacks in the county. People said that they must each weigh a ton and they were well known throughout the county for their strength and their endurance.

Mr. Brisley and some of the other plantation owners would sometimes get together at Mr. Brisley's plantation on Sunday. His was the largest and most conveniently located; about the same distance from each of five other plantations and having more open space for such activities, for a Sunday picnic and business meeting. Mr. Brisley would have Jasper's family along with some of the other plantation owner's slaves that they had brought along to prepare the food and keep the area clean. Jasper thought that was a great honor but although Mr. Brisley had always favored his family for such things, he had never acted as though he liked them enough or was interested enough to let Jasper go to town with him.

Jasper, being small enough that they paid him little attention, while the other kids were playing what he considered their silly little games, anytime he had some free time, he would stay around the men and listen while they talked and boasted about their strong teams. They would sometimes make bets on whose horses were the strongest. Jasper would snicker in his sleeve so they didn't notice because he knew whose horses were stronger than any of the others.

But the other men also knew the strongest because they wouldn't even let Mr. Brisley's horses compete with the others when they had their pilling contests. They hadn't forgotten how badly they had been beaten on an earlier occasion when they had let them compete.

As they went toward town with the big wagonload of cotton pulled by Mr. Brisley's finest pair of Pertain mares, Babe and Beauty, Jasper, having been awake since his mother had taken him to the Big House very early that morning was so tired that he was almost asleep. He was forcing himself to stay awake because since he had never been to town, he wanted to see everything along the road and to be awake as they entered town. They passed two plantations along the way, but the houses weren't near the size of Mr. Brisley's house, nor did they look nearly as pretty; having been built from plain boards instead of siding and having never been whitewashed. The plantation houses looked more like the houses that Mr. Brisley had built for the workers except that they were not built from logs. They didn't have nearly as many small houses either, but they did have families living there because Jasper could see some little kids playing along the road at the end of the field alongside the house where their mothers and fathers were picking cotton.

Then Mr. Brisley stopped at a plantation and left Jasper sitting on the wagon seat while he talked to the owner. Jasper was wishing for him to return, so they could be on their way to town. Why doesn't he hurry, he wondered?

Some little kids, not even as old as Jasper, who lived on the plantation ran to the wagon and were going around and around it, looking at the big wagon and the two mares hitched to it. Jasper could see a wagon by the cotton field next to the house and could imagine, even though they were very young, how they felt looking at a wagon so much larger than the other one.

Then one of the small boys noticed Jasper sitting on the seat. They just stared at him for a few minutes before one of them talked to him.

"Wheah y'goin wit' yo' master?" He asked. "Why don'tcha git of'n play wit' us?

"I don't have a master. I'm going to town with Mr. Brisley. He owns the Big House where my mother works. He promised that I could see the whole town and go to the cotton gin," Jasper answered. "He promised me a new pair of shoes when we get to town."

"Aw! Gee!" He replied, "None o' us e'er was t'town an' I ne'er had new shoes, only hand-me-downs from my brother."

I would like to come here and play with these kids sometime, because they want to play, not like the kids where I live, but not now, he thought. Right now I wish Mr. Brisley would come on. I want to see what town looks like. It seems like it will take all day to get there."

"you c'n still git off'n play wit' us caus' you c'n see yore master wh'n he's comin' bac'."

"These are my best clothes and my mother said that I can't get them dirty or she'll skin me alive."

Only then did the thought occur to Jasper that his mother must have known that Mr. Brisley would take him to town that day. Otherwise why would she give him his best clohes to wear when he was going outside to play and then tell him not to get them dirty? Jasper had always loved his mother but the love he felt for her at that moment surpassed any feelings of love that he had ever felt for her. He thought that she had to be the best mother that anyone could ever ask for or ever hope to have.

After they passed the three plantations they passed some timber not unlike the woods near the Big House, where they had to wind their way through timber and around swampy areas, But the road was dry in some places and having been traveled so much with wagons going to and from town, dust raised from the wheels. Jasper didn't realize that the road went through some swamps. In fact the only part of the road that he knew anything about was the part that went from the little church, past Mr. Brisley's fields, then past the worker's houses, past the barn and ended up near the Big House. There was no reason for the road to go farther because Mr. Brisley's house was built next to the river and both up and down the river from the house stood tall timber.

But he knew what swamps were like. Even though they had been told to stay away from the swamps, he had talked George into going into them many times on the plantation and they had lots of fun, wading through the shallow water, climbing over fallen timber and chasing frogs and turtles. But when they saw a snake, which occurred quite often, the fun they were having quickly ceased and they would immediately get out of the water and be on their way home.

But that was different. Almost everywhere he looked he could see either trees or water. He saw a lot of black walnut and other timber like the woods that George and he had played in for years. He could see a lot more wild persimmons along the road than there was near the Big House and he could almost taste the fruit which would be ripe enough to eat in a few weeks.

It seemed to Jasper that the swamps and timber would go on forever, he was so anxious to get to town. He just knew that town should be there somewhere and he wanted to be in open country so he could see it from a distance because he didn't know what to expect when they arrived.

While they were passing through a clearing with fields on both sides of the road he could see a large stand of timber ahead and Mr. Brisley said that they were almost to the creek. He saw the bridge ahead and was trying to keep his eyes open, but no matter how hard he tried, he could no longer stay awake.

He awoke to the sounds of the wagon going over the wooden bridge. It made a roaring sound and was bumping along going over the rough timbers. Then he heard sounds that sounded like "crack, crack and crack" and suddenly the wagon leaned to one side and stopped. He thought that they were falling into the creek, because he could look right down into the water. He was a little concerned because he had never been above water before except when they were on the raft that he and George had made and then the water was not running so fast and carrying floating sticks and limbs as it was doing as it went under the bridge.

Mr. Brisley was worried that the wagon would break completely through the bridge as he looked down into the creek. He knew that if the wagon fell all of the way through the timbers, their lives as well as the lives of the team would be in grave danger.

His first concern was for Jasper. Could he swim? He knew that he would lose the wagon and cotton and maybe even the team. But all of those could be replaced. Jasper couldn't. Then he began to worry that even he couldn't swim in that kind of torrent.

Why didn't I take time to teach him to swim while he was younger like I did George? At least he would have a chance to save himself. I should have forgotten what the other slaves might have thought and taught him, he thought.

What he didn't know was that Jasper, while George and he were spending so much time at the Big River, had become a very good swimmer; a much better swimmer than George. George was so heavy that Jasper could literally swim circles around him.

Jasper was frightened, very frightened when he was fully awake and the reality of their predicament overwhelmed him. Then Mr. Brisley helped him down on the left side of the wagon and he could see what peril the wagon was in; him being young it looked worse to him than it really was. If he had been a little older he would have noticed a similar fear and anxiety showing on the face of Mr. Brisley but he was so calm that he appeared to Jasper to be completely unafraid and completely unconcerned.

"Run to the end of the bridge, son, and wait there in case more timbers break," he said. Then Jasper watched as Mr. Brisley calmly slapped the lines down on the backs of the two prize mares and said "giddup Babe, giddup Beauty." That was definitely the largest and strongest of Mr. Brisley's teams and he watched as the two prize mares, with no other encouragement and no other action on Mr. Brisley's part, leaned into the traces. Their enormous muscles bulged as inch by inch the front wheel of the big wagon began climbing out of the hole in the bridge. Whoa he said as the rear wheel reached the edge of the hole. He knew that the brakes would not hold that much weight and he was worried that the rear wheel would fall into the hole too fast and break more timbers or break the wheel itself.

"Giddup Babe, giddup Beauty," he said as the rear wheel settled into the hole and that wheel seemed to toll out easier than the front one had.

The creek wasn't very wide at that point and there was timber on both sides, so they had built the bridge by cutting and placing three logs across it and putting timbers across the logs. It had been plenty strong when it was built many years before, but time and weather had begun rotting the timbers. Mr. Brisley inspected the bridge and determined that it could be patched temporarily with three timbers to replace the broken ones. But he knew that would be only a temporary repair because the bridge was so old.

"Hop back on the wagon, son, and we'll go on to town," Mr. Brisley said after he had examined the wheels and decided that they were not noticeably damaged. He would have the blacksmith, who was an expert at such things to examine them when he was home before he brought another load to town.

"Wait until I tell Mommy about this. She will be excited."

"She may be too excited to let you come again. Let me tell her in my own way when I think the time is right.

"She was so happy when you decided to bring me; she wouldn't keep me from coming again, would she? She seemed almost as excited as I was before we left while we were looking for my coat"

"She might be afraid for you to come again. She is awfully protective of you, but you were so scared that you may not want to come again."

"I was scared all right, but next time I won't be. I'll just sit right here and watch while you get the wagon out."

"I believe you would, but there will be no next time. When we arrive in town I'll ask the gin foreman to send some men to patch it and I'll see that it's rebuilt before we bring another load of cotton."

As they were going through town Jasper saw the cotton gin standing big and tall ahead of them. When Mr. Brisley saw the expression on his face, he began explaining the gin to him;

"That big building is where the cotton is taken first; it is taken up to the top and when it is back down again, the seeds are removed and it is pressed into bales. All of those white bales you see by the side of the gin are cotton, ready to be taken to mills which spin it and make it into cloth to make clothes and bags like the sugar sacks from which some of the girl's dresses and your shirts are made."

When they reached the mill the gin foreman stuck his head out of the door and said that he had a customer in his office and would be out shortly,

The gin foreman was a short stocky man who had been foreman since Mr. Brisley and some of the smaller plantation owners had opened it a few years before with a minimum of equipment to gin their own cotton. It was primarily to keep some of them from taking it an additional ten miles to the only other gin in the area.

Not only did they not like the extra hauling time, but also a big outfit from Chicago owned the big gin. It had been the only one anywhere near since the original gin had closed. The original gin, a few miles further from the Brisley plantation had closed shortly after the big one had opened. After it closed the owners of the big gin, the only one near enough for some of the plantation owners to haul their cotton had been hard to get along with. They could then dictate prices and terms to suit themselves; they in effect had a monopoly because the plantation owners had no other choice.

Of course some of the other plantation owners had been very happy when the big gin had been built, because it was a few miles closer to them than the one that they had hauled their cotton to for years and the owners had originally been easier to deal with. The original gin had been only a short distance further from Mr. Brisley's plantation but it was outdated and some of the timbers were rotting. They had decided that it would be more feasible to build the new one than to remodel and re-open it.

Mr. Brisley as well as the other owners had known the foreman since his days with the big gin before he had a disagreement with them and had been fired or laid off and Mr. Brisley had wanted to hire him. This caused a big rift among the other owners of the new gin that was under construction. Some of them thought that since he had quit or been fired from the other gin that he would not be a good foreman. Others had a relative that they preferred having the job, but since Mr. Brisley had the largest share in the gin, they went along with the arrangement; some of them were so unhappy, they vowed that they would sell their share when there was enough business to make it profitable so a buyer for their share could be found.

From the beginning the foreman had been a big asset to the owners of the gin helping with the installation of the equipment and later taking care of it as if it were his own and worrying about whether or not there was a profit.

Shortly after it opened other plantation owners who were not investors but lived close enough to deliver their cotton there, began doing so, partly because of the distance to the other gin and partly because the service and prices were very much better.

The other investors soon forgot their differences and were happy with the gin foreman, having seen how competent he was. The animosity toward Mr. Brisley ceased, which also helped to make the gin more efficient.

To some of the investors; the ones that needed the income for other purposes, it seemed that it would never generate a sustained profit. When extra money was earned above operating costs something would need repairing and take the extra capital or a drought would lessen their income and further complicate their problems. Therefore some of the owners were discontent from the beginning, thinking that they should be realizing more profit than they were.

When there were more customers than the gin could handle and improvements needed to be made and additional machinery bought, the other investors either didn't have the capital or didn't want to invest more money. Some didn't want to take the chance that it would ever generate a sustained profit so they began selling their shares to Mr. Brisley until he was the sole owner and it had since become not only profitable, but also a very good asset.

Even though Jasper was too young to understand business, he had heard his mother and Mr. Brisley discuss keeping the books for the gin, and he knew that was another of her jobs that kept her from teaching him to read and write better; and many other things that he wanted to learn.

When they were in town Mr. Brisley had gone directly to the gin and waited there patiently until the customer had left the office and the foreman came out to talk to him.

"Could you spare enough men to take three timbers and patch the bridge? The wheel on the right side broke through. It would be too dangerous to cross and there must have been a lot of rain somewhere to the north, so we can't ford the creek with the water as high as it is now."

"I'll start them right away and have it done by the time you start home."

"Will you see that my wagon gets moved ahead behind the others so it will get unloaded? I need to go to the store while it is being unloaded."

"Sure will," the foreman said. Then he seemed to notice Jasper for the first time. "Who is the little Indian we have here?"

"This is Jasper. Jasper, meet Alex Short."

"I'm pleased to meet you Mr. Short," Jasper said, as he almost had to bite his lip to keep from laughing. Short, he thought, they sure named him right.

Alex short was definitely short. No more than five foot four inches in his boots, but he was husky and known to be very strong for his height. He was actually a good looking young fellow with his full head of brown hair and his brown eyes that accentuated his light complexion and his prominent facial features. He had a pair of wide well shaped shoulders; some people said that he was as wide as he was tall. He wore the same type of bib overalls and plaid shirt that the other workers wore and they were clean and had been ironed. He had a good disposition to go along with his other traits. He was easy to get along with; he had what seemed to be a constant wide smile and was exceptionally friendly with everyone.

He treated the workers at the gin more like friends than employees and could get them to do more work calmly and without any excitement than most foremen could with all of their yelling and threatening ways.

"And I'm pleased to meet you Jasper," Alex said. "Where did you learn such good English instead of the slang words used be everyone in this God forsaken country?"

"I learned everything from my mother, Mr. Short."

"Since you have such good manners and everyone else calls me Alex, you can do the same, jasper."

"My mother would skin me alive if I called my elders by their first names, Mr. Short."

"His mother will let him use only proper English at all times, Alex," Mr. Brisley said.

"His mother must be a special person around here to teach him such good manners."

"She has taken care of my family for many years, almost

since she was a child herself, and I have taught her. Now she's teaching her family to respect others and address them properly. That whole family speaks English as well as you or me and they have respect not only for others, but to their own elders."

"You can come here and visit me any time that Mr. Brisley will let you, Jasper," Alex said.

"I'm proud of you son," Mr. Brisley said as they walked back toward the store. Then Jasper thought about what he had said when he was excited. But he wasn't excited just then. That was the third time that he had called him son. He decided that he would hang around when he was outside where the rest of the kids were and see if he called everyone son. Surely he didn't think of ham the same as he did George, because that was the first time he was allowed to come to town, but he had talked about them coming back with another load. That was more than he had even imagined, being able to come back.

"If I can come back may I come and talk to Mr. Short, huh, may I please?" Jasper asked. "I like him more than anyone else that I have met."

"Alex meant want he said about you talking to him, but he is very busy and you could disturb him, but I'm sure that you can talk to him occasionally."

Jasper was excited form the thought that he would be allowed to come back to town and especially that he would be allowed to talk to someone different than the ones on the plantation. He always enjoyed hearing them talk, but Alex was different. He treated Jasper with respect, something that he had never had happen before.

"Alex was right about this place," Mr. Brisley said as if he were talking to himself. If I didn't have so many ties and so much money invested here I would get out of this Malaria infested place."

Why would he want to leave where he can stay inside and do a few books and he can go to town or on a business trip whenever he wants, Jasper wondered?

And he can buy whatever he wants; even a wagonload of food. And when he talks everyone listens; not like me, when I talk around the men, everyone tries to send me away.

His thoughts were interrupted as they approached the store. Since he had never been in a store he didn't know what to expect if Mr. Brisley would let him go in, but his father had told him that when Mr. Brisley brought him, he always stayed outside and loaded the merchandise that Mr. Brisley bought. He said that he was never allowed inside of the store.

They would be there soon and he hoped with all of his little heart that he would be allowed to go inside so he could see what was in there, if it were for only a few minutes.

When they reached the store he took Jasper by the hand and led him up the high steps and inside. It sure would be nice to do like Mr. Brisley, he thought. He just walked right on inside and brought me with him.

That still being somewhat early in the morning on a weekday, there were no other customers in the store.

"Good morning, this is Jasper and I want you to fit him with a pair of shoes and put them on my account," he said to the storekeeper as soon as the storekeeper had spoken to him.

"Hello Jasper, he said. Then he turned to Mr. Brisley and asked. "What kind of shoes do you want him to have? I have two styles in his size, both come in black or white and both lace up above the ankles."

"They will be his shoes so let him pick them."

"Are you sure that you won't have every boy on the plantation wanting shoes in the middle of September? Most of the plantation owners haven't started buying winter shoes yet," the storekeeper said.

Mr. Brisley seemed to ignore the question and instead asked one himself. "Is it all right if he remains here while I get unloaded and take care of a little business? If you'll have the items on this list ready I'll pick them up on the way home."

"You know that it will be fine with me without even asking. Since my son is in school now I will probably keep him busy until you get back."

"If he wants to help that will be fine but I don't want him doing things that he is too young for."

"Kind of fond of this little fellow I see," the storekeeper teased.

"He is learning to read and write and he has no trouble counting. He may be of some help to you while I'm getting unloaded. I'll bet he can put the things on this list together himself."

"You're kidding me. This boy is learning to read and to count?"

"You've got a big surprise coming."

How did he know that I'm learning to read and write, Jasper wondered? He never pays any attention to me except to play with George and me occasionally.

Mr. Brisley and the storekeeper had grown up and gone to school together in the lower grades, but when Mr. Brisley had gone to college, the storekeeper had gone to work for the previous owner of the store.

Rumor had it that many years later, after Mr. Brisley's father had died and left the plantation to him that when the previous owner wanted to sell the store, Mr. Brisley helped finance the purchase. Some folks said that he still had a half interest in the business.

Jasper knew by listening to Mr. Brisley and his mother talk that since the storekeeper's wife had died and he was so busy taking care of the store and also his son that they were taking care of his books. They also made sure that there was enough money to operate the business. He also heard them say a few times that there wasn't enough profit for the storekeeper to pay all of his bills and that Mr. Brisley would have to pay some of the expenses incurred during the previous month.

Jasper was wondering why, when he was taking care of his little brother and playing around the study door, they didn't seem to pay any attention to him when they talked about business. Maybe they didn't think that he would remember what they said but he was determined to remember everything they talked about. Since he couldn't go to school, he wanted to learn everything he could by listening. He wanted to know more than George did. George always thought that he was so smart.

Jasper was always looking forward to the days when Mr. Brisley would go to town with a load of corn or cotton and most of the time when George was in school he would take Jasper with him. When George was not in school he would nearly always take them both.

Even though it was only a few miles to town, since it was getting late in the fall, they would need to leave the plantation very early in the morning. By the time the wagon was unloaded and Mr. Brisley was through with his business they would have to leave for home immediately and sometimes they didn't get home until dark. When they were hauling cotton and George was out of school and went along, George and he would ride on top of the load so they could sleep on the way to the gin.

When they were hauling corn George was usually in school and Jasper would have to sit on the seat and he would lean on Mr. Brisley and sleep. That pleased him very much, especially when Mr. Brisley would put his arm around him to keep him from falling off the wagon. His father never seemed to care enough to put his arm around him, usually saying that he was tired and wanted to sit and sleep himself.

Jasper wondered why, when George was along they could go outside and walk anywhere around town but when he was alone he could stay only in or near the store until Mr. Brisley was finished with his business and came for him. He really didn't care too much because the street was so dusty when it was dry or so muddy after a rain that he would get his new shoes dirty. His mother would have to clean them when he arrived home.

One day he asked, "Mr. Brisley, why can't I go outside and walk around town when I'm not with George? I would sometimes like to talk with people around town."

"You are too young to understand but it would not look right and it may not be safe."

"That is what my mother says, 'you're too young to understand'"

"Your mother is very wise and you should listen to her. Someday, when you are old enough to understand more, I'm sure that she will explain a lot of things."

"You can explain them to me now and I won't tell my mother, I promise."

"You'll just have to wait until she's ready to explain things to you. If she had left it up to me I would have explained a lot of things to you long ago."

Since Jasper had been going to town he had learned to recognize and read all of the signs over all of the goods in the general store, including the candy sign. He would really like to have all of the candy that he could eat from the candy container that was there but he never had any money to buy anything. Sometimes when he would help the storekeeper by putting things on the lower shelves or dusting what he could reach, he would be given a few pieces of candy. That would encourage him to do more.

He couldn't understand why he wasn't allowed to get things from the shelves to fill orders for customers. When customers were in the store he had to stay in the back corner of the store or in the storeroom.

"Why can't I get things off the shelves for people?" He asked the storekeeper one-day. "I know where everything is and I can read the labels, so I could get them as well as anyone."

"I know that you are strong enough and can read well enough to get things for customers, but some people are very particular; even in some cases, peculiar. I think you are too young to understand or your mother would have explained those things to you."

"But when they are outside I can load the sugar-sacks and roll the flour barrels to their wagons for them."

"You will have to get Mr. Brisley or your mother to explain those things to you."

"They will both say that I'm too young to understand."

Jasper had never been to any town except the one where Mr. Brisley took his cotton and corn, but he knew every building there. After having seen only the buildings on the plantation he thought town was a very large place, with so many buildings. The General Store was the largest building in town, except the cotton gin, which wasn't really in town at all, but just outside of town. It had everything a person would need to plant and harvest a crop, including plows, hoes, harness and it even had seeds as well as feed for cattle, horses, chickens and hogs. It also had groceries as well as patent medicines as well as alcoholic beverages, said to be for medicinal purposes only.

There were also some clothes. Jasper had never had any clothes from the store, although he could always see some there that he would like to have. He was also fond of the suits like the ones that he had seen Mr. Brisley wear when he went on business trips, but they didn't have any that would fit him. He couldn't wait to grow up so he could wear clothes like those.

His mother made all of his clothes except shoes, and during the summer months he had no shoes until Mr. Brisley bought him the shiny new ones that he was wearing, and she made him put those away until he went to town.

"Since he was good enough to get you those shoes, you should take care of them, because you can't expect him to get you another pair for winter," his mother said.

Next door to the store was a livery stable where people could leave their horses and mules if they lived a long ways from town or for some reason they needed to stay in town overnight. Since there was no hotel, people sometimes spent the night in the livery. It was a bit trying, especially for the ladies, because there was only a vertical ladder. But they could climb into the loft and sleep on the hay. It was probably softer than some of their mattresses at home, unless they had enough feathers or duck and goose down to make feather beds. It sometimes took all they could get for pillows because a pillow would sometimes split down a seam and feathers would be scattered around the house and lost.

There was also plenty of hay and grain that could be bought from the wrangler for their stock while they were in town. And some of the townspeople, including the store owner stabled their horses there instead of having their own stables.

A few work horses and a saddle horse or two were always kept at the livery for rent in case someone's horse went lame or for some reason they needed a horse while they were in town or they needed to leave their horse for more than one day to be shod.

The wrangler, Jasper had heard someone say, had been a cowboy in Texas until the year before when he had become so crippled that he could no longer work with cattle, and he had come to the little town and had bought the livery stable. Someone said that he had been fast with a gun, fast enough to have a reputation as a gunfighter. As the story went someone challenged him and he beat the man to the draw with his single shot pistol, then he realized too late that there were two of them. He came there because there was no chance that someone that knew him would find him and he never wanted to shoot it out with another person. Whatever brought him, Jasper had heard that he was friendly with everyone and was easy to get along with.

On one of the rare occasions that he had gone outside and was playing in front of the store, he saw the wrangler sitting in front of the livery on a block of wood cut from a log. He was chewing tobacco and spitting tobacco juice halfway across the road in front of the livery.

Having the natural curiosity of a boy of his age, Jasper's curiosity got the better of him and as he was playing, he was also wandering closer to the livery stable. He didn't want to do anything that would make Mr. Brisley mad, but as he played and moved closer, he was soon near where the wrangler was sitting. He wasn't quite in front of the livery, but he made sure that he was close enough to be noticed. He really didn't know what to expect, but he wanted to see for himself if the man was friendly and would talk to him.

The storekeeper would talk to him when he was not busy or had customers in the store and he had to leave, but he was the only one in town that seemed to notice him. When he was in town he was starved for conversation when he was not with George or the storekeeper's son.

Jasper loved talking to people and listening to their stories of other places and other things. He would listen to someone for hours if he had a chance. Since most of the other kids at the plantation wouldn't let him play with them he usually had plenty of time after he left the Big House in the evening. Sometimes when a group of people would be talking, he would get close enough to hear what they were saying and just listen, unless they were cursing or saying things that his mother had said were bad.

Jasper was beginning to think that the wrangler was going to ignore him like the other people in town. Maybe he wasn't as friendly as he had been told or maybe he just didn't like kids. He kept playing and moving closer until he was in front of the man, and then looked directly at him.

"They call me Wrangler. What's your name, sonny?"

"Jasper, Mr. Wrangler."

"Not Mr. Wrangler; just Wrangler. Out on the big cattle spreads in Texas people sometimes go by what is known as a handle, which they want to be called. When someone gives you a handle instead of a name, like Jasper, they have a reason to want to be called that, so you should respect their wishes."

"Then I'll call you Wrangler. Where is this Texas and what do you mean by a big cattle spread? Do you mean like Mr. Brisley has? He has a lot of land and a lot of cows, and I get to go and bring them into the barn sometimes. I like to do that because most of the time they are in the woods and I can see the animals and birds when I'm there."

"You are quite different from the rest of the workers around here and pretty sharp for your age. If I didn't know that you were from the Brisley plantation, I might have thought that you were one of those little Indians like we have in Texas. Texas is the largest state and it is mostly unsettled except for the large cattle ranches, called spreads. Where I was working they have thousands of acres and they don't know exactly how many cattle they have."

"Why can't they count their cattle I can count to a hundred; do they have more than that?"

"They have more than a thousand. Some have many thousands. They do count them at roundup time. They call it tallying, but by the time they are rounded up and tallied, new calves are born and some of the older ones die, so they never know exactly how many they have at any given time Sometimes rustlers get some of their cattle and that throws off their tally."

"Thousands; gee, but that's a lot. Someday I'll learn to count that high. But what's a rustler?"

"They are thieves; they come by when no one is around and drive away some of the cattle."

"I would like to go there someday and learn to be a cowboy just like you."

"You will never be allowed to go that far from the plantation unless you are freed. Besides, Texas is hundreds of miles from here.

"What does it mean to be freed?"

"You really don't know about freedom? Your family must be protective of your feelings and haven't told you about your situation at the plantation, so I won't shock you by telling you: how old are you?"

"I'm seven but I'm almost eight. I have been asking my mother to tell me about a lot of things, but she always says 'you're too young now' then she sends me out to play. You can tell me anything you want and I won't tell my mother who told me, I promise."

"Your mother will tell you what she wants you to know when she's ready, but I think someone should have told you a long time ago why Mr. Brisley has complete control of everyone and why they can't leave the plantation. If your mother doesn't explain things to you, you will learn as soon as old man Brisley decides that you are old enough to work in the fields. I have seen you work around the store. When you are older and if you are freed and want a job, come and see me."

"I had better get back to the store. I'm not supposed to leave there."

After that, anytime Jasper had a chance to go outside, he made sure that he found a way to get close enough for Wrangler to notice and talk to him. They became good friends and Jasper often thought that he would like to have a chance to work with him. He had been told that there was no better man with horses and cattle in the country and he would like to learn to ride like the cowboys that Wrangler had told him about but he would be afraid to ask if he could help Wrangler because Mr. Brisley would know that he had been outside talking to him and he may be mad and not let him come to town again.

Past the livery was a row of houses where the people lived that worked in the gin and did odd jobs around town. They were small houses; not much larger than the one his family lived in on the plantation; they were built from lumber instead of logs. He could see inside one when the door was opened and he could see that it had wood floors like Mr. Brisley had in the Big House. How he would like to have wood floors in their house.

Then there was the doctor's office, which was not an office at all, but a house where he lived, with a room in front where people would sit while they waited for him to examine them. Would he examine them by looking in their mouths like his mother did him, he wondered? Jasper had never been in the doctor's office so he didn't know what it was like inside, but he would really like to see some of the surgical instrument of which he had heard people talk.

On the other side of the street was the school, which consisted of one large room where one teacher taught kids of all grades, like the one that George had described near the plantation. When the kids would come outside to play, he wished that he could at least go there and play with them but he knew that he didn't even dare ask because his mother had told him that he wasn't even allowed on the school grounds. Mr. Brisley had told him not to even go near the school, but he wouldn't tell him why. He said that was another thing that his mother should have already explained to him.

Then there was the church, which consisted of one large room where people would meet every Sunday. Jasper wondered why his mother and father couldn't come to that church instead of the small one only a little ways from the plantation that Mr. Brisley had been letting them go to for quite a few weeks. Since Jasper had been going to town his father had mentioned a few times that he would like to come to the larger church in town each Sunday.

Of course he knew that very few people from the plantations could go to church at any time, even to the small church nearby, and then the ones from the Brisley plantation had to follow his family to and from church. His father had said that since the bigger church was in town; so far from the plantation, that there was no chance that they would be allowed to attend.

"Mr. Brisley, why can't my father and mother come to this church in town each Sunday?" Jasper asked Mr. Brisley one day as they passed the large church in town.

"You know that no one from the plantation is allowed to come here unless they come with me to work on the gin or haul things home. Your family is lucky that I let them and the two families that follow them go to church; that's because they are so trustworthy and can be depended on to come straight home each Sunday. Most plantation owners don't let any of their people attend church."

"But if we can go to the little church, why can't we come here? You know that in the short time that we have been going to the little church that he has become a deacon and she sings in the choir. He always helps the preacher there and they always talk about the big meetings they have here that they should come to sometimes."

"Why are you so interested in church at your age? You seem to know everything that's going on there."

"My mother hasn't had time to teach me much about reading, but I can read a few words to the kids from the other plantations that come to the little church. None of the other kids can read and they get so excited when I read to them."

"They have only the local people who live in town and the most trusted ones from the closest plantations coming here. The ones that live near my plantation that have special permission attend the little church where you go. Why would you want to come here?"

"They have people from a long ways around town coming here for special meetings and I would have a lot more kids to read to. My father said that there would be a meeting next Sunday that will be very important for him to attend as a deacon. He said that there would be some people from all of the plantations except ours."

"How does he know all of those things when he can't come into town to find out?"

"He somehow knows each time they have a big meeting. The preacher here wants him to come so he can work with him and the one at the little church said it would be all right with him."

"How does he know that?"

"I'm not supposed to tell you this, but the preacher from here sometimes comes to our house in the middle of the night when everyone is asleep and talks to my father, and sometimes I am awake and hear them talking."

"I'll think about it."

"But there is no time to think about it. The important meeting is next Sunday."

"When we get home I'll let you tell your family. They can come to that meeting Sunday."

"But if we can come this Sunday why can't we come every Sunday? We would have time to get here if we leave early, and we would be home early unless there was a special meeting. And even if my father has to get up in the middle of the night and take care of things if there's a storm, or some other bad thing, he is always at work the next day. I heard my father and mother talking about it and they said that they would have plenty of time to get back after the meetings."

"You can tell them that they can hitch up that pair of grays to a wagon each Sunday and come to church here, but they can't bring anyone with them. They may use that as a means to get away."

"Why would they want to get away? They have everything there to use and eat that anyone could ask for. And they have horses and mules that they can use every day. If they want to go somewhere all they need to do in hitch up a team and go. But they would have only Sunday. Of course they would have to ask you."

"I need to talk to your mother about telling you many things about my plantation and the people that work there. I think that she should have explained everything to you long before this."

"Why don't you explain things to me now? When I ask her something she says 'you're too young to understand,' so if you will tell me I won't tell my mother, I promise."

Jasper was always happy when they came into town for church. They would leave home before daylight and after the morning church service they would have a potluck dinner and sometimes stay for the evening service if they had a special meeting; which happened more often than not.

Between services if Jasper would see the wrangler he would go and talk to him. If he didn't see the wrangler he would play with the other kids at church. They would sometimes build a fire in the pot-bellied stove and stay until late at night. That pleased Jasper because he could never stay up late at home.

Next to the church was the large house where the storekeeper lived. It was the largest house in town, larger even than the house where the doctor lived. It was almost as large as Mr. Brisley's house, but it was not as neat and well kept. Jasper knew that the storekeeper usually had no help in the store, except when he would stock the merchandise on the lower shelves and dust everything that he could reach Maybe he was just too busy to keep his house and yard clean.

Then there was the gin foreman's house. It was always neat and clean like Mr. Brisley's house. He probably had people to come and clean and repair his house like Mr. Brisley always did, Jasper thought.

Next to the gin foreman's house was a large horse trough with buckets hanging from pegs on a post nearby to be used by a bucket brigade in case there was a fire in one of the buildings. Jasper had never seen a building on fire, but even at his age he wondered how anyone could throw enough water on a building with a bucket to put out a fire. He remembered that when they built a fire in the woods to cook something that it took a lot of water to put it out.

Past the water trough, off to itself, was a large blacksmith shop with a corral alongside in case someone needed to leave his or her horse to be shod. Jasper wasn't as interested in the blacksmith shop as he was in the other buildings because except for being larger it was like the one on the plantation; and besides, the blacksmith wasn't nearly as friendly as the wrangler or the storekeeper.

Then past the blacksmith shop, off to itself, was what was referred to as the white church which had so many more people in attendance that it needed much more room out front for parking and they had a special shed for horses.

That was another mystery that Jasper would like for his mother to explain to him; why did they need two churches in one town; especially a town that people referred to as being a small town.

Jasper couldn't understand why he could go to town with Mr. Brisley when none of the other kids could go. But he was so happy to go that he thought little of it. The other kids would tease him about being the boss' pet. He didn't mind a little teasing, but he was afraid that Mr. Brisley may hear the teasing and stop taking him.

One day while the other kids were teasing him one of them said, "You ain't lik' th' res' o'us, you don' e'en talk lik' th' res' o' us; you aint nuthin' cept a forriner."

CHAPTER 3

"What could the boy have meant when he said that I don't talk like them and that I am a foreigner? Haven't we always lived here?" Jasper asked his mother.

"Mr. Brisley said that his father had no accent of any kind, but by working with the people here all of the time while he was young, Mr. Brisley said that he was developing an accent. Then his father sent him to the schools up north where he lost his entire accent. He doesn't like the accent that all of the other people here use. He said that his grandfather had even lost most of his English accent after he came here. While I was a young girl he took great pains in teaching me to talk like him, so I taught the rest of the family. The rest of the people think of us as being different," his mother answered.

"But why would they say that I am a foreigner? If I'm a foreigner then you must also be a foreigner."

"You are too young to understand now but Mr. Brisley got your grandmother and me from the neighboring plantation when I was very young. Your grandmother and I lived in the little room out back and we did all of the housework for Mr. Brisley until the man died that lived in the house that we live in now, then your grandmother moved there. Even though I was young Mr. Brisley kept me here to do the housework. When your father and I married we moved into the house with your grandmother. I have always worked here in the Big House. Some of the others seem to be jealous because I have never had to work in the fields as they must. The only time they really associate with me is when they want me to do something for them."

"Too young to understand; all I ever hear is 'you're too young to understand,' Will I ever be old enough to understand anything?"

"Hush up child and go outside to play. You're going to get me to tell you things that I don't want to tell you now. Wait until you're older and then I'll explain everything that you need to know about life here on the plantation."

"Is that why grandma was telling you one night that she wished that she was back on the other plantation with grandpa?"

"Yes, the neighbor refused to let your grandpa leave. I don't think that Mr. Brisley would ever permit one person to leave and keep the other, and split up a family for any reason."

"What do you mean, let grandpa leave? Can't he leave and come here with grandma if he wants? Why would he let grandma leave and not grandpa?"

"You are entirely too young for those things and I have already said more than I intended, so you just go outside and play."

"George is gone and the older kids won't let me play with them and the younger ones want to play their silly little games. None of them will go into the woods with me. But I sometimes play where I can hear the older kids talk. I wish you would tell me why some of them keep talking awful about Mr. Brisley and talking about running away; why can't they leave when they want? But I remember having to get Mr. Brisley's permission to go to the church in town."

"Everyone here needs Mr. Brisley's permission to go anywhere or to do anything; even when they go to the fields each day. You have been sheltered from many of the problems and ordeals everyone else has by coming here with me each day and there are a lot of things that I haven't told you. But one of these days, to keep someone else from hurting you badly by telling you, I will have to explain by telling you things that I should tell you myself."

"Why can't you tell me now? I'm old enough to understand anything that you tell me."

"I will explain everything, but I'm trying to wait until you're older, so just go outside and play."

For years Jasper's mother had been deathly afraid that someone would explain that he was a slave and could never do anything except work on the plantation and be told what he could or could not do. Presently he considered himself equal to Mr. Brisley and his son George, but he was not. He was considered an inferior member of the human race; an asset owned by Mr. Brisley to be bartered sold or traded, as he desired.

She was afraid that if he learned his actual status that he would lose his unquenchable desire to learn and would resign himself to being like a pawn, to be moved and used at will. She knew that someday soon she would have no choice but to tell him because he was becoming so inquisitive that someone with malice in his or her heart, if they knew that he didn't know his situation would take pleasure in telling him things that would hurt him deeply.

When he was allowed to go to town with Mr. Brisley, which was not as often as when the cotton was being picked, Jasper was not allowed to roam the town freely like the kids who lived in town.

He had become such good friends with the storekeeper's son and was always helping with the work at the store, that even when there was no work for him to do, he was allowed to stay at the store while Mr. Brisley was taking care of business. Along with George and the storekeeper's son Ralph who was a year older than he was, he had become acquainted with many of the kids who would come into town and the ones that lived in town.

When he was working in the store or loading things for customers, even though he was too young to realize it at the time, he was learning a lot about business which would be a great benefit to him during his lifetime.

When George would go to play with kids of his own age Ralph would sometimes go around town with Jasper so he wouldn't have to stay at the store until Mr. Brisley came for him.

Jasper really liked Ralph. He thought that he was the smartest kid he had ever met, including George, even if George was two years older and two grades ahead of Ralph. He was also very large and strong for his age. He had brown hair and blue eyes like his father, but he was heavier built. He didn't look or act like he would be a storekeeper when he grew up.

"Why don't you help your father more at the store?" Jasper asked Ralph one day.

My father said that I have plenty of time to learn to work in a store, if we still have it when I'm older. He wants me to watch and learn everything I can while I'm young so that I don't always have to work in a store. He said that he began working in the store right out of school and that's the only kind of work that he knows."

"But you already have a store."

My father says that the store is not all his and someday he may not have it."

"He tells you all of those things? When I ask my father anything he always says for me to ask my mother. When I ask my mother anything she always says 'you're too young to understand now.'"

"You are not too young to understand. You can write and do your numbers better than me, and you can read just as well."

"Oh she teaches me those things, but she won't answer most of my questions."

Even though George was three years older than Jasper, his father had given him no responsibilities and he was free to do as he pleased. Jasper wondered why Mr. Brisley had him doing things at his age that George had no knowledge of doing. He wondered why he didn't teach George to do something; just anything productive so that he would at least know what problems the men would be coping with when he told them what to do. But on rare occasions when he would have them working together on something, while Mr. Brisley was there helping them and showing them how, George was at least getting his hands into things, but without any particular interest, then when Mr. Brisley would leave, so would George. When George was in school, when Mr. Brisley had time he would stay with Jasper and show him and explain to him in detail what he wanted done.

Jasper had overheard some of the men talking about George. They agreed that he would grow up useless and of no account for doing things on his own and they said that he would never be the man that his father was. They said that he would be foot loose and fancy free.

Even though Jasper liked to run in the woods and play with George he agreed with the men because when it came time for building things such as rafts he had to do all of the hard work because George was almost useless to him. He was always ready to play but when the play turned to work, he was uninterested, even when his help was badly needed.

When there were no loads to take and Mr. Brisley had no reason to go to town, George would be at the plantation alone all day unless Mr. Brisley would let Jasper play with him; he usually let George do whatever he wanted, so George would usually take Jasper away from whatever he was doing and they would play together for hours at a time. They would go into the woods and pretend that they were hunting; they had sticks that looked like guns and wood bows and arrows. They would sometimes just hike through the woods pretending that they were Indian scouts for a hunting party or for a detachment of soldiers that they had heard people talk about.

When they were going across ground soft enough to leave a slight depression, they would take turns, one going ahead and the other one tracking him. Although George would lose Jasper's trail easily, he would sometimes go ahead and make turns, brushing out his tracks with a limb, even crawling for a short distance, but he could never fool Jasper. They became adept at tracking each other, but George was jealous because Jasper was much better than he was at following a trail.

Jasper always wanted to go completely through the woods to see what was on the other side, but George was afraid, so they would go only to the edge of the swamp where they had seen the snakes and then return home.

The swamp was a source of fear for many of the workers; none of the other kids dared go there. They had a lot of sayings about what was there. Some said that there were panthers there that would attack anyone they saw. Some said that there were alligators large enough to swallow a man whole. Some said that there were snakes fast enough to catch a grown man. But one thing that everyone agreed on; there were places where quicksand was so bad that it would pull a man or a large animal under in a short time.

Jasper couldn't understand George being so afraid of going all the way through the woods because that's where he said that the cute little girl that he went to school with and that he was so fond of lived. He said that he always played with her when his father visited there and took him along. Jasper would like to see the cute little girl that George was so fond of. He thought that if he were as fond of her as George was, he wouldn't let a little swamp keep him from going there, but Mr. Brisley would never take him so he could see if she was as cute as George said she was.

Jasper thought quite often about his mother and Mr. Brisley as well as the other people saying that he looked like an Indian and he really liked the bow and arrows that George and he had made. But he wanted to get some real game like the workers got while they were hunting with the dogs. One day he asked George about taking one of the dogs with them that were on the plantation.

There were dogs always running lose, seeming to belong to no one in particular, but they were good hunting dogs, always ready to go with anyone that would take them hunting. They didn't have to worry about being fed because any time anyone had bones or scrap food left they would throw it out and the dogs would always find it. They were just mongrels and even though they had no real training they were good trackers.

"We don't have to hunt with dogs and cut trees like the workers, who can hunt only at night and can carry only saws and axes. We have guns and bows. You can be an Indian and carry the bow and arrows and I'll be the white hunter and carry the gun."

"I would like to have a real bow and some real arrows like the real Indians have, that will kill game. We can't kill anything; only make believe hunt."

"You can have your bow and arrows. I'll take a gun anytime, like my father always carries."

"Oh, I would like to have a gun also. When I grow up I'm going to be an Indian."

"You can't just be an Indian. My father says that you look

like an Indian but you have to be born an Indian to be as good in they woods as they are."

"I can too learn to be an Indian when I get older. You'll see."

"You can't even shoot a real arrow with a real bow."

"I know, but when I grow up I'll have a real bow with real arrows and a gun. I'll learn to shoot either of them."

"You always think about things that you will never be able to do. You'll have to do the things that my father tells you to do like the other workers. You won't be allowed to have a gun; you can hunt only with saws and axes; taking a dog along to tree game for you."

"You'll see. When I grow up I don't want to plow fields like my father and all of the other men. I want to see all of the places that Mr. Brisley and the other people have been talking about. The man who has the livery stable in town, who wants to be called Wrangler, was telling me about a place called Texas and another place called New Orleans and even a place over mountains so high that there is snow on the peaks all year called California."

"You left the store after my father told you not to?"

"I didn't really leave the store? I was only out front."

"You went and bothered the wrangler?"

"He talked to me first."

"If I tell my father you will never again be allowed to go to town."

"Then I will never, ever play with you again or help you build any more rafts or push them along the river. You can't build or even handle one alone."

"I promise that I won't tell if you'll help me finish the raft we're building. Why do you want to talk to the wrangler anyway? He's just an old cripple."

"He is not just an old cripple. He's the smartest man I have ever talked to. He knows about cattle and horses and lots of places that I had never heard of."

"What do you mean smart? He only takes care of horses and mules. You don't have to be smart to feed livestock."

"He didn't just feed livestock before he came here. He knows all about guns and Indians and he even told me about a place by Texas called Mexico, I won't tell you what he said about Mexico because you wouldn't believe me anyway,"

"So what, my father knows about all of those places."

"But he hasn't been there; Wrangler has."

"What is so smart about learning about New Orleans or Texas or even Mexico? The teacher has already taught us about those places."

"Maybe so, but I can't go to school and learn about them, and you don't teach me everything the teacher teaches you."

"He can't tell me anything about Texas that I haven't already learned in school."

"Did you learn about the big cattle ranches they call spreads? Did you learn that they drive their cattle hundreds of miles to where they sell them? Did you learn that all of the cowboys carry pistols in case they encounter wild animals or snakes? He said that a cowboy could hit a snake with a pistol. They sometimes get into gunfights and kill each other."

"He told you all of that? He was probably lying."

"Smarty, you don't know nearly as much as you think you do. I am not supposed to tell, but he said that's the reason he's crippled. Someone challenged him and he was barely faster with a gun than the other man was and beat him to the draw. That's when he learned that the man had a friend who fired on him. Now, he said, he never wants to see a gun or a gunfighter."

"You can't talk to me like that. My father won't let me whip you because you're younger, but if I tell him how you talked to me, he will be mad and may whip you himself."

"You won't tell him because you know that I will never play with you again. He can make me stay at the Big House but he can't make me play."

"Then I won't teach you what I learn in school. That's all you want me to do; teach you something."

"When I grow up I will find a way to go to school and I'll learn about everything; you'll see."

"You'll see! That's all I ever hear! I won't see because you will never be able to go to school and you will never be able to learn as much as I will."

Jasper, having been provoked until he was very mad, managed to control his temper because he knew that George was right about Mr. Brisley. He bit his lower lip and didn't say any more. He wanted to tell about a lot of other things that he had learned about Texas and about rounding up, branding and herding cattle which he was almost sure that George had never heard about, but he decided that since George was so mad, he would save that for later.

They had already gathered together small logs and built a small raft but they were afraid to venture out into the current and would paddle or use sticks to push the raft along the bank while they were fishing. Now they were building a larger one that would be sturdier and would not tilt as easily and they could handle better. Jasper was really more interested in going up and down the river than he was in fishing. He would daydream about going to faraway places that he had heard some of the workers and Wrangler talk about.

One day while they were fishing Jasper asked, "Why don't we go further out into the river? We could surely get back to the bank."

"I'm afraid to go into the current. You always want to take chances and someday you may get too far out there and drown."

"I only want to see what it would be like. Someday I would like to get on this raft and float down the river to see what the cities are like that I have been hearing about. It would be exciting to go to a city with lots of people and big stores, like Mr. Brisley sometimes talks about, someplace like New Orleans. I wouldn't care if I never got back to where I can't even go to school."

"You may as well forget that because my father says that you belong to him and you will have to stay here and work for him the rest of your life."

"I do not belong to Mr. Brisley. I belong to my father and mother."

"Do too, you just ask your mother sometime."

"I will not have to live here the rest of my life. When I grow up, after I learn to be an Indian, I'm going to Texas and learn about cattle. Then I can learn to be a cowboy and learn to ride a real horse that knows how to herd cattle. Wrangler says that the horses there are much faster than the ones on the plantation and the cowboys can rope steers from their saddles."

"You will have to live here all of your life. You will have no way of leaving."

Jasper didn't know what George meant when he said that he belonged to Mr. Brisley. He didn't believe him, but he decided to ask his mother when he got home. After all, Mr. Brisley had never acted as if he owned him. He had taken him to town and let him do almost everything he wished.

Jasper had noticed that since he turned eight years old, Mr. Brisley had been giving him more to do when he was at the plantation including splitting and bringing in kindling, repairing fences and even helping to repair the equipment. He had been wondering why he could no longer play with George as much and he was never required to help Jasper with the chores. It didn't really matter, because he was never any help even when he was supposed to be helping.

"Why would George say that Mr. Brisley owns me?" Jasper asked his mother when he arrived home.

"I wanted to wait until you were older and could understand, but you are the son of your father and me, but you are the property of Mr. Brisley. He tells you what to do instead of us and he can tell you when you can come and go. You know that I would like for you to go to town with him every trip but you can go only when he allows you to go. He takes his son George more often than he does you."

"But when we're alone he treats me as much like a son as he does George."

"You are entirely too young to understand his reasons, but you will always have to do what the Brisley's say."

"So that's why George said that I could never go to Texas or New Orleans."

"Texas! New Orleans! What do you know about those places?"

"The wrangler told me. He has told me about lots of places that he has been and lots of things that he has done. When I grow up I want to go to all of those places and do all of the things that he has done."

"You don't go bothering him when you're in town. If you get Mr. Brisley mad you will never be allowed to go again."

"He talked to me first and Mr. Brisley knows that I sometimes talk to him. But I want to know how someone can own me."

"We have belonged to Mr. Brisley since before you were born; ever since he bought your grandmother and me from the neighbor. He can tell us what we can do. He may someday tell you to go the fields and work, like all of the others and be treated like the other slaves. He has already mentioned sending you into the fields so that while you're young you can learn what will be required of you, but I have resisted. I have talked him into letting you work with the stock and repair things so you will have experience with the equipment and will be a more valuable slave. As long as Mr. Brisley is in charge you should be able to keep busy in the shop or with the stock and not have to work in the fields with the other slaves. When George is old enough to take over who knows what will happen? He may be lenient like his father, but on the other hand he may continue getting meaner."

"What do you mean slaves? Why didn't you explain such things to me a long time ago? So that's why one man said, 'old man Brisley couldn't make money if he had to pay his help instead of having all of the slave labor.'"

"Yes, a slave belongs to his master. He can sell him, trade him or even set him free. Some plantation owners want to be called Master and are very mean to their slaves, sometimes beating them as if they were no better than animals. Sometimes if a slave does not do his master's bidding he will be tied to a post and whipped like some people whip horses."

"Why didn't you tell me of those things before? I could have made Mr. Brisley mad and he could have whipped me with a horsewhip."

"I don't think he would whip you. Even though Mr. Brisley acts mean sometimes, he is actually a kind and gentle man, not wanting to mistreat anyone. Only when a slave disobeys a direct order or is caught shirking his duties does he punish him, and usually he or she is only restricted. To my knowledge he has never whipped anyone."

"One day while George and I were going fishing we heard

Mr. Brisley talking to one of the men. He said, "I should take the horsewhip to you for leaving without permission, 'please don't whip me Mr. Brisley. I only wanted to see my lady friend that I met the last time we had a picnic. She came with her owner from the next plantation. I'll never do such a thing again without permission,' the man said."

"Then Mr. Brisley said 'I think you have learned your lesson. I'll let you go this time but the next time that happens, no matter who it is; he will get the whipping of his life.'"

Then Jasper said, "George said; 'if I were Dad I would whip him until he couldn't walk so the rest of the hands wouldn't try the same thing.'"

"I've heard that's the way most of the plantation owners treat their slaves. Someday George will be in charge and I hope when that day comes that he will treat you as Mr. Brisley has until now, but he has a mean streak in his character. You should be careful when you're with him because even though I can see no reason for it, he seems to be very jealous of you."

"I'm not afraid of George. He has done nothing until he's weaker than I am. In another year I'm almost sure that I can whip him. But if I'm a slave they you're also a slave."

"Yes, I have always been a slave; first as a child for the neighbor, until Mr. Brisley bought your grandmother and I, and then for Mr. Brisley. No matter what is asked of me, no matter how much I dislike doing what is ordered, I can't refuse his bidding."

"Then how can you talk him into letting me go to town with him and do things that the other slaves can't."

"There are things that I can't explain to you now. When you are older you will figure out a lot of things yourself. But for now I will only tell you that I have been coming here for so long and bringing you that I think that with our relationship like it has always been, he really doesn't want to send you out in the fields like the other slaves."

When Jasper was bringing in wood or repairing things around the house, he could sometimes hear Mr. Brisley instructing George on how the plantation should be managed in case he should be in charge someday. How Jasper would like to have that kind of training. He felt that he would be the best boss there ever was. He would run things just like Mr. Brisley because even though he was very young, he knew that he was a good boss.

"Leave that for later and come with me," George said one day while Jasper was repairing the corral fence.

"Mr. Brisley wants the corral fence repaired so I'm going to finish that."

"You will do what I told you."

"No I won't. Mr. Brisley is my boss."

They were getting into a heated argument until Mr. Brisley came out of the house and stopped them from arguing.

"George will be in charge someday. He must learn how to keep the plantation running smoothly before he takes on all of the responsibilities himself, so while he is out of school he may as well be learning. You may as well get used to having him give you orders." Mr. Brisley told Jasper.

Jasper felt that his whole world had ended. George and he had been in their own little world for years, doing what little kids would do together, but he could no longer feel that he was equal to George, but as if he were inferior. Suddenly he vividly understood what George had meant when he said that Mr. Brisley owned him.

After that every time Jasper would start a job George would come and get him to do something else. Jasper knew that he was doing it to show his authority, but he could do only what George said.

"Why do you move me from a job before I'm finished? I never get through with a job."

"My father told me to plan and have people to do the jobs that need to be done, but he only lets me tell you what to do."

"Your planning is not very good. I already have five jobs started and have completed nothing."

"You can't talk to me like that or I can make it a lot worse for you."

"Then I would leave and you would have no one to work."

"We would find you and then it would really be bad for you."

"If I leave you will never find me."

"Just for that you can go into the fields and hoe cotton and corn."

"I am only nine and no one my age hoes cotton or corn."

"You will work with your grandmother. You will hoe all you can in front of her and she will finish cutting the grass when she comes behind you .When the hoeing is done I may let you come and repair things until cotton-picking time and then you will pick cotton. That will teach you not to argue with me."

Jasper loved his grandmother and even though that job was too hard for someone his age, he was glad that he had been placed with her. After the cultivator had ripped up the grass between the rows, they would take the hoes and cut the grass from between and around the plants

Jasper's grandmother was a big woman, as tall as his mother but heavier. She had a much darker complexion than his mother did. Her hair was not completely black but had a slightly reddish tint. Her eyes were a dark blue gray, almost black color but otherwise she favored her daughter. And she was strong. She was much stronger than any other woman in the field and she was able to hoe all day alongside any of the men, and with what seemed like very little effort she could leave most of them behind.

In keeping with George's mean personality he told Jasper to hoe well ahead of his grandmother so they could not talk to each other. When she came along behind him she could hoe the weeds and grass that he had missed. Jasper was glad when George was not in the field because he could hoe close enough to his grandmother to ask her questions. She would usually answer more of his questions than his mother, and especially his father, would. His grandmother would hoe very fast until she was well ahead of the other slaves, then Jasper would slack off until they were close enough to talk where the others couldn't hear them. They didn't want to give anyone anything to gossip about.

"Grandma," he asked, "Why can't grandpa come here and work so you can live together like my mother and father?"

"You are too young to understand why now, but I was doing the cleaning and cooking at the neighbor's plantation until he came to me one morning and said; 'you and your daughter have been sold to the neighbor, Mr. Brisley, but your husband will remain here.' With no further explanation he told me to pack our few belongings and load them in a wagon, and then he brought us here."

"Do you know why George is getting so mean to me and making me hoe corn and cotton?"

"I heard that you was arguing with him and threatening to leave. You should be careful with him because your mother and I both know that he has a mean streak in his character. He will probably be even harder to work for when Mr. Brisley puts him in charge of the whole plantation. Besides, you are much too young to be thinking about leaving. Where would you go? What would you do? Even if you were old enough to work for a living no one would hire you. If you asked for a job they would bring you back here hoping there would be a reward offered."

"He makes me so mad! I know that I couldn't leave; I would have no place to go except in the woods, but if I did leave he would never find me. If I had a real bow and some arrows and a knife and hatchet, I could live like the Indians live."

"You know, you are so independent that it wouldn't surprise me if you did try to leave, but it would be much worse for you when they did find you."

When George was in the field watching him, although to Jasper's knowledge his father had given him no authority to do so, he was usually also watching the other slaves; prodding them to do more work and keeping them upset.

Too soon to suit Jasper, the day came that Mr. Brisley became more ill and put George in charge of the whole plantation. His son, who wanted to be called Master George, began changing the way things were done. That was when things really changed for Jasper. From that day forward he was never allowed to go to the Big House and he was only rarely allowed to repair things, but was kept in the fields with the other slaves.

One day while Jasper was following the old mules, he was daydreaming about the times that he was allowed to go to town with Mr. Brisley. He missed those trips; those were the highlight of his younger years, and he resented having to work like the men at his age. At thirteen he was the strongest boy of his age, even stronger than most of the older boys. He could handle the plow as well as most of the men. But he couldn't understand why he was required to plow that year especially with a double moldboard plow, which was called a middle buster pulled by two mules when the other boys his age only cleared away brush and helped their fathers or carried water for the crews.

Another thing that had started bugging him lately; his mind had a tendency to run away with him. He had all of those daydreams to contend with every day while he was working; dreams of going places and doing great things. Dreams that he could not squelch even if he tried; he was that intelligent and ambitious; delving into any mystery and trying to solve any problem that came to mind. Not only was he learning to read better and learning some arithmetic, but also his mother had talked Mr. Brisley into letting him have a book at a time to read and he had been studying everything that he could get his hands on. Learning would be much easier if he had a teacher to answer his questions, but he had studied some spelling as well as geography and other things that he had time for after work.

He knew that was one thing that Mr. Brisley would not let Master George do; interfere with his reading and studying. As long as he did his work during the day, his evenings were his to use as he pleased.

Even if it took until well after dark to take care of the stock, milk the cow and do the other chores, since the other boys would have nothing to do with him, he had plenty of time to himself. He had conditioned himself to need very few hours of sleep so he could study late at night; until someone yelled for the lamp to be blown out.

Master George had become so distant and aloof that he had nothing to do with the slaves and seemed to be afraid to come near them at night, so he had no worry about Master George seeing him burn the midnight oil.

He liked all of the other subjects but geography and mathematics were his favorite topics; geography because he wanted to go to all of the faraway states; especially Texas and California. Arithmetic because he had been reading about banks and bankers in the large cities; about lawyers who represented people for a fee; about doctors, not merely like the one in town, but the ones in the cities, said to be able to cure almost anything.

He had decided that almost everything that he had studied

about involved knowing about business in one way or another. Even at his age, he had decided that he wanted to learn whatever he could about business, but he couldn't decide if he would like to be a lawyer, a doctor or a banker. He had seen a doctor and a lawyer come to Mr. Brisley's house, but he had never seen a banker, but from what he had read he knew that they were all good professions. He had also read that they all made money, lots of money, and for years he had daydreamed about having money,

He had also seen Mr. Brisley shell out money to people; had watched neighbors and Mr. Brisley when they had their Sunday picnics make marks on the ground and throw dollars at them. Whoever was the closest to the mark with his dollar picked up all of the dollars; he imagined that a handful of money would last him forever. But he had no way of getting money. Oh, he had a couple of pennies that he had found but he was afraid to show them to anyone, thinking that they may take them away from him.

He had already decided that when he grew up that he would leave the plantation and do something different. Somewhere else! Anything different! Anywhere else!

It had been bad enough the last few years when he had to hoe cotton and corn and was forced to keep up with the men, but this was ridiculous. Why would even a mean minded man like Master George expect that of him, he wondered? Why only him? He could understand if he had been obnoxious toward him but he had not argued with him or threatened to leave since he had been sent to the fields. So why had he been singled out to take the brunt of Master George's wrath? Could he be jealous for some reason? What possible reason could he have for being jealous? Someday he would ask him.

When they had a chance to be alone he would ask his grandmother why she thought that Master George would be jealous or why he was so mean to him. He thought she had almost told him when he was younger while they were hoeing cotton and he asked about his grandpa, but she suddenly changed the subject and would not discuss it again.

"Why did you want me to plow this year when I'm only thirteen? I am the youngest one out here and this is awfully hard work, even for me." Jasper asked Master George one day.

"Why should you get any special privileges? You're nothing but a slave, just like the others."

The reality of him being a slave and that he would forever be told what to do suddenly overwhelmed Jasper. He had merely been doing what he was told to do to the best of his ability, keeping himself out of trouble. Then he well remembered what his mother had told him many years before after George had told him that Mr. Brisley owned him.

Until Master George was in charge of him he had given little though to being a slave because he had been doing repair work and working with the stock, which were both things that he enjoyed. He had felt more like a son to Mr. Brisley, just doing what was asked of him. They had been more like requests than orders.

Then Master George became his boss and put him in the fields and he realized what being a slave really meant. He was supposed to have no mind of his own and do only what he was told, but he definitely had a mind and he was determined to use it. He went along with Master George in order to get along, but he resented every minute of his mistreatment.

Jasper remembered when he was younger and had been treated so much differently. Had he not been able to play with George when he was young and not been allowed to go to town with Mr. Brisley, and have been treated like the other kids he may have been more content to do what he was told and have paid no attention to how he was being treated. But he had learned that there was a better life and he yearned for the day that he would be free to come and go as he pleased. There were many places that he wanted to go and so many things that he wanted to see. Someday!

"Do you think that we will ever be free?" Jasper asked his mother.

Since Mr. Brisley and George were late getting home and his mother had to stay at the Big House until they came home, he had sneaked in so she could teach him more about reading and begin teaching him about keeping books.

"Where did you get the idea of freedom? You shouldn't even mention freedom when Mr. Brisley or Master George can hear you."

"All of the talk among the slaves is that they will be freed soon, and they will be getting paid for their work. Some of them think that they will be instantly rich. They think that they will have their own horses and wagons and can travel wherever they want and buy whatever they want to eat and won't have to eat only the type of food that Mr. Brisley provides for them."

"I'm afraid it won't be that simple. Since I have been helping Mr. Brisley with his books I know that it takes most of his income to buy supplies and food for so many slaves. He doesn't know that I understand everything about his books, but I have been studying in his library when everyone is gone and I have my work done. If I needed to I could do his complete books quite well."

"I have heard rumors that the north is trying to free the slaves."

"Mr. Brisley usually knows a lot about what is happening and he usually shares what he learns with me because he knows that I don't gossip, but he has said nothing lately to indicate what he has heard. He did say once that it looked like there would be a war between the northern and southern states before long."

"Has he said how he feels about the slave situation? Will he be able to continue hiring the crew that he has if he has to pay them?"

"He doesn't say if he has enough money saved to continue operating the plantation during a transition period, but I know that he has never completely recovered from the money he spent trying to cure his wife before she died. I accidentally discovered that he has some funds that he never mentioned, but I don't know how much money is involved. He doesn't share all of his financial information with me. I do know that his reserve operating funds are lower than they were when I began helping with his books."

CHAPTER 4

Each year Jasper had become more and more discontent with life on the plantation and at sixteen he was thinking more about what would happen to him in later life. Would he forever be under bondage to the Brisley's and be tied to that plantation as Master George had said so many years before, and always be told what to do or would the day come when he would be able to make his own decisions? After all, the other slaves had been talking more and more about rumors they had heard that someday soon they would be freed.

But how would they hear rumors when they could not leave the plantation for any reason. He knew that the pastor from town would still sometimes come during the night to confer with his father about some problem in the church that needed to be tended to that they had no chance to discuss during meetings. But he knew that his father was no gossip, even if the pastor had mentioned freedom. So how would they get the idea that they would be freed, especially in a short time?

But would that ever happen or were they only rumors possibly started by one person from their wishful thinking. If it did happen would he know enough about things other than working on the plantation to make a living somewhere else? He knew that he was much better than any of the other slaves when they were doing mechanical things; repairing the equipment such as wagon wheels and he had repaired a wagon bed once and Mr. Brisley had complemented him saying that it was as good as new, which made him proud.

But he also knew that he would never work for Master

George if he were no longer a slave. If he should ever be freed all they would see of him would be his backside as he left the plantation. They wouldn't even see that much if he left before he was freed.

The more deeply he dwelled on the subject, the more he wondered how they could hear so many rumors because now that Master George was in charge, they couldn't leave the plantation without his permission and he would never permit them to leave for any reason. He had become awfully mean to them; punishing them in ways that Mr. Brisley would never have done; either whipping them until they begged or making them work many extra hours, and sometimes both punishments, for any infringement of the rules that he had set for them since he had taken over the operation of the whole plantation.

Some of the rules would be almost impossible to comply with on a daily basis; some rules that he seemed to make up when he wanted to punish someone. They were afraid to do anything without being given a direct order. If they did anything and everything went as it should, Master George would have nothing good to say, but if anything went wrong, no matter how trivial and no matter how many good things they had done in the past, they would be punished.

He was afraid for them to leave even for a Sunday meeting at the little local church, just a short distance away; for fear that they would escape. He wouldn't even take a person to town to load for him; he would go alone and hire someone in town to load the supplies that he would buy for the slaves and he was more conservative in the goods that he bought for them; withholding any special things that Mr. Brisley would sometimes bring them.

Jasper wasn't sure but he thought that he could see a slight bulge under his clothing, indicating a concealed weapon, of which he was sure that Mr. Brisley would not approve. With his mostly uncontrolled temper, he thought, that would be an act of violence waiting to happen; and Jasper was sure in his own mind that if it was a weapon, someday it would happen.

He was not afraid for them to go hunting at night because they were so afraid of the swamp that they would never go by there at night and they would have to come by the Big House to leave without going through the swamp. But he was so afraid that they would leave that he would not let them go out to collect black walnuts, hickory nuts and pecans or to pick wild persimmons, which grew in profusion around the house. For them to go for that purpose the foreman had to accompany them; the foreman being the only one that Master George seemed to trust and for whom he seemed to have any compassion.

Surely Mr. Brisley didn't condone that kind of treatment, Jasper thought, but he had sometimes been confined to the house for days, sometimes for a week or more at a time.

The only ones that could leave the plantation for any reason was Jasper's family when they went to church on Sunday and Master George had threatened to stop them. But Jasper was sure that Mr. Brisley had given him no authority to stop them from going each Sunday or he would have enforced his order and would keep them on the plantation.

Being allowed going to town for church on Sunday was a thrill for the rest of the family and Jasper enjoyed it as well. He was especially grateful for the opportunity to talk to Wrangler, but he yearned to go other places and to see other things and since he had been treated so badly it was awfully tempting to leave from town. But they would surely catch him and then his family as well as he would forever be restricted to the plantation. If he left and did get away his family would be restricted or worse yet, punished, so he would feel that he would in effect be punishing them.

Jasper couldn't understand how the wrangler could resign himself to staying in the little town and taking care of the livery after being so many places and seeing so many things. But Jasper could see that since he wasn't under bondage, staying there might not be so bad especially since he had been crippled. Anyway, if he was happy there, Jasper was happy for him, and he was happy that the wrangler had taught him so much.

Some of the slaves from he neighboring plantation had already escaped to the north, but no one had heard from any of them, to know whether or not they had been able to find work that would permit them to make a decent living in the cities to the north. Since Master George had been in charge some of Mr. Brisley's slaves had tried to escape but they had always been caught before they were hardly out of sight; then brought back and whipped by Master George. That discouraged the others so there had been no attempts recently. The ones that had left had then been more restricted and could go only to the fields to work and then come directly home and they could not leave their homes after dark even to go hunting. That put an additional strain on Mr. Brisley's budget because they had always eaten everything they caught.

Jasper had heard of some instances where, if a slave had served his master long and well, he would set him or her free and let them leave the plantation. If a slave got too old to do farm work or was not needed anymore, especially if his master was short of money and couldn't afford to feed him, he would give the slave a letter setting him free. There was no chance of that happening on the Brisley plantation because since Master George had taken over, even if he didn't need all of the slaves, he was so hungry for power that he would never set one free.

Before dark one evening Mr. Brisley came home with a person in the wagon that Jasper felt sure was a slave. He was plowing near the road when they passed and he was wondering why they would need another slave because they were almost finished with their early spring plowing and they would have plenty of help for the summer hoeing and the fall harvesting and there were always more slaves than they needed during the cold winter months. When they stopped, Jasper could see him get out and he was just walking around and looking at everything when Jasper left the field. On his way to the barn with the mules he happened to meet the man. He really didn't just happen to meet him; he was so curious that he made sure that their paths crossed.

"My name is Jasper," he said, extending his hand.

"I'm Rufus. You the onliest one talk t'me. Been hyar two hour'n nobody see me," he said as they shook hands.

"Oh, they must have seen you but Master George is so strict on them that they are afraid to even slow down until the stock is taken care of and the chores are done."

"But they don' e'en say hello."

"Come into the barn with me while I take care of these mules, then I'm going in for supper. Are you hungry?"

"I'm stahved. Your Mistuh Brisley was th' onliest one offer me food."

Not only did the man go into the barn with Jasper, he helped him take care of the mules and feed them. He had been working them hard and they were wet with sweat. While he was removing the harness, Rufus threw in some hay, threw in a few ears of corn, and with an old rag, began rubbing them down. Jasper had never seen anyone more efficient when they were taking care if stock, None of Mr. Brisley's slaves ever bothered rubbing down mules, or horses either, for that matter, unless they were Mr. Brisley's personal stock, and then they did it while complaining. Of course they had a habit of complaining about almost everything.

When they were washed and at the table, after Jasper's father said grace, his mother told Rufus to dig in and they more or less watched as Rufus ate. It was a good thing that his mother had cooked plenty of food because he was not only good with stock, he could put away turnip greens, cornbread and sweet potatoes faster than anyone Jasper had ever seen. He could swipe a chicken leg through his mouth and suddenly there would be nothing except bone. He ate as if he hadn't had any food for a long time. When they were through eating they pushed their chairs beck from the table, as was customary with them, waiting for dessert.

"It must have been a long time since you have eaten," Jasper said.

"Been three days now. Don' let ennbody set you free less'n you got a way up nawth. Been free three week'n near stahved three times. Nobody'l pay you ennythin' 'n won't e'en let you work fer keep. Don' know how far nawth is but I been walkin' fer thar hopin' fer a job thar iff'n I e'er get thar."

"How did you ever manage to get here?"

"Hitched a ride wit' a man wit' a load o' cotton. Was in town hungry an' your Mistuh Brisley say if I work fer a few days he'll see I'm fed 'n give me food fer my tote sack. He say he hev plenty help 'n don' need me but he'll do it ennyway."

"That's our Mr. Brisley. He always helps when he sees someone in trouble."

"He shore don' good fer me."

"You say you're free? Have you got something to show in case you're stopped?"

"Got my paper rat cheer, but I'se so ol' nobody notice me." He said as he produced a piece of writing paper from his pocket. "Know ennybody kin read?"

"Yes, I can read."

"Howd'ja learn t'read. Ain't ne'er seed a slave kin read."

"Mr. Brisley taught my mother and she taught me. She can read, write and do arithmetic better than most people."

"Rat proud o' yore mommy I see."

"I'm very proud of her. If we are ever freed she can operate a business and take care of the books like anyone else. Maybe someday that will not be only a dream but a reality; someday!"

"Iff'n I was aroun' an' yo'all got freed I'd work fer nuthin' 'cept a place t'stay 'n vittles."

"We can't promise you anything because we may never be free," his mother said.

Jasper glanced at the paper and found that it was indeed a letter from his former master releasing him.

"Pleas' read it t'me. My master say, 'hyar yore walkin' paper, now git fore I change my mine.'"

"Do you know why he released you?"

"My master say; money too hard t'git. He say he cain't keep e'er'body. Said I'se too old t'cut th' mustard 'n let me leave."

Jasper read, "This letter is to serve as official notice that Rufus is hereby set free from this plantation to come and go as he pleases." It was signed and dated by his former owner.

"Mr. Brisley always says 'when someone gives you a paper that you don't want to lose, you should take it to the county recorder's office and have it recorded.' You should do that in case the original gets lost or destroyed." Jasper's mother said.

"You folks shore know lots fer slaves, but I don' e'en have a dolluh. But I'll 'member that iff'n I e'er git up nawth. My master say e'er thin' different up nawth an' I c'n work fer pay n' make a livin' up thar. Don' really know wh't workin' fer pay would be lik' but iff'n I git thar I'll try."

"Since you have your bedroll along you can stay here if you don't mind sleeping on the floor."

"I thank'ee Mam. Rat now I'd sleep a'standin' up iff'n I had to. Ain't had a good night's sleep fer weeks."

"At your age are you sure that you want to go north and try making a living in one of the large cities?" Jasper's mother asked. "No one here knows how hard it is to get a job there or how much money they pay, but we have heard that it is hard to make a living there."

"Reckon not. I wouldn'tve lef iff'n I warn't run off."

"I'll talk to Mr. Brisley. He needs someone to take care of his horses and other livestock. He has some prize stock that needs special care and he doesn't have anyone to spare now that is good enough with stock to suit him. Jasper has already told me how good you are with livestock."

"I'd be in yore det'."

"Mr. Brisley left on the boat down the river to see his doctor and take care of some business after he brought you, so you can start tomorrow and I'm sure that when he returns he will let you stay. He will be gone for a week so when he returns if he doesn't let you stay you will have worked enough to earn your food to take with you. You can go ahead and move into the room alongside the stalls. You can come here for your meals until you can get a table in there. You probably noticed a small stove in one corner."

"I'm forev'a in yore det'."

"We will enjoy your company and since Jasper is the most particular person on this plantation about the treatment of livestock I'm sure that with his recommendation that Mr. Brisley will be impressed and let you stay if you decide you want to." His mother said.

"You folks don' treated me rat nice an' yore Mistuh Brisley'll have t'run me off t'git rid o'me."

"Are you sure that won't make Master George mad when he finds out?" Jasper asked.

"I'll take the chance. I won't turn this man out with no place to go and no food, especially at this time of night and with a storm coming."

"Since Master George took over from Mr. Brisley he is much stricter with the slaves but he still allows us to go to church. Do you want to go with us to church in town Sunday? Since you don't belong to Mr. Brisley, they won't care if you go," Jasper's father asked.

"Shore would; we warn't 'lowed t'leave; our master ne'er let us go t'church."

"We leave before daylight and sometimes we don't get home until after dark."

"S'all rat wi' me. I'll be ready."

During the times that they didn't have plowing or harvesting to do, when the weather permitted, they were constantly clearing new fields, sometimes adjoining previously cleared ground. They would find a fairly level place, sometimes only a few acres in size where the trees were not too large. It would sometimes be completely surrounded by woods with only a road from a field that had been cleared to the new one. If a person didn't know the clearing was there and go on that road, he would never see the new field. It would grow better crops than the soil that had been planted to cotton year after year. They would cut the trees, clear and burn the brush, pull all except the largest stumps and plant cotton or watermelons the first few years.

One day while Jasper was plowing in just such a clearing, completely alone, he noticed a young rabbit near the edge of the clearing where he was working. He needed to let the team rest anyway, so he decided to try catching it. After all, he had been working since daybreak and he thought that he needed a break himself. So he tied the team of mules and started stalking the rabbit. It would go into a pile of brush and he would sometimes be reaching for it when it would bolt for the next pile. He was so engrossed in his stalking that he hadn't noticed how long he had been in the woods. When he came back to his plow, Master George was waiting for him along with Mr. Brisley's foreman.

Mr. Brisley's foreman was a big burley brute of a man over six feet tall, weighing over three hundred pounds and he was black; as black as the ace of spades someone had said. His arms were as large as some people's legs and there seemed to be no limit to his strength. He was a bachelor whom everyone was afraid of because he looked so mean. Everyone that is except Jasper and he felt something approaching fear since Master George had been in charge. They were almost always together while the slaves were working. Jasper wondered if Master George didn't always have the foreman with him in case he needed protection because the slaves would have had ample reason to get violent because he had been so mean to them. Jasper wondered why he had never married, but, he thought, maybe he is too mean.

Feeling that the foreman was mean was new to Jasper because he was also the plantation blacksmith and he could remember when George and he would go through the blacksmith shop. The foreman was always friendly and would do almost anything that they wished of him including making straps and bands for their projects, rawhide strings for their bows and to tie their rafts together.

He would also let them stay where it was warm while he worked. Jasper would watch him when he would throw coal and coke or clinkers into the forge, turn the crank that operated the bellows and stick the end of a piece of steel in the fire until it was red hot. He could then shape it into almost anything. He was so strong and handled large pieces of steel so easily that Jasper always had the feeling that he could crush an ordinary man with his bare hands.

He seemed to be proud of his abilities and he was usually showing them how to do whatever they would need to know in order to do their own blacksmith work. Even though Jasper had been young then he had never forgotten what he had learned, but George never seemed to be interested. To Jasper it seemed that he never wanted to do anything except to play in the woods.

Jasper remembered when George and he were watching the blacksmith shoe a horse that had never been shod. When he would try to pick up a hoof the horse would try to kick him. He couldn't move around much because he was tied to a post, but that didn't affect his hoof.

"Why don't you tie his leg to a post and make him stand?" George asked.

"That would scare him so bad that you would always have trouble getting shoes on him."

"How will you ever get him shod?"

"You two just watch and don't make any fast moves to scare him and he'll settle down in a few minutes."

The blacksmith grabbed a hind leg and he was so strong that when the horse tried to kick, he hung on and let him kick. When the horse stopped kicking he straddled the leg and the horse settled down and stood still.

He cut away the excess hoof, shaping the front of it round, he then used a rasp to smooth the edges. He took a horseshoe and put it on the hoof and looked at one side of the hoof, then the other side. Then he took it to the forge and heated it until it was red-hot. He took it to the anvil with the tongs and hit it a few times with the hammer. When it cooled it fit perfectly.

"How did you know how many times to hit it?" Jasper asked. "It looked like it fit the first time you put it on his hoof."

"You learn only be experience. The first time you might have to heat it many times before it fits. It has to fir perfectly or it will get dirt and stones between it and the hoof and sometimes come off when the horse goes through a rocky area. You call that throwing a shoe."

Jasper worried about the horse. He wondered what would happen when he grabbed some square nails that had been tapered to a sharp point. Would he drive a nail into the middle of the hoof? Instead he bent the nail slightly and turned the bent point out. When he drove it into the hoof the bent point came out of the side of the hoof. He clinched the end against the hoof.

"When you shoe a horse clinch each nail after you drive it, because a horse's hoof, if he should kick with a lot of nails sticking out of his hoof, could tear a man up," the foreman said.

"What were you doing in the woods when you should have been working?" Master George asked Jasper before he was even near his plow. He gave the impression that he was so anxious to make an issue out of the situation that he couldn't wait, and Jasper was sure that he had a pleased look on his face as he questioned him. Master George's expressions always showed his feelings in a matter and Jasper had been with him so much in their younger years that he could almost read; "Ah-hah, I finally caught you doing something wrong."

"I saw a baby rabbit and I was trying to catch it."

"You know that you are not to leave your plow for any reason, so you will have to be whipped as an example to the other slaves"

"What's so bad about stalking a rabbit? I needed to stop for a few minutes to let the mules rest anyway. I have been plowing more every day than any of the others."

"That's not the point. I know that you plow more each day than the others do. If you had just stopped to let the mules rest, that would have been different, but you have set a bad example for the others by leaving your plow."

"There's no one that can see me."

"That's not the point either. You broke one of the rules that I have set for the slaves of the plantation. You left your plow and now you are arguing with me. You know better than to argue with me. My father protected you while he was in charge, but now I decide who will be whipped."

"Suppose that I only plowed at the same speed as the others. I would get a lot less done. I have already plowed more today than any of the others will have plowed by the end of the day."

"Then you would be whipped for not trying."

"Then why don't you whip everyone each day because you know that some of them are not trying very hard?"

"You will be whipped and that's final."

Jasper knew that there would be nothing gained by arguing with Master George, even though the offense was not so bad as to provoke a beating. Besides, there was no one close enough to see him leave his plow, but he had decided that he would take a beating rather than to plead with Master George as he had heard others do. Pleading had never, to his knowledge, changed the punishment they were to get, but he could see that the pleading had thrilled Master George.

Jasper remembered how Master George had whipped some of the others in the past and he knew that it wouldn't be a pleasant experience. But he thought that since they had played together and had been such good friends for so many years that he wouldn't be too hard on him. After all what was so bad about taking a few minutes off? Usually they would be whipped because they would leave the plantation trying to run away or would sneak away to another plantation to see someone they knew from the days when they had the Sunday meetings at the Brisley plantation. Mr. Brisley had been so much more lenient with the slaves than Master George was; they seldom did anything for which to be punished.

When all of the men were finished with their work that evening, Master George told them to wait for him at the barn before leaving for home. When everyone was gathered and Master George came, he told the foreman; "Jasper is in the rear stall. Take his shirt off and then bring him here and tie him to that post for me. Put a gag in his mouth because I don't want to hear him yell and plead."

"I'm sorry that I have to do this, Jasper, but you know that I have to do what Master George says," the foreman said as he was getting him ready.

"I know it's not what you would rather be doing now, and I understand. You don't have to gag me to keep me from pleading with George and he knows it. That is just to humiliate me in front of the other slaves or he would whip me in private."

"Master George never whips anyone in private. That would never satisfy him. Be careful about not calling him Master because he gets awfully mad if someone just calls him George."

"Master George is always mad at someone. He seems to enjoy whipping people."

"Just be careful and don't upset him. The more upset he gets the harder he whips."

If Master George was trying to humiliate Jasper he did a good job. He was not only humiliated but as he was being whipped he was thinking more and more about being free.

Free? Free from Master George? He may get loose but he would never be free from him. He would hunt Jasper forever if need be and he knew it. The only way to really be free from Master George was if they were all freed or Master George died, and then he wouldn't be completely free; if he died then he would have Mr. Brisley to contend with again.

But he remembered that he had always liked Mr. Brisley and he was sure that he would never whip anyone for such a trivial offense. If he did anything it would be to talk threateningly to them and maybe restrict them for a few days, but nothing as harsh as a beating. He may not be thinking so much about leaving if Mr. Brisley was still in charge partly because he would not have that beating to think about, he thought.

With every step the old mules took young Jasper's feet and legs became more tired. He was looking forward to sundown when he could quit for the day and head for the barn. After feeding the mules, since his brother had taken over the milking and other chores, he would be through for the night. He was plowing near the barn and if he could get the old mules to hurry, he would have time to go down to the river and do some more work on the raft that he was building, he thought, as he was heading for the barn. With any luck at all, Rufus would still be at the barn and he would usually take care of the mules for Jasper and he could head for the river immediately. He knew that his mother would save some food for him.

The rafts that George and he had made were crude and even though they had improved the second one, it wouldn't be safe to take out on the swift current of the river, especially since he weighed more than both of them had when they were building the first two. The one that he had started would be better and stronger and he thought that it would stand the current no matter how far he got away from the bank, so maybe he could see what it was like to drift down the river for awhile. In fact he thought the one that he was building would be strong enough to take completely across the river, but it would be lots of work with only the homemade paddle.

After leaving the mules in the care of Rufus that evening, as Jasper was walking along the riverbank on his way to the raft, he was wondering what it would be like to actually go across the Big River. He had been thinking so much about leaving lately that someday, he thought, he would venture across and find out what was over there, because all he could see was a wooded area and it intrigued him so. As with any young man, he had no thoughts about all of the problems and perils that he would encounter if he left. But getting away was so strong on his mind that he began planning and wondering how he would ever get enough time alone, and get enough supplies and equipment together to accomplish his goal.

Jasper had heard many stories about what was on the other side of the river, but no one that he knew had ever been across it and he could only dream of the day that he could find out for himself what was over there. He knew every inch of the riverbank alongside the plantation and almost as far as the woods went, both north and south, between there and next plantations on the east side of the river because he had been fishing there since he had been a small child and had become a good fisherman.

"Do you know what is on the other side of the river?" Jasper asked his mother that night.

"All I know is what the slaves have said that they have heard and the few things that Mr. Brisley has said about it. They say there are not as many people there, and that they become scarcer as you go west. Mr. Brisley seldom talks about that area except to say that there a lot of thieves there."

Jasper had not heard much about thieves, because they were a long ways from another plantation and from the town. They hadn't had any problems with people stealing things. Oh, there had been a few times when a few of their chickens had disappeared but they blamed it on people going along the river and coming ashore at night and stealing them. Every time some would disappear someone would say; "it's those Indians again. They can come in at night and steal chickens and never make any noise."

Jasper would feel bad about the people accusing the Indians because they really had no idea who the thieves were. After all, he had always wanted to be like an Indian and he had decided that he would never steal anything. Besides, it could be a raccoon that had raided their chickens. They were known to be fond of chickens and were adept at catching them, especially at night.

"What kind of thieves are there?"

"Horse thieves mostly. There are still a lot of Indians past there and they can trade them horses for furs which they can sell in the cities up north."

"What would a person do with furs? We have a lot of them here when people catch game. Why haven't we been selling them?"

"Mr. Brisley has a book on furs and I have been reading it lately. They are not very good here because it's not cold enough, but as you go west and north there are tall mountains where it gets colder and the furs are much better, especially in winter."

"I would like to see what its like on the other side and I would like to go north and see for myself if it's like people say."

"You could ask Mr. Brisley what it's like across the river. He has been there before."

"I wonder why he would go there. He would never take a boat over there and walk around the area, and there's no way you could get a horse across the river."

"There's a ferry down the river. You can get a ticket for it and take it across. You can put a horse on it and take it across if you can coax him or her onto the ferry."

"But why would he want to cross the river?"

"A long time ago when his wife was sick and he needed the money, he caught a slave that had run away from a plantation over there and had somehow gotten across the river. He took him back for the reward that is always offered for their return."

Jasper knew that he couldn't ask Mr. Brisley because if he decided to go across and see for himself what was over there, and if he decided to keep going after he crossed he would have given Mr. Brisley an idea of where to begin looking for him, he would surely remember him asking what it was like over there. Then he would be over there searching the whole country until he was found.

"Why are you asking all of these questions? You know that you can never go anywhere without permission and you could never get permission to cross the river."

"Maybe if the slaves are freed I will try to get across the river and see if I can get to Texas."

"All you ever talk about is Texas or some other place. You had better not mention those places to the Brisley's because you may be restricted even more."

"Don't worry; I only mentioned them to Master George once when we were younger and he made me mad. He knows that I could never go there and so do I, but I can dream about someday being free from the Brisley's and I can come and go as I please."

Between the Brisley plantation and the neighboring plantation was an area about ten miles across that was heavily wooded and contained the swamps that everyone was so afraid of, and there were also some small hills. There were hardwoods such as hickory, oak, pecan and black walnut as well as softwoods such as pine, cedar and cottonwood. That's where the slaves had gone in previous years to gather nuts and also to pick berries. There were so many small logs that had been felled by wind and by hunters; cut to get the game their dogs had treed at night, there was no problem in getting enough small logs to build any size raft. Jasper settled on a raft about twelve feet square and two small logs deep. He was sure that he could go wherever he wanted in the river, but it would be hard to control.

Mr. Brisley and the neighbor had been the best of friends for years and they would sometimes loan slaves back and forth when they needed extra help temporarily and they would each take care of the slaves as if they were their own; making sure they had food and places to sleep.

That was before the neighbor became so mean to his slaves. Everyone knew that he had gotten so mean over the last few years that some of them had begun leaving. He had not always been mean, but when his character changed and he began getting mean, when one slave would leave, he would get meaner to the others, punishing them and trying to keep them from leaving because of fear, but more of them would leave. Soon most of them were gone; to the point that he had too few to keep the plantation running efficiently. Then most of Mr. Brisley's slaves were afraid to go there on a loan basis because they were afraid of him.

"Why don't the neighbors slaves come and have a party like they did in the past?" Jasper asked his mother.

"He's afraid for them to get out of sight for fear that they will run away."

"I wonder why he's so mean to them. If he treated them like Mr. Brisley always treated us maybe they wouldn't all run away."

"Yes, but all slave masters are not like Mr. Brisley."

"I know, because since Master George has been in charge, everyone talks about leaving."

"Don't you get any of those ideas because when they caught you it would be worse for you than it has been."

"If I decide to leave I will get away so fast that Master George will never find me. He won't even know which direction to start looking."

"He would find you alright. He would never stop looking.

You have become so popular among the slaves that he would want to make an example of you in front of the others. That would discourage them from leaving."

During the last few years, since the neighbor had lost so many slaves, Mr. Brisley had loaned him money to operate with, gotten the storekeeper to extend credit to him at the store and paid the bill for him when he could not pay it himself. Since he had been so short of help, Mr. Brisley, instead of trading labor, had sent slaves to work for him. He charged him by the acre or by the day, depending on the job done. He owed Mr. Brisley so much money that his place was no longer his, but Mr. Brisley's anytime he wanted to take it for the debt. But in his condition he didn't feel that he could operate another plantation and Master George had all he could handle, taking care of one; his responsibilities were already well above his ability.

In accordance with Mr. Brisley's wishes, because he knew that Jasper would do much more plowing than the others would, and also because the others were afraid to go, Master George had been sending Jasper to work for the neighbor for the last two years. Jasper was sure that he didn't want him out of his sight, but he had never said anything about him running away. That year he had acted differently than he had before when he had told him to go there.

"Master George sure acts different this year toward me going to the neighbors' plantation to work," Jasper told his mother.

"It may be because he whipped you last fall and thinks that you may want to run away."

"He did whip me awfully hard. I think he was trying to get me to plead with him to stop, in front of the other slaves, but he didn't get the satisfaction. I don't think he would have stopped when he did, but the others started yelling and leaving. I think he is still mistreating them because they started leaving while he was still whipping me."

It was early spring and as usual the neighbor didn't have enough help for his plowing and even though Master George was reluctant to send Jasper, he told him to go and help him get his plowing done.

"You will leave here after daylight and leave there before dark so you'll be here shortly after dark or I'll be out with the dogs, looking for you. You will walk so I know that you can't get far before we could catch you."

"If I wanted to leave I could go anytime."

"You wouldn't get to town before we would catch you."

"If I ever decided to leave you would never catch me. I would disappear so fast that you wouldn't know I was gone until I was across the state line. Then you would never find me."

Jasper was only baiting Master George into looking to the north if he should leave. He had already decided that if he left that he would not go toward the north like everyone else had tried doing. That had been how they were caught. They would have no money so they would have to try stealing food or asking someone for it. When they would stop and ask for food or were caught stealing, they would be returned for the reward that was always offered for their return. He also knew that there were some rivers to cross to the north and they would surely be caught there.

"I would catch you all right and you would wish you had never tried leaving. I wouldn't send you this spring but my father insisted. He knows that you can plow more than any of the other slaves and we will get paid by the acre. The neighbor has plenty of spare mules so you can change mules when you go in to eat and you can plow more during the afternoon.

"You just remember to plow every acre you can. I don't

want you to do a good job like you do here; just get the acreage plowed. Then once the harrow goes over it he won't know the difference."

"Whether or not he knows the difference, I will. I'll plow like I always plow."

"You will plow like I tell you. Here you plow narrow furrows to break up the soil better, letting one overlap the one before it. There you will plow wide furrows to get as much plowed as you can each day; then pull the harrow over it before you leave."

"If you want that kind of work done, then send someone else because I won't do that kind of work. He will be paying for a good job."

"You had better do what I tell you. My father said that he owed him a lot of money already and the plowing will only add to the debt, so I want it kept to a minimum."

"Does Mr. Brisley condone such behavior? I can't believe that he agrees with such deception."

"Never mind about whether my father agrees or not. I am running the plantation now. You will do as I say."

Jasper managed to control his temper before he said something to make Master George so mad that he wouldn't let him go and help the neighbor. And above everything else, he wanted to go so he could do more work on the raft as he came back through the woods. He had graduated from thinking that he may cross the river to thinking that he would cross. Master George had played right into his hand by authorizing his leaving before dark because he knew when a normal day's plowing would be done and he could leave long before dark. He was thinking that if he ever left for good he wouldn't know where to start looking for him. "I would get away so fast that he would never catch me," he said aloud.

Since he was plowing by the acre he would really push the old mules, plowing all that he could in the short time he had in the morning after having to walk to work. He would change mules at least once each day and if he were plowing near enough to the barn, he would change them three times and sometimes four times by picking out the fastest mules and keeping them separated so that he could get them fast. He would have so much work done early that he could leave in time to be through the woods long before dark. That pleased him because not only could he work on the raft, but he could also see the animals that were nearly always out before dark. He still had some fear of the swamp, but he had been crossing near it for so many years that he was not deathly afraid unless it should get dark before he was past it.

As he was working he was thinking more and more about the bad treatment that he had been getting from Master George. He would find all of the worst jobs to give him. He knew that he did it out of spite or jealousy because he could see it in his eyes when he would find an exceptionally bad job for him. So he decided to make the raft he was building about a foot larger than he had planned so he could be sure that it would take the strong current even with the extra weigh he would be taking across the river. He picked out logs that were completely dry so they would have their maximum buoyancy as an extra precaution.

While they were younger George and he had made a small playhouse in the woods by bending small saplings over and tying their tops together. It was not like the tee-pees that Wrangler had told him about because they had no skins to stretch around it to make it waterproof, but they had put cedar boughs with their needles pointing down all around it and there were places that were always dry inside. Since they had no extra covers for their beds he began by taking some old clothes and rags that he could use for a bed and storing them inside the playhouse. He also took a small axe, a razor, some scissors, a knife and some hooks and fishing line along with all of the food items that he could get his hands on. He even found an old shovel with no handle.

Even though the other slaves would seldom let him go with them hunting at night, he had learned to roll matches in a rabbit skin, and then roll it in an oiled piece of cowhide to keep them dry. Mr. Brisley was very conservative with the matches he gave them, but he took all that he could without his mother noticing.

What if Master George should come there and find the things he had been storing? Or found the raft he was building? He had to take the chance because he had few places that were practical to build the raft. The bank where he was building it was sloped toward the river and it was so large that he put two logs under it so he could launch it alone by prying it into the water with a pole. He wasn't very concerned about him finding anything in the woods because he had become so obsessed with finding the slaves doing something wrong so they could be punished; he seemed to have little time lately for anything else.

He was also unconcerned about any of the slaves finding anything because lately they had been restricted to their homes at night and they never fished that far south. Even though he had been strongly considering leaving and not coming back, he at first planned it only as an adventure. He wanted to find out what was on the other side of the river in case he ever wanted to run away. His original plan was to leave Saturday after work, spend the night, and the nest day he would make a place to hide his equipment so he would have it stored anytime he had a chance to go there. Then he would have time to explore some of the country before he returned, but as he worked to prepare for the crossing, he began thinking more about venturing farther west. He knew that once he made it across the river, if he couldn't make it back in time for work Monday morning, it would never be safe for him to return. If he went farther west and was caught he would be returned and beaten.

He also knew that if anyone recognized him, they would bring him back for the reward that Master George would surely offer for his return. Being seventeen years old and full of natural curiosity, he decided that it was worth the risk to find out what it would be like to be free of Master George even for a short time and even if he were caught. Unlike his father, Master George seemed to have no compassion for anyone. And to Jasper, even though he had not whipped him again, he had become almost unbearable, using every opportunity to harass him.

Jasper had known for a long time what it would be like when George was in charge. He remembered once when he was feeding the stock and he overheard Mr. Brisley telling George that someday soon he would have to be in charge because of the illness that he had that was keeping him inside most of the time.

"When that day comes I will not be as easy on the slaves as you have been," he heard George say.

"You can't mistreat them or you'll have them constantly trying to run away like the neighboring plantation owner's slaves have been doing. We can't afford to lose any because during harvest time we'll be short handed," Mr. Brisley said.

Remembering that Jasper decided to get everything he needed ready in case he decided to leave the plantation and not return. He began taking other things that he would need for the trip, including his extra clothes, and old half worn out pair of shoes, a few potatoes, beans and other food items as well as an old cast iron pot and skillet for cooking.

"I seem to be missing my extra pot and skillet," his mother said one day. "Have you taken them for some reason?"

"Yes, I have built a small house in the woods and I need to be getting on my own so you don't have to do things for me, so I'm taking things that I need. I will practice doing everything for myself."

"I can't find your other clothes. Do you plan to do your washing?"

"Yes, I need to be able to survive alone. Someday I want to be just like an Indian. They can get along with what they catch with snares and shoot with their arrows. They don't need stores and houses like we have."

"Who told you that?"

"The wrangler did; he said that they sometimes have adobe huts, but they sometimes live in tee-pees made from limbs with animal skins stretched over them."

"All I hear is Wrangler this and Wrangler that. When Mr. Brisley stopped taking you to town I thought you would forget about him. That's probably where you disappear to between church services when we're in town."

"I'll never forget about him. He has taught me more in the short time I've known him than I could learn in many years alone."

"You shouldn't be too concerned about doing everything for yourself, because when you marry, your wife will wash your clothes and do the cooking for you after work while you do the chores."

"I haven't seen anyone that I would marry. Besides I wouldn't want a wife that had to work in the fields every day like everyone here. I will probably be like the foreman and be a bachelor."

"You will never escape the girls here. I have seen them eyeing you and following you around like a sick calf."

"All of my thoughts now are of when the slaves are freed and I can leave and continue my education."

"I think I know what you are planning and I hope you make it without being caught, but if you don't tell me I can't tell anyone where you went. When you get up north maybe you will find a good wife."

CHAPTER 5

Jasper knew that if he was going to leave that he should leave while the weather was good, and he was afraid to tell anyone, his mother even, that he was going across the river for fear that she would somehow be forced to tell. Then they would know exactly where to start searching for him and that would give him little time to disappear as he told Master George that he would. He knew that she would never tell the Brisley's anything unless she was somehow forced.

He assumed that they would first search all of the area to the east and to the north of the plantation on the east side of the river because runaway slaves always tried going toward the big cities of the north. Besides, he had planted a seed of thought in Master George's mind that if he left that he would go toward the state line. He hoped they would assume that he meant the one toward the north. If he went that way, and he hoped they would assume that he did, he would have to cross the river near Memphis on a ferry and he had no money for the fare. That would be a place for them to catch him if he couldn't sneak in and stow away. Of course he would know that he had crossed the state line when he went across the river to the west, but he did not think that they would suspect that he tried crossing the river on a raft. The only raft that Master George would know about would be the one they had built and it would seem impossible for him to cross on one like that. It even bucked and jumped when they were only a few feet from the bank. Besides, if they did check, it would still be tied to a tree on the bank.

When he was younger and Master George made him mad

he had told him that if he left he would leave so fast that they would never find him, but even though he felt and sounded confident when he said it, he nevertheless was then filled with anxiety. If he got away and crossed the river, that alone should give him time to get further away to the west before they started searching for him anywhere there.

He also thought that his mother knew that he would be leaving and they would be the only ones that would miss him and he thought that they would go ahead to church as if he were there so nothing would look suspicious. He was hoping that would be the case.

While he was on his way to the neighbor's plantation to work on the Saturday morning that he planned to leave he stopped at the river and loaded the raft; he was determined to go ahead with his plans. He had thoughts that he may change his mind about such a bold adventure alone when he was actually on his way across the river and return before he was late enough to be missed. If he did return, since he was plowing by the acre, the neighbor never kept time or even noticed when he came and went, so if he returned and did a decent day's work, no one would notice that he was late.

He had overlooked one little thing. Even though he had built the raft on two poles so he could slide it into the water, he had not considered how heavy it would be and how hard it would be to launch compared to the ones he and George had made. He pried one end and then the other with a long pole, moving back and forth, until he finally got it started into the water. Then he brushed out what evidence that he could before actually launching the raft. He slid the raft into the water with the long pole and then threw the ones he had used for slides into the water. He quickly boarded the raft; taking the pole with him to push it out as far as he could and then threw the pole into the water to float downstream. He could see that there were a few marks left on the bank that had been left when he had to jump on the raft before it drifted too far out from the bank, but maybe they would be missed by anyone looking for evidence.

With only the homemade paddle that he had been seasoning so it would be strong and light, he moved into the current. He had never been very far from the bank before because George always refused to leave the bank and he didn't realize that the current was so strong until he was well away from the bank. With the extra size of the raft compared to those that he and George had built, before he was halfway across he realized that he would be miles down the river when he landed on the other side. Then he realized that the east wind that had been blowing that had been a hindrance to him while he was loading was then helping to push the raft toward the west bank so at that point, if he changed his mind and wanted to return, he would have a hard time returning to the east bank, paddling against the wind. He would have to wait until the wind was not so strong to come back across and then he would be more miles downstream, maybe past one of the towns that Mr. Brisley talked about, before he was back across.

He realized then that if he did manage to get back he would have to hike for miles upstream and he knew that he would be in trouble and if he went ahead, with the waves that the wind was causing, he may have trouble getting across, but he had little choice; if he made it across there would be no coming beck; unless the slaves were freed as those on the plantation thought would happen soon.

Then the wind suddenly ceased and although it was a lot easier to stay on the raft, he had to work hard with the paddle to keep going toward the bank.

Then it suddenly became evident to Jasper that he was going to make it across and with that thought also came sudden elation; all of his anxieties disappeared and although he had thought that he had a happy childhood there was always that feeling of restraint, but now that was gone and he realized that he was experiencing the happiest day of his life.

When the wind had ceased it had left the prettiest day a man could ask for and he was free from Master George, if not forever, at least temporarily and he would take his freedom one day at a time.

Then a thought came to his mind; how would the neighbor ever finish his plowing? But he had caused his own problems by being so mean so he would think no more of it.

Then another thought came to him; how would Master George finish his commitment to the man since the other slaves couldn't be trusted and were scared to death of the man anyway. He wouldn't worry about that either.

Then another thought came to mind; as the old saying goes "let George do it."

Then he could just visualize George out there, following a single moldboard, a turning plow, behind a big mule, maybe falling down on the big clods and rocks, plowing his wide furrows, maybe two or three furrows across the whole field and then trying to get a harrow to smooth the whole mess.

Then for once Jasper let himself go and if they were listening they may have heard his laugh at the plantation.

When he was approaching the opposite bank he was in a very swift current when he ran headlong into a stump barely under the water. He suddenly found himself in waist deep water, fighting to get back on the raft. He knew that at all costs he had to save the meager supplies that he had brought, even though they were then wet. And he knew that he must take the raft apart and hide it or let the small logs float down the river, because Master

George would immediately recognize one built like their earlier ones, especially if he were looking for his method of escape.

Instead of getting back on the raft he began trying to get it to the bank. He pushed and pulled and heaved until he was utterly exhausted but he finally freed the raft from the stump and got it to the bank. When he finally had the raft tied to a tree on the bank and had time to assess his surroundings, he found that he was in a wooded area that seemed not to be inhabited. He considered himself very lucky, because on his way down the river he had seen some houses near the bank, and he could have just as well hung up on a stump near one of them. He wouldn't want to go out into the current again and drift further downstream to get past a house. After he had rested a short time he rolled up his possessions and threw them on the bank. After deciding that he would never voluntarily go back to that plantation unless the slaves were freed and that he would never need that raft again, he took it apart to the point that Master George could not recognize it and let the logs float downstream, keeping the ropes that he had it tied together with to take with him in his tote sack. The vines that he had used to supplement the ropes, he chopped into small pieces and let drift with the loose logs.

Without even waiting for his clothes to dry he threw the wet burlap bag containing his possessions across his shoulder and immediately started through the woods heading west. He soon came to a plantation, but he skirted it, making a wide semicircle through the woods to the south, giving it a wide berth. Then he continued southwest staying as much as possible in the woods and making as little noise as he could through the sometimes almost impassable undergrowth.

He hadn't liked circling so far around the plantation but the fields that he would have crossed were open and he could have been readily seen from the house, especially by an alert dog.

The nearest woods were to the south and Wrangler had told him that Texas was to the southwest and that's where he wanted his quest to end.

He wanted to put as much distance between himself and the river as possible, so he traveled as long as there was any daylight. Then he waited for a short time at the edge of the woods until the moon was high enough to light the way before crossing the first clearing that he had encountered that he could see no way of skirting without going a long ways to the south.

He had been so intent on getting far away from that river that he hadn't stopped to eat anything and he suddenly realized that he was hungry, very hungry. When he was in the woods again he was afraid to light a fire so he ate some of the biscuits, by then wet and soggy old biscuits that he had brought with him. By then the clouds had blanked out the moon so he crawled into a dense thicket, and throwing his still wet bedroll on the ground he tried to sleep. Sleep didn't come for a long time as he tried to get comfortable on the ground. Tomorrow he would stop in time to make a better bed. George and he had many times used pine boughs to make beds while they were pretending to be Indians and hunters but he didn't even take time for that.

When he was ready to leave the next morning he remembered how terrifying the night before had really been for him because he was in a very dense forest and he could hear sounds of animals breaking small sticks and rustling leaves around him. Although he had spent many hours in the woods, many times at night he was usually with George or some of the men. When George and he had spent the night in the woods they were barely out of sight of the Big House. He had never spent an entire night alone in the woods. He had felt very much alone, more alone than he could have imagined. It had seemed that everything he heard was out there waiting for a chance to pounce on him.

Even though he had vowed the day before that he would never voluntarily go there again, he had many thoughts that night of going back to the comfort and security of the plantation even though he would have to face the wrath of Master George.

He was thinking that if he were there he would be in the warm house and he would have finished eating a good meal before that time and it would be nice to get into his own bed with a feather mattress and pillow. He knew then that by morning his fear of the unknown that he felt in the forest may not be gone, but the fear of being beaten and forever being mistreated by Master George would far outweigh any other fear that he may have. And the thought of the adventure that lay ahead would keep him going.

He wondered what his mother, and his father as well, was thinking. He knew that they would be worried when he didn't come home after work. Although he was almost sure that his mother knew that he was leaving she would probably have been sitting up most of the night, waiting for him to come home.

Come home?

That was not his home anymore and he was convinced that it could never be his home again. He could go back again if he wanted to face the wrath of Master George and endure the harassment to which he would always be subjected. He might be able to talk to Mr. Brisley and appease him of his anger, but not his son. And Mr. Brisley would not interfere with his punishment at the hands of his son. He had not interfered when his son had whipped him and he was almost sure that he knew when it was happening. Then again, as he wanted to believe, he didn't know about the beating at the time.

As soon as it was daylight he took the scissors and by feeling all over his head, he cut off all of his hair, every last tight kinky curl. At least his hair with the tight curls all over his head would not identify him as a slave.

That day was rough on him because he was going through some swampy areas and through some dense brush and he estimated that he had gone no more than ten miles.

When he came to a wooded area away from the swamp, even though it was not dark, he decided to stop for the night. After all, he thought that he was far enough from the river to be safe and he was tired, so awfully tired. He could hardly put one foot in front of the other. And he was hungry, so awfully hungry. He found a place where he could lay his old clothes that he used for a bed in the sunlight so they would finish drying by the time he was ready for bed. It would be awful to have to try to sleep with them if they molded,

Jasper built his first fire; a small fire stoked by hardwood limbs so there would be very little smoke for someone to see and cooked some of the food that he had brought.

How much better he felt. His stomach was full, the evening was warm and pleasant and he felt free for the very first time in his life. The only things that bothered him were the mosquitoes and he vowed that they would not dampen the feeling he had. After he had extinguished the fire so there was not even a glow in the night, he lay down with his tote sack as a pillow, pulled an old shirt over his face to discourage the mosquitoes and was almost instantly asleep.

He had always been able to go to sleep in short order, but was also easy to awaken. That came from being a slave and having to get up early and sometimes being called on during the middle of the night to take care of some emergency, such as sometimes occurred during a bad storm. It seemed that his family had always been the ones to be called on to take care of such events; his parents having the most level heads and the best judgment of any of the slaves. And Mr. Brisley knew without a doubt that they were the most dependable and trustworthy.

In fact they didn't even have to be called upon for such things. They had taken care of emergencies for so long that Mr. Brisley and the other slaves as well, almost always stayed in their houses and depended on his family to respond. Then if they needed help they would sometimes almost have to drag the other slaves out of their houses if the emergency was because of bad weather or if it required considerable work.

He awoke during the night to the sound of barking dogs and he knew from experience that when they sounded like that, they were tracking something or someone trough the woods. Had he been fully awake and thought more about the situation, he may have done differently. He knew that dogs, when they are tracking game would pay no attention to a person and if they were tracking him, he could never run fast enough to get away from them. All he thought of was that there was a pack of dogs coming directly toward him through the woods, and he knew that when dogs are tracking something there are usually people not far behind them.

How could Master George determine where he had gone and have gotten a pack of dogs across the river so soon? Or if it was not Master George, how could he be unlucky enough to stop right in the path of a pack of dogs, he wondered? A pack of dogs that sounded like hounds; they were the best dogs for tracking known to man.

He was surprised. When he went to bed there had been some moonlight lighting up the area, by then it was almost totally dark. The trees, and the clouds that had drifted in while he had been asleep had completely obscured the moon.

He jumped up and grabbing his tote sack, ran in the direction that he thought was west, but he had gone only a few steps when the dogs, only a few yards away, were coming directly toward him through the woods. In his excitement he threw his tote sack down and when he ran headlong into a tree he climbed it as fast as he could.

He could barely see the dogs down there jumping as far as they could up the tree and barking furiously. He thought that they were trying to reach him but he was on the second limb, well out of their reach. Suddenly the woods around him seemed to be full of people carrying torches. When they were close enough for him to see them well, he could see in the light from the torches, there below him was a group of six slaves, one carrying an axe and another carrying a crosscut saw, looking up at him sitting there on a limb, holding onto the tree; he then realized how foolish he had been in climbing a tree instead of trying to get away. He knew that they were out with the dogs hunting small game and the dogs were actually paying no attention to him, but were tracking a small animal that must be in the same tree that he had climbed.

"Come down hyeah, you," a command was spoken.

Jasper had no other choice but to come down among them. He was sure that he would be taken back to the plantation when they discovered that he was a runaway slave, but he started down the tree anyway.

"What you doin' in a tree wit' a 'coon our dogs don' treed?"

Jasper then realized how foolish he must look to them; thinking that the dogs were after him when they were actually after the raccoon. Then he wondered how he could have been so unlucky as to run in the same direction the 'coon had gone and climb the exact same tree in a heavily forested area.

"While I was half asleep I thought your dogs were chasing me, so I climbed the first tree that I came to."

"Whils't you up theah shake that 'coon out'n theah."

When the dogs had the raccoon caught, Jasper climbed

down among the slaves. They were in a tight circle around him in a threatening manner and for a moment he thought of trying to break out of the group and run. He knew that he would have no chance of getting away in the dark, since they had torches and knew the area and he didn't.

"You jus' a boy; where you goin' wit' a tote sack in th' middle o' th' night?" One of the men asked.

"I was just exploring this country."

"I c'n see you 'splorin'. You can't splor' at night. You from cros't th' riva?"

"Yes." Jasper answered. He had thought about trying to convince them that he was an Indian, but he was sure that they knew that he was a runaway. He decided that there was no point in trying to deceive them. He had been told that one slave could recognize another one a mile away.

"Howd'ja learn t'talk thataway?"

"My mother taught me."

"I'se goin' act lik' you'se a white boy caus' you'se brave 'nuf t'be in th' woods at night by yo'self, tho y'aint ver' smart comin' by this place. This's th' bigges' place this side o' th' riva' an' they's mean people. You betta be gon' plumb out'a th' country by mawnin'. Bes, not wait fo' daylight. Bes' to go wes' caus' iff'n you go nawth you haf'ta pass our place."

"I had better grab my tote sack and be on my way as fast as I can."

"Hyeah', take this hyeah pine tawch. You two boys take 'im cros't the swamp 'caus he'd neva make it 'cros't theah by hiss'elf in the dawk."

"I sure appreciate the help," he said. He didn't know it but he was on the verge of entering the swamp; he decided that he must have stopped on a little dry island in the center of a large swamp. When he had his first glimpse of that part of the swamp he knew that the man was right; as dark as it was, even with the torch he wouldn't know where to start.

"Don' mention it, I hope y'git clean away."

The two boys, who were just a few years younger than Jasper, told him to follow them and started picking their way across the swamp. Jasper knew by the way they were going back and forth, sometimes holding their torches near the ground, that they were looking for a trail, but he was so happy for the help that he didn't question them. They were lucky that the clouds parted into groups and then drifted away letting the light from the moon shine through among the few trees that were there. Jasper couldn't remember when the moon looked better to him.

After a short time they found the trail and then it was easier for them to find their way through the swamp grasses and the occasional trees. Then they came to swamp that it was hard for the boys to pick their way through. The trail dwindled to nothing except a trace, with vines that they had to push their way through; blackberry vines that seemed to reach out and tear at them as they went forward. Then water was all around them. They had to weave back and forth, left, then right, then left again to find ground hard enough and solid enough to hold their weight.

Jasper had not talked to them while they were trying so hard to find their way through the very bad trail, but when they came to a better trail, he decided to question them to get information about what lay ahead.

"How far do we have to go before I'm off your master's land?"

"Bout two mile."

"How far is it to the other side of this swamp?"

"Bout two mile."

"What is the country like past the swamp?"

"Don' know. We don' hunt off'n the masters lan."

"Do you hunt here in the swamp?"

"Don' hunt hyeah at night caus' they's 'gators hyeah. Sometimes hunt 'gators on Sunday when they's no work in the fiel's. Gotta watch fo' 'gators t'night."

Jasper knew that they resented being sent away while the hunting was going on, because he sometimes had the same thing to happen to him when he was younger. He remembered being disappointed many times by being left behind or being sent back for something that had been forgotten, once only for matches so they could build a fire. Usually only when his father went along would they let him go along with them, and that was seldom because his father worked so hard during the day and had so many things to do in the evenings that he seldom went with them on their hunting trips.

"Do you go hunting with them often at night?"

"They don' let us go mos' times. Fust time this yea' fo' us," one of them answered and Jasper could detect a lot of disappointment and some sarcasm in his voice. He understood because he would not really appreciate being taken away from a hunt merely to guide someone across a swamp, especially a swamp as spooky as that one; and with alligators as well.

"Sorry I took you away from your hunting, but I could have never made it across here at night."

"You'se right theah; Maybe not in the daytime eitha."

"I know that you're anxious to get back to your hunting, so when we get to where I can find my way, let me know and you can leave."

"Be no place lak' that. Trail gets wors' 'fore we git out'en the swamp."

Jasper soon found out that he had been right. The trail did get worse; as bad or worse in fact, than any place they had been before. The upside of the situation was that it could only get better as they progressed. I hope we get out of here soon before we do find some hungry alligators, he thought. He had heard that all alligators were always hungry. He had heard that there were some alligators in the swamp where George and he had played near the Big House. They had seen many snakes, but they had never seen an alligator. If they had, as much as the snakes scared them at their young ages, they would have probably given them the whole swamp and not come back again."

"You two are really good at traveling through this swamp at night," Jasper said. "I really appreciate you bringing me through."

"Y'don' know how lucky y'are. Jake mus' feel sorry fo you. He's 'pose t'take you t'our master, then y'hafta work fo' him or he c'lect money fo' you Iff'n somebody tell 'bout you bein' let go jake'll git whuppin'."

"Do you think anyone will tell?"

"E'er'body like Jake; he's or fo'man; nobody'l tell."

"Tell Jake that I plan to get an education and make something of myself. Someday I would like to do something good for him. He has done for me what no man could expect of another."

I thot you not ord'nary slave now I know you not. You c'n make it iff'n enny'body can."

Jasper knew that he had been paid the best compliment the boys were capable of bestowing on someone and he thanked them again for their help.

When they were out of the swamp and Jasper was alone again, he only went until his torch burned down, then he found a place in a thicket to sleep a few hours, but sleep didn't come for some time because he was thinking about whether or not Jake would get into trouble. He knew from experience what it was like when a slave had to endure the wrath of his master; not only the punishment but then the harassment that would follow during the foreseeable future.

He left at daybreak the next morning and was going through some partly open country where he could make good time. He wanted much more distance between him and the river. He was so happy that he could put some miles behind him and so intent on getting as far away from the plantation as he could that he had forgotten about caution and was making more noise than he normally would as he was going through the woods. He was not being as careful and watching where he stepped as he had trained himself to do. But even though he thought that he was fairly safe, he couldn't seem to keep from looking over his back-trail often because he knew that if Master George even suspected that he had crossed the river he would be across the river himself, and would be on his trail by then.

He also wanted to get far enough away so it would be safe for him to take the time to build a trap and set some snares to catch a rabbit or some quail. His supplies were short and he had nothing with which to get larger game. He had brought some rawhide strips with him but it would take a long time to find a suitable limb to make a bow and then find wood hard and straight enough to make arrows. And then he couldn't be assured that he could bring something down with such a bow larger than a rabbit.

Suddenly a man stepped from behind a tree directly in his path.

"Lookee what we have here," the man said. Jasper found himself looking straight down the barrel of a rifle; a rifle barrel that, while he was looking from the front, looked like a cannon to him.

He was so frightened that his first impulse was to run and

take a chance that the man wouldn't shoot or that he would miss, but there were few trees to cover his retreat and his better judgment told him that he should stay where he was. What a fool I was he thought, to stumble into another trap, the second one in as many days. He thought that his only chance would be to bluff his way through the situation. Maybe he could convince the man that he was an Indian traveling through the area, seeking the rest of his tribe.

"Where were you going in such a hurry?" the man asked.

"I' m with a hunting party and when I made a circle looking for game they went ahead of me. I'm trying to catch up to them," Jasper explained.

"Are you tying to tell me that you are an Indian; an Indian that was almost running through the woods, without a bow and arrows or weapons of any kind; an Indian with a tote sack? I think you're a runaway slave. You just come closer so I can get a better look at you; come a little closer yet. Now I can see that you have ordinary clothes and shoes instead or buckskin clothes and moccasins; you look just awful."

"I was to the east of the river staying with some people. When I left, I left all of my other things with them and am wearing these clothes until I rejoin my tribe. Since I have been looking for the hunting party, I fell into a swamp, have been chased by a pack of dogs, caught by a group of men and got away, lost all of my equipment except this tote sack and I was moving as fast as I could."

"You don't talks like any slave I ever met, but then again, you don't talk like an Indian."

"All Indians don't talk alike. I am not all Indian; I was raised among the whites."

Jasper remembered Wrangler talking about half Indians that had lived among the whites and could speak English as well as anyone else and had lost their ability to speak the Indian dialect; sometimes neither Indians nor whites liked them. But he decided that he would try anything to get the man to think that he may be an Indian and not a runaway and put him in better standing with the man. He soon realized that he had made a serious mistake.

"One of them 'breeds, huh? I hate 'breeds more than anybody; they aren't anything. You just do as I told you and come closer."

Jasper tried to act as if he was not afraid and walked right up to the man. But he seemed not to be impressed with his show of bravery.

"So you claim to be an Indian, do you? An Indian with no hair; most of the Indians that I have met have long hair," the man said when Jasper was near him.

"I had a reason to cut it off right down to the scalp."

"Did you have those little bugs? I had to cut mine off down to the scalp once."

"I don't mean any harm. I'm just passing through looking for the hunting party."

"I still think that you're a runaway. My boy can understand some Indian. He will know if you're a runaway or not. He went into town with some hides to sell and he should return soon, maybe this evening."

"Furs are not very good in this area because of the warm weather, and there's not much of a market for them," Jasper said, trying to impress the man by acting as if he knew about furs and trapping.

"Our furs come from west and north of here. We trapped some and traded horses to Indians for the others. There's a man in the town to the south that buys furs and ships them north. My boy is due back soon, so you just go into that woodshed and make yourself at home until he gets back."

Jasper knew that it would be useless to try convincing the man to let him go. He also knew then that his first impulse to run was probably a good one because he now knew that the man couldn't see very far and if he could get away for a short distance he would probably be safe. But his chance for getting away had evaporated. The man was staying right behind him; close enough to hit him with the rifle barrel if the need arose.

As Jasper was going into the shed he noticed a corral in the edge of the woods that had a dozen horses in it. He decided that if he were there when the man's son came back he would soon be dead, because they were probably horse thieves. That's probably how they get furs from the Indians, by trading stolen horses to them for furs, he thought.

The man threw his bedroll alongside the shed and latched the door on the outside.

"Lord'ee what do I do with that boy? If he is a runaway and we take him back for the reward he will tell about the horses and we'll be in trouble. If he is an Indian and we turn him loose he will tell the tribe about us holding him and they won't trade with us any more so we have no choice except killing him. I'll take care of it tomorrow morning," Jasper heard the man say, as if he were talking to someone, from inside of the cabin.

Jasper found that he was in a woodshed with a dirt floor, with walls made from logs and he saw that there was a portion of one bottom log where the ground had settled and there was a space under it with no dirt. But there was not enough room for his escape. He decided that he could move some of the wood toward the front and begin digging with a pointed stick, behind the woodpile. He didn't dare get in a hurry because the wood might roll and the man may hear the noise. Although he could hardly contain himself, he would need to wait until the man was asleep because the shed was in front of the cabin and he could hear the man moving around inside through the open front door. He might even hear him if he made much noise while he was digging. While he was waiting for the man to go to sleep he realized that since he had been short of food that he hadn't eaten anything that day and he was very hungry, but what little food he had left was in his tote sack in front of the woodshed. Even though there was very little food left, at that moment he thought that it would look like a feast if he could get his hands on it.

He remembered what it would be like if he was back at the plantation. His mother would have supper ready about then and he could almost taste the cornbread made with rendered out pork skins, called crackling bread. Then came the home churned butter, the baked sweet potatoes, the blackeyed peas cooked with salt pork, the turnips and turnip greens, the fried chicken or pork chops and glass after glass of fresh churned buttermilk.

"You two eat all of your food so you will grow up strong like your father and Mr. Brisley" he could almost hear his mother saying as she had when he and his brother were younger.

When it was dark enough to be safe he moved the wood from the back of the shed and with a sharp stick, began digging. He found the ground to be hard and he was afraid that he was making enough noise to wake the man, but he could hear his steady snoring. He knew that if he wasn't out of that woodshed and gone by morning, even if the man's son didn't come and question him, the old man would take the responsibility of Jasper's fate in his own hands and he would soon be dead. That left him no choice but to work like he had never worked before.

While he was digging he was thinking about taking one of the horses from the corral so he could travel faster, but there was a chance that if he approached the corral, the horses would make enough noise to awaken the old man. Besides, there were two other things wrong with that idea. First: he could be followed much easier and that would assure that he would be followed. Second: Wrangler had told him that if a person got caught with a horse with another person's brand on it he would be hung from the nearest tree. He said that they wouldn't even wait for a trial.

Sometime just before daylight he managed to crawl through the hole that he had been digging, and grabbing his tote sack from in front of the shed, he went as fast as he could through the woods. He knew that the old man had seen that he didn't have a gun, so he would be no threat to them if they followed him. Why didn't I grab the rifle, he wondered? He had seen the old man put it beside the door just inside the cabin and the door was wide open. And it was just standing there for the taking, only a few steps from where he picked up his tote sack, but he didn't think about that until he was long gone. Even though he had never fired a rifle he was sure that he could use one: but that would be stealing and he had been told that nothing that was good ever came from stealing anything. But on the other hand the man would be reluctant to follow him if he had a gun. He decided that it was too late to think about that. He had to look forward, not back.

He was so happy to be free of the man and so anxious to get far away that he forgot about being hungry and continued going as fast as he could until dark. When he stopped that time he was so tired and sleepy that he could hardly stay awake long enough to eat the little bits of ham that he had left in his tote sack.

Jasper didn't remember how many days he had hurried through the woods since he left the Big River but he knew that it had been long enough for him to be out of food and very hungry. He wanted to make sure that he didn't wind up traveling in circles so he kept to his course through the woods even though he sometimes had to get down and crawl through the brush and vines. He came to some woods like the ones by the plantation. He knew that there must be a stream nearby and where there was a stream, he thought that some houses and plantations also may be near and he didn't want to get caught like he did before. He began picking his way along, going from tree to tree and being as quiet and inconspicuous as possible. He was also watching every step, avoiding all sticks and limbs; making as little noise as possible in case there was a plantation house situated beside the river like the Brisley place was.

At least, he thought, the ordeal with the old man taught him to be more cautious. But as hungry as he was it was hard to contain his emotions. His instincts told him to be cautious but his stomach told him to hustle some food of some kind quickly. When he came to the stream and found no danger there, he stopped to rest while he thought of what to do next and he suddenly realized that he was hungrier than he had noticed being. His food was gone except for a few dried beans and they would be gone except that they would take a long time to cook and he hadn't stopped long enough to cook them. Then he realized that he should have given more thought to distance. If that stream hadn't been there he would have had to stop anyway and cook the beans and there would not have been enough of them to appease his appetite. Of course distance had meant little to him because he had only been away from the plantation when he went with Mr. Brisley and to the church in town and that seemed to him to be a long distance.

He had given little thought to how long it would take him to get to Texas or some other place where he would be safe; or at least where he would feel fairly safe from Master George.

Even though he was tired and very hungry and the only way

to get food was to go fishing, he decided to work on a raft until almost dark and then go fishing. He knew that if there were catfish in that stream, they usually would bite better near or even after dark. Then he could build a small fire and cook the fish, assuming that he was lucky enough to catch some. To his way of thinking the most important thing: building the raft would be well underway and he could finish the raft and cross the river the next morning.

He found some small timber that was down, probably from high winds, and began building the raft. He was so intent on getting it done that he was really not being careful about noise because he could see that there was no house nearby and the old man would surely not have followed him that far. Besides it would be impossible to track him through the woods that he had just come through.

"So hyeah y'are," someone said behind him.

Jasper was almost afraid to turn around because the first thing that went through his mind was, "not again." He slowly turned around to find five men whom he was sure were runaway slaves watching him with home made spears in their hands?

"Ye'makn' a raf? Heered ye' makin' noise wit' yo' ax an' sneaked t'see; no need t'make a raf. They's Injuns ova theah, whole passel o' Injuns. They's fires at night. When we start wit' rafs' they's jus' lookin' at us. Jus' standin' theah wit' rifles'n bowns'n arrys, lookin'. We been walkin' fo'days an' ever night they's theah jus' waitin' fo' us t'come acros't."

"Do you mean there are Indians following you up the river? That seems odd because they could come across and find you if they wanted to harm you."

"They ain't got no boats. They's jus' keepin' up wit' us I tell you. We cain't get acros't so we jus' gon' walk nawth til' we fin' a town wit no slaves."

"Unless I'm mistaken, from my memory of the map, if you crossed this stream you would be on the west side and you need to be going upstream if you're going north. You should stay on this side and go up the stream. You may need to leave the stream and go northeast to get to the large cities of the north.

"Y'mean we'da been goin' th' wrong way? We'un'll jus' stay ovah hyeah an' go nawth?"

"Unless I'm mistaken you should stay on this side of the stream and continue north. I'm going to take a chance anyway and cross because I want to continue west or southwest. I'm leaving as soon as I get this raft built. But I am fresh out of food and I need to catch some fish."

"We'uns'll hep you. Take us no more'n a hour, but you'll fin' Injuns ever' wheah theah."

"Where are you from?"

"Cain't tell you thet, but we been comin' fo' days from down near New Awleens. Iff'n we didn' sneak in'n get thet hawg weed'a ben' stahved by now."

"How did you manage to get a hog with a spear without him squealing and alerting everyone?"

"No botha a'tall wit' th' moon shinin' t'otha night. One o'them war in front whil'st I sneak up behin'n hit his haid wit' a rock. He jus' laid down."

As they were helping him with the raft one of them was cooking some of the pork. Jasper had never smelled food that smelled better. He was so hungry that he thought that he could eat the whole hog.

"I appreciate the help," Jasper said as they were finishing the raft. "And I also appreciate the food. I was nearly starved but I didn't want to take time to fish until dark because I wanted to get as much done on this raft today as I could."

"Iff'n we gon' make it up th' riva 'n get t'where no slaves are, we gon' hav'ta stick t'getha an' hep one 'notha. You kin go wit' us iff'n you want to."

The offer was tempting to Jasper because he knew that he would have trouble obtaining food with the few things that he had to work with. He knew that under ordinary circumstances more people meant more safety, but nothing about that situation was ordinary. They would have a better chance of getting game with six of them together, but if they were seen they would be looked at as bigger game for whoever could collect the reward. They would have no chance of escaping because with the prospect of more reward, there would be no problem for the person who saw them to get enough help to capture them.

Jasper decided that he would have helped them any way he could except going up the river with them. Not only did he have no idea of what was up there, he would not consider going any way but west or southwest, away from the plantation. He was happy for the help because he could see that, even though the current was not very strong there, it would be almost dark when he reached the other bank. Being almost dark when he got there would make him happy. Although he had been straining his eyes to see Indians over there, he had yet to see any, but he had no doubt that they were there. He could hide out until dark and then take the raft apart enough to float it down the river. Then he could pick his way through the woods and avoid the Indians that he was sure were over there waiting for him to cross.

CHAPTER 6

"I'm awfully worried about Jasper. How could he have disappeared so completely without a trace? He has been gone for more than two weeks now and Mr. Brisley has been asking me every day if I have heard anything from him. I don't know why he would think that I would have heard anything unless he thinks that he may be sneaking back home at night. He may have been thinking that when he first disappeared because for the first few nights I was awake most of the night, worrying about him. And as I told you at the time, when we agreed not to discuss him, in the moonlight I could see men that looked like the foreman and Master George apparently taking turns slinking around outside keeping a close watch on our house. They would even come to the wall so they could hear anyone inside. I'm not sure that they have completely stopped yet," Jasper's mother said to his father on their way to church; the first time they had gone since the day after Jasper left. They were reasonably sure that they could discuss him along the road by the swamps without having eavesdroppers. "I have been getting more worried each day and so has Mr. Brisley.

"Contrary to his normal 'so what' attitude when a slave has left and Master George caught him and whipped him, he seems to be more concerned about Jasper's welfare than he is in merely catching him. Even though they had been watching for him to come home, by the way that he acts and talks, I'm sure that he had no confidence in that happening. He has been informing me each day of what is happening. He has gone to all of the nearby plantations himself, in his condition, and worn himself out.

"He has sent Master George to all of the plantations within a day's ride, informing them to be on the lookout for him. He also has had him posting notices and has had him riding all day every day inquiring of people and looking for him," his mother continued. "He seems to have vanished. I have been hoping every day to find out that he is alive and well."

"I know that you can't help worrying about him, and I am also, but I feel confident that he is alive; not only alive, but doing well wherever he is. Contrary to our attitude that he is still our child, he is a grown man. Not only a grown man, but also a very strong man, much stronger than I am now. He can take care of himself in any situation wherever he has gone," his father said.

"I know that you have been worried about him also and you have done everything you could to find him, short of leaving the plantation, but that doesn't relieve my mind.

"I didn't say anything to you or anyone else about what I'm going to say before this because I was afraid that Master George would somehow find out, but long before he left he had been taking clothes and food into the woods when he had a chance. When I questioned him about things disappearing, he said that he wanted to learn to fend for himself. He has a pot, an old skillet and a few other items with which to survive. I'm afraid that he tried to cross the river and drowned, but if he made it across he could survive because he had almost everything he owns with him including a few tools," his mother said.

"I was afraid to tell even you before, in case Mr. Brisley or Master George found a way to put pressure on you to tell, but I found evidence enough to be almost positive that he went across the river because he would have never gone down the river. What you just said explains the recent activity in a small shack that I found in the woods. Mr. Brisley had all of the slaves scouring the woods looking for any sign of him and I was lucky enough to be alone when I found the small shack where he had everything stored before he left. He was in such a rush that he left marks where he had everything stored, but I took a limb and brushed out all evidence that he had ever been there."

"Don't say a word to anyone about that because word may get to Master George and he may get the idea that he crossed the river and go across the river looking for him. I think that you're right about him crossing the river. From the first, I thought the same thing, but I can't help thinking that he may have drowned trying to cross on a tiny raft," his mother said. "I knew that Master George and he had a raft somewhere because he talked about it when he was younger, but I was afraid to say anything because I was afraid that Master George may find it missing."

"Don't worry about that because I sneaked away from the other searchers again and found a raft that didn't look like it had been used for years, pulled up on the bank and tied to a cottonwood tree. I was then almost sure that he had left by the river. He had destroyed almost all evidence, but he had built another, larger raft and left that one tied to the tree for Master George to find. Don't worry about anyone finding any evidence because I took a branch and brushed out every speck of evidence down to the last footprint before I left. I knew that the first rain would obliterate the tracks, but I didn't leave anything to chance."

"Since you mentioned another raft I remember now that he had been staying out every day while he was working for the neighbor until after dark. Don't mention that to anyone because Master George may start questioning the other slaves and put pressure on them to tell."

"That's why I went to the shack by myself and went to the river alone. If Master George would have gone there himself he would have found the raft tied to the tree but no trace of Jasper. He would have never suspected that he crossed the river."

"I still can't help but worry about where he went and if he is safe, although we both are almost sure that he went across the river. There are some plantations there and when he runs out of food and has to steal or ask for something, they will surely bring him back for the two thousand dollar reward that Mr. Brisley has offered for his safe return."

"Two thousand dollars; he didn't say that he was offering that much. I have never heard of anyone offering that much for the return of a slave. With all of the talk of slaves being freed and all of the discontent and unrest among slaves in general he should be able to buy another one for less money than he is offering."

"I have no doubt that he could, but a man to compare with Jasper could not be bought. There is no one to compare with him and since he has been gone, the slaves here have been doing much less. No slave could ever replace him. I know that you have always set the pace and they followed your lead, but since you have been gone while you're looking for Jasper they are much more discontent and have slowed down immensely."

"He was popular and set a good example for the other slaves. He would be hard to replace," his father said.

"He had only a few food items that I know of and I can't help worrying that he is over there somewhere right now, hungry and cold, with no place to sleep. I can't seem to cook without fixing enough for him also. Just think of the baked ham or fried chicken, the turnip greens, the sweet potatoes, the cornbread and butter that's left every night, and all of that buttermilk that we can no longer use. Although I am happy that he is no longer under the thumb of Master George, I miss him and wish he were here. I just hope he is doing well wherever he is."

"Although I am glad that he got away and hope they never catch him, I also wish he were here with us, but we can't have it both ways. I can't help but think that he is better off no matter where he is or what he is doing than being here and being mistreated by Master George," his father said.

"I have also been told that there is a tribe of Indians across the river near the coast and since he always talked about Texas and cattle ranches, he may have headed straight for trouble," his mother said. "Indians are still known to kill people and take their scalps. Suppose he ran into them? They could do him harm."

"Unless there were a lot of them they wouldn't want to encounter Jasper. He surely has an axe and the knife that Mr. Brisley gave him, and for all we know he may have a bow and some arrows that he has made. Anyway he is good enough in the woods to sneak right by them. He could be past them before they knew that he was near. He can take care of himself in almost any situation imaginable," his father said, but even though he had a lot of confidence in Jasper's abilities, he was saying some of those things to appease his wife's fears but he was really worried himself.

"But suppose he was there and they sneaked up on him? He wouldn't have a chance."

"He would have a chance alright. Knowing Jasper and his way with people, he would probably end up being friends with them. Maybe even getting them to help him on his way to Texas or wherever he wants to go."

"That would be too much to expect, even for Jasper," his mother said.

***

"I have checked everywhere that I can think of, Dad, and I have posted reward notices on every building all around the countryside. I have also ridden for many miles around asking questions of everyone I met, but I have had no clues about Jasper," Master George said.

"While you had everyone checking the woods along the riverbank did you think about him crossing the river?" Mr. Brisley asked. "I was so worried and frustrated; trying to find him that I forgot about the raft that you and he made several years ago. He was always so fond of the river that he may have tried crossing on the raft."

"I thought about that and I sent the slaves to check and they found nothing. I didn't trust them, thinking that they may have been happy that he had left and would not tell me if they found something. I went into the woods myself and checked everywhere that I could think of that he could be hiding; then I checked the riverbank. The last raft that we made is still there tied where we left it the last time we were at the river together, but there were no tracks anywhere. Then I checked the little house we built in the woods in case he was hiding there, but there was no indication that anyone had been there for years. He seems to have vanished into thin air."

"You are probably wasting your time posting the reward notices. Do you remember telling me that when he was mad he said that if he left that you would never find him? You are wasting your time looking for him yourself because you will not find him. He is too smart to leave a trail to follow. I told you not to be so hard on him and the rest of the slaves or they would continue trying to leave. The others will be much harder to handle now because Jasper was their idol; he was so strong and showed a lot of independence.

"After you whipped him and couldn't break his spirit, they looked to him for strength, even though he was younger than any of the other men."

"Since he left, if there is a group of them together, they have

THE ECSTASY OF FREEDOM

begun to question me when I tell them to do something and are a lot slower to take my commands. By showing strength and allowing them no chance to question my authority I had complete control over them and I will get control of them again if I have to whip every one of them," Master George angrily said.

"You should start treating them like men and women and stop being so mean to them. Maybe it's not too late to undo the harm that you have done.

"I want you to take Jasper's father along and make one last effort to find Jasper. I want his father to have complete freedom to go where he wishes and question whomever he wishes. In other words, give him a free rein, because they think somewhat alike and he may have some idea of where he went."

"Then you will be taking a chance of both of them being gone. You know that I have been having trouble lately with them trying to run away."

"No, there will be no trouble from his father. He can be trusted, especially since Jasper is gone and his family is still here. All I need is his word. Tell him that none of his family will be harmed in any way. Tell his father that he has my personal guarantee that no harm will come to Jasper. No, on second thought, I'll go and tell him personally. He may not believe you, thinking that you just want to get your hands on Jasper but he knows that he can trust me to keep my word. Even before Jasper was so popular with the slaves he was our best man and he and I understood each other. That's why he was allowed to go to town with us and why his family has been allowed to go to church in town for so many years.

"If you find him don't try to capture him. Let his father talk him into coming back of his own free will. When he returns I don't want him touched. I want him brought to me immediately."

"Why would you say a thing like that? I always thought that you paid too much attention to him when he was younger, giving him the run of the plantation, letting him go to town with us and letting him do whatever he wished. After all, he is just one of the slaves."

"I was foolish to let things get so out of control that he found that he had to leave. He was the smartest one on the plantation and showed more judgment than anyone else. If you find him and he will return he will be second in command, even ahead of the foreman of which you are so fond."

"Do you mean that you would put a young inexperienced slave ahead of our foreman? He has been in charge since before I was born."

"I knew that you were jealous of Jasper but I never knew how much until now. Your jealousy has caused out best man to leave; a man that we can never replace," Mr. Brisley said with a lot of disappointment in his voice, but he loved his son George and there was no malice in his voice.

***

"There is that group of runaway slaves again," the brave Running Deer said as him and another brave stood on the riverbank. "I have been watching them every day. They have been keeping up with us as we go up the stream. Almost every other day they build a raft and start across; then when they see us they go back. I wonder why they don't come on across instead of turning back every time they see us."

"They may think that we are waiting to do them harm," the other brave said. "How could we let them know that we wouldn't harm them? Surely they wouldn't think that we would want the meager supplies that they have. I can see only some homemade spears, an axe and some fishing poles along with what few clothes they may have in those bags, which would not be as good as the buckskin clothing that we use. If they only knew it, when they landed on this side of the river on those awkward rafts they build they would be a long ways downstream."

"According to the missionary there is still some fighting among the races; in some areas Indians are still killing settlers and taking their scalps. Those people may be afraid of us. Let's get back from the bank and maybe they will come on across. Too late, they have already seen us and turned back. Our hunting camp should be set up and we'll be there tomorrow. When they are past the camp and don't see us anymore maybe they'll cross."

"I wonder where they could be going. Maybe they think that by coming across they will be able to travel faster and safer as they go up the stream," the other brave said.

"According to the missionary they run away from plantations to the east and if they can get far enough to the west or north they can stay and work. There they are slaves and are forced to work in the fields. He said that they are sometimes treated very badly by their owners."

"What do you mean owners? Do you mean they are like horses and dogs?"

"The missionary says that they belong to a master and can't leave the plantation. They can't travel up and down the river like we do each year," Running Deer said.

"Missionary! All I ever hear is missionary. Why do you spend so much time there? All he ever teaches you is English and you can only use it when you are with palefaces."

"You just answered your own question. The reason that I spend so much time there is so I can carry on a conversation with the palefaces that I will meet. One of these days, and not many moons from now, he says that we will be seeing many palefaces. If we can't talk to them, before they learn that we are not hostile toward them they may think that we are dangerous and kill us. Why don't you go with me this fall and learn English? You will have plenty of time between hunting and guarding the horses while they graze to learn when we return to our winter camp. I will help by teaching you what I have learned."

"You heard the chief. He only tolerates you and Early Flower going because you are both young. He doesn't want everyone to waste his or her time. He thinks it's foolish to spend so much time to learn only English."

"Right now is a good example for you. If I spoke English you would have no idea of what I was saying. And how about the trappers that pass our summer camp on their way to where it gets very cold in winter. You wanted to talk to the one named Jim and I had to interpret for you. It will be worse when the palefaces come in large numbers because they will speak only English; Since so many of them are going to Texas they are passing closer to our village every year. Some day not far in the future, the missionary predicts that they will be in our winter village; before many moons have passed."

"Where is this Texas that you speak of? And what is it? Is it a big village somewhere near? Did the missionary tell you about that?"

"That is another reason that you should go to the Missionary school; to learn what is around us. The palefaces have sectioned off different parts of the land and call them states. Texas is one of those states. They are traveling to Texas and other states by the thousands. He said that they are looking for someplace where there are fewer people that they can call home and where they can farm and raise their families."

"The chief said that there is no need to worry about the palefaces. He said that they would never bother us if we don't bother them. We know they are there when they pass because we can see their trails."

"There they go again. They're on the bank and I think they decided to just walk because they didn't take the rafts apart to get the ropes that the logs are tied together with."

"Look at them go. They're almost running. They will slow up soon because two of them are carrying something between them hung from a pole. It looks like a hog. We should be getting along toward our hunting camp. There has been so much noise that there is no game left here."

"You go ahead. I'm going to circle around and hunt on the way," Running Deer said. "I need to get some game on my own so the chief will see that I'm a good hunter. Maybe then he'll recognize me as a man."

"You are not a man yet. You will have to wait a few more years for that."

"From where did the chief get that rule? If I can hunt like a man, work likes a man and if trouble comes I will be expected to fight like a man, I should be considered a man. I will speak to the chief about it," Running Deer said.

"It will do you no good. The chief has those old fashioned ideas carried on from the chiefs before him."

The brave discouraged Running Deer by his negative comments about him being called a man, so he decided to do an about face and go back down the stream again for a mile or two on the chance that some game would come down to the stream for water. He would show the brave that he was as good at hunting as any of them were. He would find a place and wait until full dark and then if nothing came he would spend the night, and then hunt the following morning. Surely something would come for water the next morning as he wandered back toward the north.

That afternoon, since it had been a warm day and Running Deer had been traveling fast through the woods desperately trying to get some game, he had gotten dust all over his body. Since it was still early and he would have plenty of time to bathe in the creek and still be ready for any game that should come for water, he went down to wash himself in the stream.

Running Deer was a young man of about seventeen. He had no way of knowing his exact age because they had no way of keeping track of births, but he had the appearance and build of a young man of that age. He was tall and muscular, with no fat showing anywhere, as were most of the braves of the tribe. He had black hair that reached to his shoulders and very dark eyes. He wore buckskin clothing and his shoes were moccasins made from a buffalo hide. He was a striking young man with long slim fingers that were very adept at handling bows and arrows as well as a knife which he could use as well as any of the braves; a lot better than many of

them that were older than he was.

CHAPTER 7

When Jasper and the slaves had completed the raft they were building, Jasper thanked them again and was saying good-bye, ready to leave when one of them said, "Y'all sho' yo' don' wanna go wit' us up nawth? Mo' men'd be safer. We'd be free an' cud work up yonder."

"I don't want to go any direction except west now. As far from this river as I can get. I'm planning to end up in Texas or farther west," Jasper said. "I don't ever want to be under bondage to anyone again."

"Dat's how we figger, only we's goin' nawth. Mebbe all th' way to Phillydelphy," the man said.

Jasper said goodbye again; shook hands all around and immediately, with their help, shoved off from the bank. He was hoping to get across the river before dark. He knew from experience on the Big River that it could be dangerous on the water at night.

He could tell by seeing a limb floating downstream that the stream was not nearly as swift as the Big River and not nearly as wide. He decided that he would not drift nearly as far downstream, but if there were actually some Indians waiting over there he would be well south of them when he reached the other bank.

It wasn't nearly as hard getting the raft to move toward the other side as it had been on the Big River. He could see that he would be there before complete darkness closed in on him, but he knew that it would be a close race; he would have little time to spare.

When he had almost reached the other side and while the raft was rounding a bend in the stream, he ran headlong into the branches of a tree that had fallen into the water. His first thoughts were that if he didn't have bad luck, he would have no luck at all. It was almost dark and while he was trying desperately to free the raft so he could get it to the bank, he noticed something hanging in the branches of the tree. It looked like leather. Now where would leather come from here, he wondered? He hung onto a branch and leaned into the tree as far as he could, then he could see that it was a person lodged there.

He jumped into the water and by working himself between the limbs he managed to get near enough to reach the person. Just as he was reaching for him he slipped from the tree and was going under the water. Oh no, he thought, I'm not going to lose him after all of this trouble, or am I? By struggling and fighting branches he managed to get one arm around the person. Then he was alongside the raft again with his arm around the person while he fought to keep his footing. After a struggle he was able to lift the person onto the raft. From what he could see in the semi-darkness, he could tell that he was a young man, of about his age. He checked the depth of the water between the raft and the bank and found that he could wade and push the raft to a point near the bank. He pushed it as close as he could get to the bank and with a lot of effort he got it anchored behind the tree stump that was partly in the water and solid enough that it would stay there until morning. Then by wading between the raft and the bank, he got the man off the raft and threw him onto the bank flat of his back. Then he found that the bank was high enough and also so slippery that he had to dig into the bag and get the broken shovel and he worked feverishly to dig part of the bank away so he could get solid enough footing to climb out of the water.

In the failing light he checked the man as well as he could and discovered that he had apparently hit his head on something or something had hit his head. He had been knocked unconscious and seemed barely alive. But he had no time for the head wound then, he had more important things to check and do. And those things had to be done quickly.

When they had been young Mr. Brisley worried so much because George and Jasper played at the Big River so much, making rafts and pushing them in the water, that he taught both of them how to handle a drowning person. He had them to practice on each other by putting the other one on his stomach and by sitting on his back, to push over the chest area. He called it artificial respiration. He had explained that they had to do that fast in case the other person's lungs were full of water.

He rolled the man over, turned his head to one side and began pushing on his back. The water just gushed from his mouth, but he showed no signs of reviving. Then Jasper rolled him on his back and blew air into his lungs a few times. I may be too late and he may already be dead, he thought as he continued working on him. But when he stopped for a second and checked his pulse he found him to be definitely alive. And he had begun breathing ever so lightly, and Jasper was happy that he was at least breathing.

Since the moon was rising and the clouds had opened up he could see a little better. He moved the person away from the water and laid him on his back and tied a rag over the cut on his head. Then he managed to get a fire going to dry them both. By then the young man was beginning to arouse. He looked frightened and was trying to get up.

"Easy, easy, don't try to get up now. You have had a very bad fall or you were hit on the head and you almost drowned."

When the young man was more awake and was becoming

more alert, Jasper asked him how he fell into the river, but he seemed frightened and was reluctant to talk to him. After a few minutes he tried to talk even though Jasper knew that he must still be groggy from his ordeal.

Jasper knew that he was different from him, but he had been so busy taking care of him and getting a fire started that he hadn't really noticed his appearance. In the light from the fire Jasper could see that he had shoulder length hair and wore buckskin clothing, as well as shoes. He thought that those must be moccasins that he had heard so much about. That was when he realized that he had rescued an Indian.

Jasper didn't even consider that he couldn't speak English, as he kept talking to him in a low voice telling him to lie still and quiet for a while longer until he had recovered from the ordeal that he had experienced.

Jasper had always heard that Indian braves always carried a tomahawk and knife as well as a bow and arrows. He wondered why this Indian had no weapons of any kind and why he was in the water. He may have fallen out of a canoe when it had turned over. He may have hit a snag and torn a hole in his canoe, which Wrangler had told him, would be made by stretching animal hides over a framework of wood. He may have lost his weapons when he fell into the water, he thought. Then he realized that he was letting his imagination run away with him as he sometimes did when he was dealing with the unknown.

He had been constantly talking to the Indian softly to keep from frightening him more than he already was until he was fully awake and more alert. He couldn't understand him being afraid; all he felt for the young man was compassion; as much concern as he would feel for any other person that had been through such and ordeal.

No one had told Jasper that few Indians could speak English, so when the brave seemed to be fully awake he began talking to him in a normal voice.

"How did you get into the river? How did you lose your weapons? Does the cut on your head hurt badly? Do you feel like sitting up now?"

When the brave decided that he meant him no harm and began trying to sit up, Jasper helped him up to a sitting position.

Then he explained in somewhat broken English that he had gone to the river's edge to wash and when he stepped on the edge of the bank it broke off and he fell into the water. Jasper wondered about the cut on his head.

"You must have washed down the river and lodged in that tree," Jasper said as he pointed toward the stream.

"The last thing I remember is falling. Now I remember, something hit me on the head when I fell."

"My name is Jasper."

"I don't speak very good English, but my name is Running Deer."

"You are doing fine. I have no trouble understanding you."

"How did I get here?"

"When I found you, you were hung in the branches of that tree in the water but I managed to get you on the raft and then on the bank."

By then Running Deer was able to walk so he went with Jasper to the riverbank and by the light of the moon, looked at the tree where he had been lodged. He wondered how Jasper could have freed him and gotten him upon the bank in that much current.

"Where was I hung in the tree?"

Jasper pointed out his location as well as he could in the darkness and said, "You must have washed up on that limb head first with your legs over a limb underwater, because all I could see was your buckskin shirt. Your head was partly in the water."

"In that much current how did you get me loose and on the raft?"

"I almost lost you once. If your legs hadn't been over that limb I couldn't have held you. You must have washed there while I was coming down the river because you were barely hanging on those limbs."

"You took a chance on your own life to save mine. Among my people when you save a person from certain death, that person is forever indebted to the person who saved him. My life belongs to you; I could never repay you. Even if I saved your life many times it would not repay you."

"You don't owe me anything," Jasper answered. "I'm sure that you would have done the same for me."

"I don't know if I would have before this happened, but I would after this. Now I would never pass up even a paleface if he needed help."

When they were back at the fire Jasper had him to lie down and rest to further recover while he went to the stream, and contrary to the luck he sometimes had, in a matter of an hour he caught and cleaned quite a few fish. When he had them cooked for their supper he apologized for not having more.

"Sorry there is nothing else, but my supplies are all gone and it seems that we will have only fish. The last of my biscuits went to mush when I fell into that last river. That night I had biscuit soup."

"Many times I have had less that these fish and sometimes I have had nothing."

When they finished eating it was getting late and they needed to wait for morning before leaving, so they decided to stay where they were. Since Jasper's other clothes had gotten wet in his tote sack he needed to keep the fire going to dry both of their clothes.

Jasper offered to share his meager covers with Running Deer but he refused them, seeming to be embarrassed, so Jasper chopped off a few pine branches and brought them to where they were and made a bed for Running Deer, and they both went to bed. Jasper was dead tired and wanted nothing more than to sleep but Running Deer was curious and said, "You look like an Indian and act a lot like one, but I am sure that you are not. Where are you from?"

"I can't answer that now. I can only tell you that my name is Jasper, and you are right, I am not an Indian, but I want to be enough like an Indian that everyone will think that I am one. I want to learn to shoot a gun and bow as well as any Indian. I want to learn to stalk and track game as well as any Indian. I want to learn to take care of game as well as any Indian. I really want to be the same as an Indian. But it is also very important that I go farther west. Tomorrow morning I will leave early and go on the way I was going."

"I can already tell that you know how to take care of yourself, but it will be very hard for you if you go alone with no supplies of any kind. There is some very desolate country after you leave this stream," Running Deer said. "If you will go with me, I'm sure that when my people learn that you saved my life, they will let you stay with us, and I will make you as much an Indian as I am."

"Are you sure that your tribe will let me stay with them? I have heard that most Indians don't like people that they call palefaces. I wouldn't want to cause you any trouble by upsetting the rest of your tribe. Maybe I should take a chance and continue going west as I planned."

"We have never had a paleface to live with us, but I'm sure they will be happy to let you stay."

"I have no way to repay them for letting me stay and I wouldn't want to be a burden on them."

"You have already shown that you will be no burden. When I get through teaching you the few things that I have learned you will be able to live on what you will get by hunting and fishing."

Even though Jasper was dead tired he lay awake for hours thinking about his situation. He thought about what Running Deer had said about them letting him stay with them. He tried to visualize what life would be like with a tribe of Indians. He had no reason to doubt that he could stay with them because Running Deer would vouch for him and surely he would be able to earn his keep.

He thought about his chances if he went alone, to where he knew not, with the problems of getting food with no equipment except a knife, an old axe with a decaying handle and some fishing gear. At best a few hooks and some string that he had salvaged from their scrap.

Then he thought about what life would like with him living that close to the plantation. Did he really look enough like an Indian not to be recognized as a runaway slave? If one of the Indians learned his real identity and got mad at him, would he or she betray him to someone that would take him back to the plantation? He knew that there were a lot of chances he must take no matter what may be his decision.

He had never heard much about how Indians lived. Of course that was except a lot of what he thought were wild tales from some of the other slaves on the plantation. He doubted seriously if they knew any more than he did about them. Mr. Brisley may have told what they said to them in order to scare them into not running away to the west where many Indians were.

Then there was a possibility that they had heard it from the slaves from another plantation that had been brought to the Brisley plantation for a picnic, whose master had scared them by telling stories about killings that they themselves had only heard about. But in any event they had some bad and frightening opinions about any and all Indians. They said that all Indians were mean and that they would kill anyone they met and scalp them.

They said that all Indians would even kill and scalp people from another tribe on sight: that no one except someone from the same tribe was safe among the Indian tribes. They said that anyone, black or white, didn't dare even be in the woods where there was an Indian tribe because they would surely be killed and scalped.

The truth was, he believed all of those tales and knew nothing about Indians until he talked to Wrangler.

Wrangler had told him that Indians were the best trackers and hunters that there were; they could hunt with bows and arrows, knives, tomahawks and even guns when they had them. They could sneak through the woods without making any noise until they were close enough to use their bows and arrows. They could skin and clean game faster than anyone. He also said that some of his best friends were Indians and that when you had an Indian friend you had a friend for life.

He had absolutely no doubt that Running Deer meant what he said and that he wanted Jasper as a friend; and he had instantly formed the same opinion of Running Deer; he felt that they would be each other's friend for life.

Why not take a chance and go with Running Deer? What did he have to lose because if they would let him stay he would be able to hunt and at least he would eat regularly again, which he hadn't done for the last few days? And he would be learning to be like an Indian, as he had wanted to do since he had been a small child.

Besides all of the other considerations, who would think of looking for a runaway slave living and traveling with what he had heard described as a dangerous and dreaded tribe of Indians? And who, if they should see him, would think of him as anything except one of the Indians?

The next morning Jasper went to the stream to start taking the raft apart. He had to get into the water to take it apart and he thought about pushing it past the tree and letting it float downstream, but it may hang up on some other obstacle: much better to destroy it. Besides he could always use the ropes that he had sneaked out of the barn to tie his two rafts with, along with all of the leather straps that he had sneaked out of the blacksmith shop.

When he was in the water he found that without asking any questions, Running Deer had joined him. Within minutes they had it apart and it was floating down the stream, a log at a time so there would be nothing to indicate that they had ever been made into a raft.

Jasper saw the curiosity in Running Deer's eyes and said, "for reasons that I can't explain now I don't want anyone to know that a person on a raft ever landed here. Taking it apart was the only way to be sure that someone wouldn't recognize it as one that I had made."

"If anyone outside of the tribe ever asks, I have no idea of who you are or where you came from. I know you only as a man named Jasper," Running Deer said.

When the last of the raft had floated out of sight and Running Deer was ready to travel, just as if there was no doubt in his mind that Jasper would follow him, he motioned to Jasper and started up the trail by the stream. Just as if it was the most natural thing to do, Jasper grabbed his tote sack and followed him.

"Where are we going?" Jasper asked.

"We have a summer camp many miles to the north of here and we are going toward it. Our winter camp is down the stream near the coast. We go this way in the spring and go south to our winter camp in the fall."

"Where is the rest of your tribe?"

"Some are a few miles ahead where we have a hunting camp being set up along the trail. They should have the camp set up by now and we should be there by tonight. The squaws are very efficient at setting up camps and since the braves that went ahead didn't hunt in that area the braves there should already be bringing meat in to dry.

"I was with a hunting party coming behind looking for game that may have wandered back since the tribe passed. Some have already gone ahead to the summer camp to repair anything that the winter has damaged and get everything ready. Some of them will start planting our summer crops while the rest, including the older and slower ones will hunt and fish along the way."

"I have heard that Indians never walk; that they always ride a horse."

"Our horses were so tired and hungry from coming so far that they were taken ahead where there is better grass. We will ride when we leave the hunting camp."

"Will your people come back looking for you?"

"Since I didn't come last night there will be some looking for me but they really won't know where to start looking. I want to prove that I can hunt as well as any of the braves, so when the others started on toward our camp I stayed behind to hunt. They only know that I'm south of our hunting camp. It seems that I bungled everything and didn't do a good job of finding game."

"Did you lose your bow and arrows when you fell into the water?"

"I leaned them against a small tree when I went to wash in the stream. I thought that I was far enough from the edge of the bank not to fall in but when the bank gave way and fell into the water, I fell with it. It was a very stupid thing to do and the rest of the braves will laugh at me when I tell them how I fell. I will know the place when we get there and then we will be able to kill game if we see any."

"Don't feel badly about falling into the water. I did exactly the same thing many years ago and had to fight like mad to get back onto the bank. It's an easy situation to get into and I wouldn't doubt that some of the other braves have done the same at one time or another. Besides I won't tell anyone if you won't."

"Now I don't feel so bad."

"Do you think that your tribe will want to teach me to hunt since I never had a chance to learn, or will they just make fun of me because I don't know how?"

"We would never treat a person that way, but you don't have to worry about that. I have a lot to learn, but I will teach you what I know and we can learn the rest together. I wouldn't think of letting someone else teach you."

They soon came to the place where Running Deer had fallen into the stream and he picked up his bow and quiver, which was full of arrows, along with his knife and tomahawk.

They were hunting on their way toward the camp. They would make half circles through the woods, keeping the trail in sight most of the time, then come back to the trail in case some of the braves should be coming back looking for Running Deer. Then they would circle again, but the game must have been scared away from the stream by all of the activity of the tribe.

After about an hour they met a group of Indian men who were coming back in an effort to find Running Deer and to hunt along the way. After they had talked in their language for a few minutes, they gathered around Jasper, looking him over while they talked in their language. He didn't know what they were saying but he knew that they were grateful that he had rescued Running Deer. After they had given Running Deer and Jasper some dried meat they started along the trail heading north.

"Now that they know I'm safe and on my way to camp we can spread out and hunt for some game along the way." Running Deer said after the braves had left them.

"Do your people agree that I can go with you and stay with your tribe?"

"That was only a hunting party but they not only agree they want you to go and stay with us. They are very happy that you saved me from drowning, but the chief will have to make the final decision."

"Only a hunting party! Isn't a hunting party an important part of the tribe?"

"All braves are warriors and hunters, but aside from fighting, a hunting party is our most important group of braves."

Jasper had still experienced some reserves that morning about going with Running Deer but they had dissolved when the hunting party had said that they wanted him to go with them. He decided that he would be safer with them than he would be in the woods alone. Besides with all of his supplies gone and with very little equipment for survival, it would be hard for him to obtain food because the largest thing that he could kill would be a rabbit. And if he went with Running Deer and stayed with the tribe he would be learning what he had always wanted to learn, so he decided that if the chief would allow him to stay, he would stay with them; at least for the present time.

Besides, he thought that learning the Indian ways and skills might be a very good asset for him in later years.

The only thing that bothered him was that he would have no teacher and no books to learn from, so if he stayed with the Indians, for the present time he would have to forego his education. But given his present options if he went ahead toward Texas or some other state, he may still not have a chance for an education and he could very well soon be dead.

Later that afternoon they arrived at a camp where there were a lot of Indians, including women and kids. They had made lean-tos by the trees and had some tee-pees set up. At first Jasper didn't know why they would need such a large camp in the middle of what to him seemed to be nowhere, but he soon noticed that they had game hung on trees and some of the women were cutting it in strips to dry. Some of the women and kids were fishing up and down the creek. In a sunny area near the stream he saw deer meat and fish hanging on limbs and lying on rocks to dry. He knew that this was the hunting camp that Running Deer had been talking about.

He was later to learn that this was common for them. They would go to the lower country where it was warmer and stay during the winter; sometimes they would stay there as many as six months, depending on the weather.

Then they would go to their summer camp where they would stay until time to return to their winter camp and stay during the winter months. Some of them would go directly to their summer camp and prepare it while some of the braves, along with some of the squaws and papooses that couldn't travel as fast would stop there and set up a hunting camp. There was always a lot of game around the camp when they arrived in the spring. They would gather all of the herbs and roots that they could use and kill and preserve enough game to help tide them over until the buffalo migrated by their summer camp, which Running Deer said was still many miles farther north.

Jasper remembered when he had been younger; he and George had made their first playhouse in the woods by taking limbs and tying them together at the tops and tying cedar branches around it to make a tee-pee. But they didn't have skins to stretch around it and it hadn't been nearly as dry inside as the ones the Indians made. But the second one they had made was much better and was good enough to keep his equipment dry while he was preparing to leave the plantation.

The Indians had made theirs from hardwood limbs tied together at the tops, with skins sewed together and stretched around them so there was just a small hole at the top for the smoke to escape through from the fire they built inside, making it act as a chimney.

Running Deer and another brave not many years his senior had been sharing a tee-pee. Jasper recognized him from the group of braves that had met them along the trail earlier that day; the one that, according to Running Deer, had told him that he was not a man yet and therefore could not be called a brave. Although they couldn't understand each other Jasper sensed right away that they would get along famously. They had Jasper to move in with them.

There was very little moving in to do. All he had was the tote sack that he had brought from the plantation. And it only contained the few rags that he had used for a bed each night while he had been traveling, his change of clothes and a few beans along with his pot and iron skillet and his old axe. He would have been hard pressed to explain why he had brought the iron skillet. He had no lard and nothing to cook in it and it had only been extra weight, but then it would be an asset as well as a novelty because none of the Indians had a skillet. His other supplies had long since been depleted.

Running Deer noticed that he carried his axe in his tote

sack and told him that he should carry it behind his belt for protection in case an animal should attack him. He had never had that to be concerned with on the plantation; his very first lesson in survival, he thought.

Jasper had heard about Indians building fires in tee-pees and he wondered how they would build one and still stay inside; when George and he had built one in the little playhouse they had built the smoke ran them out. They didn't really need a fire inside but when Jasper asked about building one. Running Deer took great pains to explain and show him the art of using the fine inside bark of a tree and using flint to make a spark to get a fire started. Then they showed him how to keep a fire small enough so that it would vent out of the top without filling the tee-pee with smoke. Jasper quickly learned which wood burned with the least smoke and how to feed wood into a fire and keep it small enough for the tee-pee. He also learned that the wood that burned with little smoke also didn't pop and throw sparks all over the floor.

Running Deer didn't ask again where Jasper came from nor did anyone else seem to care. They just accepted him as if he were one of them and let him come and go as he pleased. In fact he couldn't have been treated better if he were one of the braves. He was soon learning their ways and was learning a few words of their language, and he was teaching Running Deer to speak better English.

Within a few days Jasper and Running Deer became in-separable and would hunt and explore together as if they were brothers. Jasper was learning to use a bow and arrows but he hadn't mastered it well enough to take a chance of wounding a deer; he left that chore to Running Deer while he practiced on rabbits and other small game. They gave him a better knife that they had gotten by trading furs to a trapper the past year. Having had some practice when he was young, he could soon skin animals as well as Running Deer.

On the day that they were leaving for their summer camp Running Deer said, "In case someone questions you being here they would never make my brother leave." He took his knife out and cut a slit in the palm of his hand, then cut a slit in Jasper's palm and put the two slits together.

"Our blood has flowed together so now we are blood brothers," he said.

Jasper thought they looked like a scroungy lot as they traveled along the bank, carefully picking their way among the trees as they traveled north. There were a few horses with large packs on their backs and some braves riding horses and scouting the way through the woods in places where the timber was thick and there was no definite trail. There were women and kids and even some older men walking, and a few horses with poles tied on each side of them with the ends dragging, with hides between the poles. They had supplies loaded on them, including their bedrolls, which consisted mostly of hides taken from animals. There was also some food items, and material used for their teepees. Then Jasper saw the old squaw. She was very old and she was loaded on one of the sliding paraphernalia. He decided that she must be too old to walk and keep up with the tribe.

Jasper was curious and wanted to know what that thing was called, but he didn't want to seem foolish by asking. His curiosity finally got the better of him.

"That is a handy thing that you use." He said pointing to the slide with the old squaw.

"We call it a travois," Running Deer said. "Without those we would need many more horses and the old ones would not be able to go with us. The missionary told us that some tribes abandon the old ones when they can't keep up, but we never do that."

"I can see now why you need so many horses, even though most of the younger people of your tribe are walking. Walking so far up and down the stream must be awfully hard for the older and also the younger ones."

"Yes, we do need a lot of horses. Those are the old and slow ones that are not suitable anymore for the braves. We do not hurry on our way north or south, so it is not too tiring for the walkers. They have a lot of practice walking even when we are in camp."

"How do you keep feed for so many horses? There is very little grass in these woods and it would take a lot of grass for so many horses."

"There's plenty of feed near our winter camp. It's close to the shore of the Gulf of Mexico, where the swamps begin, and it's not good for farming so the settlers should not bother us. When we arrive at our summer camp all of the horses that are not needed then are taken far from camp and herded so there is always plenty of feed near camp for the ones that we keep there for our everyday use."

"Do you know an old man and his son who trades horses to Indians for furs?"

"Yes, they usually come by our winter camp before we leave in the spring. They came this year but they were disappointed because we had very few furs and they left with most of their horses."

"Did you know that they are horse thieves?"

"We suspected it because the horses all have different brands, but they say that they bought them from ranchers. They show us papers but none of us can read so we believe them."

As they were traveling they stopped early enough each night for the squaws to cook their evening meal and for everyone to prepare for bed before it was completely dark. They would make several small fires and hang pots over them to cook their meals. Jasper learned that there were lots of things that they ate that he didn't know were edible.

"How can you tell which roots and herbs are edible?" Jasper asked Running Deer.

"We have been coming here for so many years that we know everything that is edible. It has been passed down through the generations. For an example, we make our bread from corn when it's available, but when it's gone we use acorns or acorns and nuts together. Near our winter camp are many acorns and nuts so we usually have enough left from the year before to last until the corn is ready at our summer camp."

Since it was still early spring and the nights were cool, they kept the small fires burning until late into the evening. Jasper noticed that they built several small fires so they could get close enough to them to cook and they could still stay warm. He decided to keep that in mind, because when he was young and they went into the woods they would build a large fire and if they cooked fish or roasted an animal they would have trouble staying close enough to the fire to cook.

Jasper soon noticed that where they camped each night, they apparently had camped each year as they went up and down the stream. He thought that if Running Deer and he left earlier than the others and went far enough ahead to where there would be no noise, they might see more game. At least they would have a better chance of stalking game if they did find some.

When Jasper mentioned that idea to Running Deer he said "that's a good idea but we won't see many animals by the trail unless some has wandered back since the rest of the tribe went by. They would have killed the ones they saw and the others would have gone farther away from the trail because of the noise. We can go much faster than the others so we can make circles through the woods where there should be more game."

They left early the next morning and they were well ahead, but they hadn't begun to circle and hunt, so they were just riding along talking about their future. Since almost all that Jasper talked about was an education and about wanting to go to other places, he had gotten Running Deer interested and they talked about those subjects often.

"You are really learning English fast," Jasper said. "Since you can learn so fast, maybe you can get an education and you wouldn't need to go up and down this stream each year. All of my thoughts are of getting an education and being able to choose what I want for my future."

"Can you read and write?"

"Yes, I can read and write very well and for the last few years when she had time my mother has been teaching me to do arithmetic much better. I haven't been able to go to school so I need to get started soon. Are you learning to read and write at the Missionary School?"

"No. The missionary was beginning to teach a few of us to read and write. He taught me to write my name but he didn't come last year. Since I have been traveling and talking with you I think that I would like to have an education like you are planning. When you get to where you can finish your education, then what do you plan on doing?"

"I haven't decided yet. I first wanted to be a doctor, but lately I have been thinking of being a lawyer. Being either one will take a lot of studying."

"Do you mean that you can choose what you want to do when you finish your education?"

"A person who has been a lot of places and done a lot of things told me that you could do whatever you want to if you work at it hard enough."

"I don't know what a lawyer is but I have heard of doctors.

We have a medicine man but the missionary said that kind of medicine wouldn't cure anything. When I was sick he gave me some bitter tasting stuff and I got well very fast. I'm beginning to think that kind of treatment is much better than what the medicine man does."

They weren't expecting to see any game along the trail but Jasper knew how bad Running Deer wanted some game and it had made him tense. Although they both wanted to see some game they had let down their guard temporarily. On an impulse they tied their horses and started through some thick brush intending to make a large half circle through the woods. They were talking about their future and paying little attention, thinking that they were too near the trail to see anything, when they suddenly heard a loud grunt beside them and a large wild boar came out of the brush running straight toward Running Deer.

"Climb a tree fast." Running Deer said as he stepped aside and jumped on the boar's back.

Running Deer had his knife out and the boar killed before Jasper had time to do anything. It had happened so fast that Jasper hardly knew what had happened. In the future I will have to pay more attention to what's going on around me if I want to have a future, he thought, as in his mind he thoroughly chastised himself.

Jasper remembered when they would butcher hogs on the plantation. They would wait until the weather was cool in the fall of the year; then again before it was hot in the spring so the meat would keep longer. The children's job was to fill some large pots with water, then build a fire around them and heat the water until it was boiling. The men would then pour the boiling water into a barrel that was mounted on an angle so they could put the hog in it easily. Then when a hog was killed they would put it into the barrel and roll it over to loosen the hair on all sides. After they had scraped off all of the hair, they would finish butchering it and cutting up the meat.

They kept everything that was edible including the liver; the lights and they even kept the entrails to stuff the sausage into, as well as rendering some out for lard and to make chitterlings. They thoroughly rubbed most of the meat with salt, and then they hung the hams and side meat in the smokehouse and kept a small fire going for days to make smoked hams and bacon.

Jasper didn't get into the hog killing and butchering often because he was at Mr. Brisley's house every day until Master George sent him into the fields and then he was too busy to help. But there were few more expert at putting it away after it was cooked so he was already looking forward to some good meals.

"Look at those tusks! One slash from those and a person could be disabled for life," Jasper said. "How do you get the hair off a hog here in the woods?"

"We'll have to skin it like any other game. When a person who is called a boy does something that can be called a great deed, he becomes a man. This should be important enough to get the chief's attention. Maybe now they will treat me as a man."

By the time they had the boar dressed out the others of the tribe were there and they were amazed that Running Deer had killed the wild hog with nothing except a knife.

CHAPTER 8

While the Indian tribe was traveling along the stream Jasper and Running Deer would sit by the stream and talk long after the rest of them had gone to bed. They were learning more about each other's language and talking about Running Deer's accomplishments as a papoose growing up with the tribe and his training as a young brave.

Jasper was encouraging him to go into details about his youth because he wanted to learn all that he could about what life was like with an Indian tribe. Then he would know more about what to expect while he was with them.

He told Jasper that his father had been the chief's brother and that his father had died while he was young. His uncle had more to do with his training as a papoose than anyone else in the tribe did and the chief had been very lenient with him, allowing him to do almost anything that he wanted to do. He furnished him with the best horses, the best bows, the best arrows and the best knives. In essence he had the best of everything available to them, which gave him the best chance of success in whatever endeavor he chose. He didn't realize while he was growing up that he had such an advantage over the rest of the tribe, but it made little difference in a competitive nature because he was the only one in his immediate age group. The other braves' boys and girls as well, were either older or younger than he was. That left him with no real competition.

He had no peers so he was a loner.

He wouldn't have had to be a loner if one of the older

braves with papooses would have assumed the task of training him along with their son. But they were busy teaching theirs to hunt with the hunting parties and didn't want to bother with a youngster. The chief was always busy at one camp or the other and did not accompany the hunting parties so he had little time for Running Deer's personal training.

There were two boys only three years older and they could have associated with him while he was younger, but with him being the chief's nephew and sleeping in his hut they didn't want him tagging along with them. They thought that he may tell the chief everything they did, and they did a few things of which the chief wouldn't approve.

Therefore he had spent most of his youth as a loner; until he reached an age when age differences meant little.

He played the hunting and tracking game and even learned to hunt small game alone. He would even ride long distances alone.

Although that didn't meet with the chief's approval, given the circumstances he didn't disapprove very heartily. He was always busy and although he disagreed with some of Running Deer's antics, he was powerless to change him.

He was different from the rest of the tribe; as different in fact as Jasper had been from the rest of the slaves. Jasper could identify with him in as much as their earlier life as far as activity was concerned was similar; their lives had been on about an equal plane. But Jasper would say nothing about his earlier life for fear of letting Running Deer know where he was from. Running Deer, he thought, already knew or had an idea of where he was from, because the missionary had taught him well, even though he gave no indication that he knew or even cared.

Jasper didn't try to estimate how many miles they traveled each day but there were so many older ones along and they would tire so easily, he knew it was very few. By the time they reached the next campsite that they had used year after year, some of them were physically drained. When they stopped each day, as soon as the tee-pees were set up, some of the squaws would begin fishing while others built fires and began cooking. Some of the younger braves scouted the area around them for game, but most of the older ones, after walking most of the day, fell on the ground and rested until time to eat.

And they did eat. After a full day of traveling with only a short break at noon they consumed an enormous amount of food, although it didn't seem like so much because many of the squaws cooked food at their own campsites. But they had acquired a large pot and they always had a large pot full of stew cooking for the ones who had no families or for anyone else that wanted to dig in. Jasper usually ate from the big pot with the other young men. He always had a good appetite and liked any food that was available.

Jasper thought that all people were basically the same. He remembered on the plantation that when the day was done the slaves were required to do the chores, they would go through the motions, but what they were really doing was encouraging the children to do the work.

Jasper was glad that they stopped before dark because Running Deer and he would make their own excursions through the woods and then join them at the camp about dark. They would sometimes get a deer, but he considered himself still learning to use the bow and arrows they had given him. Oh, he knew how to use them and he would kill smaller game, but he was not confident enough to take a chance of wounding the larger game and running it away, but Running Deer would encourage him to try. After a few days he would shoot at any game and was usually successful.

Jasper felt right at home there because they were passing through country like that on the plantation except for the size of the stream. That stream was much smaller than the Big River but still too deep to ford with horses without them having to swim. But they had no need to cross.

After many days of travel they began passing through partially open country, and soon came to where there was a few trees for shade and the prairie spread out before them. As far as they could see was open country with grass over knee high, with here and there a clump of trees. Jasper, seeing that country for the first time thought that must be the prettiest place in the world.

"Before I saw this country I wondered why you came so far north instead of raising animals for food and staying at your winter camp all year. Now I can understand. This is the prettiest place I have ever seen," Jasper said to Running Deer.

"During the summer the mosquitoes are really bad where we spend our winters and if we stayed there the feed would become scarce for the horses, but here we have much more feed during the summer months. We don't raise any animals except colts. They are born in the fall at our winter camp and by spring they are strong enough to travel north. The ones here are born in the spring and by fall they are old enough to travel south. But we never seem to raise enough for our own use and constantly need to trade for other horses.

"The missionary said that the reason that our horses do not last as many years as the palefaces' horses is that ours don't get the care that theirs do. They don't consistently have good feed and an Indian is more likely to ride a horse until his wind is so badly broken that he is no good anymore. He called it riding the horse to death. I have been trying to explain that to the braves but they think of me as a boy that knows nothing and none of them will listen.

"The soil at our winter camp is not as good as it is here, and even though it is warmer there, we don't raise any crop except a little hay for emergencies. Here we can raise all of the corn, squash and beans that we need. We take most of the corn and some of the beans and squash with us when we go to our winter camp. We also dry enough buffalo meat here to last most of the winter; then we don't have to kill all of the alligators and turtles there during the winter."

They had long since left the large stream and were alongside a large creek that would furnish them with plenty of water and all of the fish the tribe would need during the summer months. But it wasn't so deep that the horses had to swim.

"How long have your people been coming here?" Jasper asked.

"Since long before any of us were born," Running Deer said. "No one here can remember when they began coming."

There were buffalo tracks and chips everywhere mostly from the fall before when they had migrated south for the winter and there were a lot of deer tracks indicating that there would be plenty of game for the tribe for the summer. But that could change fast if there should be no rain and if it should be an exceptionally hot summer. And there were what Jasper thought were a lot of recent buffalo tracks, but according to Running Deer there were far fewer tracks than normal.

"There are fewer buffalo here every year," Running Deer said. "We know that a lot of palefaces come every year and kill them for their hides and leave the meat to rot but we have had little trouble with them here. That is done mostly to the north where there are vast herds of buffalo during the summer but it doesn't seem to matter where they kill them because they are essentially the same herds. There are more to the north because they go there from different directions."

"From the tracks it looks like a lot of buffalo came through here lately," Jasper said.

"It does look like a lot of sign but a few years ago there would be buffalo here now because there were so many that a lot of them stayed here all year, wandering by in large herds. We didn't need to dry meat until late in the fall before we went downstream to our winter camp because it was available all of the time. Last year we barely got enough for our use during the summer. We got lucky and a small herd came by late in the fall and we were able to dry some for the winter. We have to hunt further away from camp each year. If they keep killing them for their hides there will soon be no buffalo."

"What would your tribe do if they saw someone killing them for their hides and leaving the meat to rot?"

"We have never had that to happen here but I heard that up north they attack them and kill them or run them out of the country."

"Do you think that your people would attack?"

"We have always been peaceful with everyone but once when a small tribe from the north invaded our territory, we had them outnumbered and could have killed them all, but the chief only wanted to make them leave. Every brave gathered and surrounded them except for one place where they could escape. The threat worked and when they saw the break they left and never came back."

As Running Deer had said, the rest of the tribe had arrived and was busy planting corn, beans and squash and they were readying their camp for summer. There were tee-pees and straw huts, some of which had been there for years. There were also a few adobe ruins that no one remembered using, but they were beyond repair. Jasper was thrilled to be in their main summer camp where, Running Deer said, few palefaces had ever been, since they were too far south for the wagon trains that the missionary had told them about that were heading west. Only a few trappers had passed that way on their way to or from the higher elevations. They would come by in the fall heading west and in the spring heading east after trapping all winter. Surely no slaves had ever been there.

Jasper noticed that when they planted corn they put a fish under each hill they planted and when he mentioned it to Running Deer he was told that the fish would make the corn grow larger. Strange, he thought, with all of the buffalo chips lying around everywhere they would have enough natural fertilizer for their use.

"Don't you ever use buffalo chips for fertilizer?"

Jasper asked Running Deer

"We only use fish under the corn. The beans and squash grow with nothing under them."

"They will grow much larger and make more beans and squash with fertilizer. You would need to plant only half as many hills. If you will tie a travois to a horse I will go with you and we can get enough chips to fertilize everything."

"That would be work for the squaws and papooses. Braves do only the hunting and fighting if we're attacked. When we leave here this fall there will be no buffalo chips for a long ways around this camp. The squaws and papooses go into the woods and bring many loads of wood. Then they bring buffalo chips to burn with the wood. They can't bring many loads of buffalo chips at one time and make a pile, because if it should rain it would ruin them so they couldn't be used for fires."

"Sorry I mentioned it," Jasper said. "I should have known that you would have a use for everything. I have seen very few things that you don't use."

They were planting their crops near enough to the creek to

carry water and they were pouring a pouch full around each hill of corn, beans and squash as they planted them. Some of them were constantly fishing for food as well as a fish to put under each hill of corn. Everyone seemed to be busy every moment, including the very old squaw who was sitting on the bank fishing, tended by some very young papooses.

Jasper knew that they could use the creek for transporting game from upstream while they were there if they wished, but they had no canoes. He also knew that they could use the water to transport their goods down to their winter camp because Running Deer had told him that it went right by camp. They could build rafts for the trip down and then use the wood when it dried.

"Why don't you stay here during the winter instead of going so far downstream?" Jasper asked."

"Because during the winter it is cold and windy here, with some snow, and some of the animals that we use for food don't stay here in winter. I was told that many years ago, before they found the winter camp, that the tribe stayed here all year, but it was hard on the old squaws and papooses and they lost some of them from the cold weather."

"Then why don't you use the stream for transportation for game here and when you leave here going south?"

"Some people don't like Indians. We could be attacked easily while we were on the water and couldn't defend ourselves," Running Deer said. "Some of the people would have to go on land to bring the horses with their loads anyway and we would have to unload each night so we could make camp. If we had canoes to transport meat here, we would have no place to leave them when we left. Besides, most of our meat is killed away from the creek."

"How far do you go that way?" Jasper asked pointing north.

"We only go three days north. You will soon learn how far we go and what is there, but there is another tribe far to the north and we don't want to take a chance of going onto their hunting grounds. If one tribe goes onto another's hunting grounds they will be attacked. We are lucky that our ancestors found this place before some other tribe claimed it."

"How far do you go west?"

"We never go very far into the evening sun because it is very desolate after a few miles and there is another tribe far to the west. The trappers that sometimes pass here have told us that there's not only a tribe there, but past them there are high mountains where the snow gets very deep and it sometimes gets very cold in winter. The hides are much better where it gets cold, so they stay there and trap all winter and come this way in the spring season on their way to where they can sell their pelts. We sometimes trade them any pelts that we have gotten during winter for knives, pots and pans and sometimes a rifle and ammunition. We got one rifle that was not very good and has to be loaded through the barrel, but the last one is better and faster and is loaded at the back."

"I have heard of mountains that are so high and so rough that you can cross them only in summer when there is not too much snow. Somewhere a long ways over the mountains, according to the maps, is a state called California, and that's where I would like to go someday."

It seemed so far and such hard traveling that he could hardly imagine being able to endure the hardships that would be encountered on such a trip. After all a long trip for him had been when Mr. Brisley would take him to town, but he had already decided that as soon as he could he would be on his way to Texas or some other place farther west, maybe all the way to California. He still wanted much more distance between him and the plantation. He knew that he should be able to cross the mountains because settlers were taking their families to California and Oregon every year by wagon train.

As soon as they were settled in their new camp, Running Deer took Jasper out with their bows and arrows and continued teaching him how to use them.

"You are learning to use the bow and arrows fast," Running Deer said one day as they were practicing.

"I should learn fast because I have the best teacher there is and we are practicing almost all day every day."

"If I am to be called a man at my age, I have to be better than the other braves."

"Don't worry about that. I have seen some of the other braves shoot and they are no match for you."

"Then how could you get better than me in such a short time? I have never seen a brave use a bow like that."

"You're only being nice. I haven't had enough practice on game to know how good I will be; anyone can hit a target."

"The chief has been watching you while we are practicing around camp. He thinks that you will be good with the rifles as well as with the bow and arrows. He will let you practice with one soon."

Since Jasper had ridden horses and mules on the plantation, almost always bareback as the Indians rode, he could soon ride with the best of the braves.

One day the chief brought out the two rifles that they had traded furs for and gave them to Running Deer so he and Jasper could practice. He showed them how to load and fire them and then gave them only a few rounds of ammunition because it was so scarce that they could only use it occasionally. Usually, Jasper later learned, they used it only to hunt buffalo when they came by the camp on their way north or south.

Jasper had never fired a rifle, but Mr. Brisley had brought his rifles outside a few times and taught George and Jasper how to hold and aim them. He also taught them the safest way to handle a rifle and told them to treat every firearm as if it was loaded because you couldn't tell by looking at one if it was loaded or not and that every firearm was a dangerous weapon to everyone within range if it was not handled properly.

Jasper also remembered the example Mr. Brisley used; he said to calmly decide where you wanted the bullet to go and place it there as if you was throwing a pitchfork full of hay into a manger; if you miss the manger you must throw more hay and you may never get the manger full.

Remembering all of the lessons Mr. Brisley taught them Jasper was sure that he would have no trouble hitting game with a gun of any kind. He was naturally a good woodsman and was putting all of the effort he could into trying to be one of their best hunters.

Jasper and Running Deer had only three rounds of ammunition each for the rifles and after Running Deer fired his three rounds, hitting the target each time it was Jasper's turn. After he had fired it and hit a target once he told Running Deer that he wanted to use the other two rounds for game. The next morning they went west of the camp looking for game and he managed to bag two deer.

All of the braves envied Jasper when they came back into camp that evening for bringing game back on his first time out with a rifle. The talk around camp centered on him: how he went out with only two rounds and came back with two deer.

One day the chief sent one of the braves to tell Running Deer and Jasper to come to his hut. He had the largest hut in camp and Jasper had never been inside it. In fact he had only met the chief face to face once; when he had brought the rifles, but when he had seen the chief from a distance, he had always been dressed like the braves. He seemed to have a down to earth approach to everything with the tribe, so Jasper was impressed when he saw all of the hides and feathers the chief had collected over the years.

He had also never seen the chief with his headdress on. He had seen some of the braves with a few feathers sticking above their heads from a headband, but he didn't expect to see a full array of feathers like the chief had on his head. They were hanging in rows from the top of his head to the middle of his back. Very impressive, Jasper thought. He was wearing a full set of buckskin clothing and a belt with a silver buckle. There were beads and ornaments tied with buckskin thongs along with leather moccasins with beads and silver on a band across the top.

He was tall, taller than most of the braves. And husky, which made the clothes he was wearing look more impressive than they would on a lesser man. He had gray hair showing around the temples but the back of his head was completely covered by the headdress.

"The chief never wears his headdress or those clothes except when he meets the chief of another tribe or when someone of great importance is present," Running Deer said. "That display of finery is for your benefit. You should feel honored."

"I have never seen anything like that in my life and I doubt if many people have, except members if the tribe and I can't help but feel honored and impressed."

The chief stood there looking at them with his hands folded over his chest until Jasper began to feel restless, wondering if he would ever speak. When he finally spoke, even though Jasper couldn't understand everything he said, there was no doubt in his mind that the conversation was to be about Running Deer and him.

"He said that he is glad that you decided to come here with me and stay with us because you have taught me to speak much better English and while the braves and I have been teaching you, you have taught us many things," Running Deer said.

"Tell him that I could never repay him or the rest of the tribe for permitting me to live as one of them for the last few weeks. I have learned more about hunting and surviving with your people than I had during all of the earlier years of my life."

"He has heard that you want to go over the mountains to the west, but he wants you to stay with us. He said that you have earned the right to be one of the tribe."

"Tell him that it makes me very, very happy that he asked, but I have missed so many years of studying that I must soon find where I can finish my education. I have been thinking about the many places that I have been told about to the west and southwest and I must soon be on my way, maybe on to California, as soon as possible."

"The chief says that we have a lot to celebrate tonight: they will honor me for becoming a man, celebrate the coming of summer and drive away the evil spirits that may interfere with the buffalo that should be here in a few days. Since you don't want to be one of his braves he wants you to join us as guest of honor while we celebrate."

Running Deer could see by the look of embarrassment on Jasper's face that he would rather be somewhere else.

"No one outside of the tribe has ever been asked to take part in such an important event, but we consider you one of us now. Will you come as a favor to me as my blood brother?"

"I wouldn't miss it for the world."

When the slaves would get together to play music and dance on the plantation, they would build a fire and someone would say that they were having a pow-wow just like the Indians did. Sometimes George and he would dance around in circles and imagine that they were Indians. They really didn't know what real Indians would do at a pow-wow. Had Jasper not been there and seen and taken part in the celebration that evening there was no way that he could have imagined such an event.

Jasper had been out by the creek where he spent much of his time reminiscing about the past and thinking about the future. He was enjoying himself so much with the tribe; learning so many new methods of doing things and enjoying being with Running Deer and the rest of his new friends that he was wondering if he really wanted to go west; knowing all the time that he must. Time was fleeing from him; time that he should be using for his education. Then he noticed that it was getting dark and decided to return to the village. When he met Running Deer he was surprised to see that he was dressed only in a cloth tied around his waist, especially since it was a cool evening. He had paint on his face, arms and body. He gave Jasper a cloth to wear and began painting his face.

"The chief has changed his mind about you being a guest," Running Deer said. "Since you are my blood brother he wants you to be one of the tribe. We will both not only be considered men and be braves, but will both be warriors.

"The chief traded some hides for alcohol last year and he has been saving it for an important pow-wow. Although we are to be known after tonight as men, he thinks that we are still a little young to drink alcohol, so we will wait until the older braves have danced and drank what he will allow them to have. Then after they have decided to accept us as men we will join in the celebration."

Jasper had not heard them beat drums before but he had been hearing them for an hour before he headed back to camp.

He had some idea of what to expect, but when Running Deer finished painting him and they came into camp he was almost shocked by what he saw.

The chief was sitting in front of his hut in his full dress as Jasper had seen him earlier that day, along with his squaw, also in buckskins with ornaments around the bottom of her skirt. The other squaws were in a circle around the braves who were going in a circle around a small fire. They were chanting as they danced. They were all wearing cloths around their waists as Running Deer and he were wearing: they had feathers sticking up from their headbands and were painted as Running Deer and he was, so from a distance each one looked like the others.

Then Jasper looked at Running Deer and realized that, except for the feathers, which came with time for the deeds they had done, he looked exactly like the others and he could imagine himself looking the same.

As they watched from a distance the chief stood up and said something, which Jasper couldn't understand, and all of the braves cheered.

"Let's go and join them. We have been accepted as braves now and will be treated as men," Running Deer said.

Jasper couldn't understand the concerns of Running Deer about not being known as a man. He hadn't noticed them being treated any different than the braves. Besides, he had been required to work since he had been very young and had been required to work alongside the men and had been treated like a man since he had been thirteen years old, which had been for about five years.

But he knew how important it was to Running Deer to be known as a man and accepted as a brave so he was very happy for him. As for himself he couldn't help but be proud that they had accepted him as one of the tribe: him not being an Indian and only related to Running Deer as a blood brother. It was the first time that honor had been bestowed on an outsider, according to Running Deer; not even an Indian from another tribe had ever had that honor bestowed on him or her.

They had been scouting every day for Buffalo and each day seemed like an eternity to Jasper, he so wanted to see some of them. The day finally came when one of the scouts reported seeing some buffalo coming toward the creek from the south along the far side. The Indians knew from experience that if they were left alone to feed and wander along as they normally would, they would cross the creek near the camp and continue their migration north.

They waited patiently until the buffalo were across the creek, taking their time as they browsed along as if they were in no hurry. Then one morning they decided that it was time to begin their hunt.

"Since this is your first buffalo hunt you are to come with me ahead of everyone else and get into that clump of trees that you can see ahead. The chief said that the braves with bows and arrows would stay at this end of the trees and get arrows into every buffalo they can before they stampede. He said that you are the best brave among us with a rifle, and he considers me as being good, so you will take the best rifle and I will take the other one and we will bring down all that we can as they run north."

"Shouldn't that be reserved for the braves?"

"Whether you realize it or not you are one of our braves and will always be. No matter where you go or when you come back you will be one of the tribe."

"I would like to someday come back and find that your tribe could all speak English so I could talk to everyone here. I feel like I'm part of your tribe, but since I can't speak much of your language I feel like an outsider."

The buffalo herd was peacefully grazing and slowly moving toward the grove of trees far to the north, so they planned the hunt so some of the braves would be on one side and some on the other side of the herd. Some of the braves went ahead and stationed themselves in the timber.

"It's time for us to go," Running Deer said to Jasper. He took Jasper with him and they made a wide circle and settled themselves in the timber ahead of the other braves. Some of the other braves were near them but they had bows and arrows and they stayed south of them since Jasper and Running Deer had the only two rifles. The other braves slowly rode along each side of the herd; far enough away not to get them excited so they would stampede, but close enough to slowly guide them toward the wooded area.

When the buffalo herd was near the timber they split up and part went on one side and part on the other side of the timbered area. When they were close enough the braves that were hidden in the south end of the timber began firing their arrows. Then when they were near Jasper and Running Deer they began firing their rifles. Then they stampeded and were gone in minutes. They brought down eight of the larger ones and then Jasper and Running Deer mounted their horses and brought down three more that had been wounded by the braves with bows. Running Deer said that much meat would last them until it would spoil. They would also have a lot of meat that they could dry for jerky.

When the stampeded buffalo were past the men and the dust had settled the squaws and papooses came with knives, baskets and pots and pans and began skinning the buffalo and cutting up the meat. That was intriguing to Jasper because he had never seen such a co-operative effort among a bunch of women and kids. Then he noticed that the braves began riding back toward the camp to take care of their horses, leaving the squaws to take care of the meat and get it to camp the best way they could, and they apparently expected him to do the same. Jasper knew that it would take the squaws many hours to carry the meat on foot, a basket at a time. The braves were paying no attention to them and were in a jovial mood talking about how they had made some good shots.

Jasper had stopped his horse near where they were taking care of the meat and loaded all that he could, tying piece after piece in front and behind him and then he discovered that he was the only man helping with the heavy work. But he decided that even though the braves had left that he would help until the meat was in camp. Not only that load but he was determined to continue until it was all at their camp.

They were saving everything that was edible and they would later stretch the hides out to dry, after scraping all of the meat and fat from the insides of them. They were cutting a lot of the meat in strips to hang in the sun to dry.

Jasper remembered when they cut up meat on the plantation. They would set aside all that would be used fresh including what they would grind for sausage and all of the bones that would be boiled and used for soups and stews. Then they would grind and season the sausage and stuff it into the cleaned entrails so it could be kept until it was used. Then they would rub salt on everything else, because otherwise it would spoil in a few days.

Although the braves had ignored the squaws and had gone to take care of their horses, Jasper's mother had taught him to help out whenever and however he could and he was determined to help with the meat. When he had his horse loaded and was on his way to camp, he saw the young girl.

When he went around a bush and saw her, he saw that she

was looking directly at him with an unwavering gaze, with her pretty brown eyes. He thought that she was a little younger than he was, but she also looked very grown up in her buckskin clothing. As he approached her he found that he had trouble keeping his eyes off her. Then he found that he didn't want to. He wondered why he had not seen her before because he had been at the pow-wow when Running Deer and he had been declared men instead of boys and she must have been there. He had been around camp for weeks then and she had to have been there all of the time. He had never seen a girl near his age except the ones on the plantation and they were somewhat younger than him and were always dressed in sugar sack dresses, some with the writing still on the cloth. But she couldn't have been much younger than him and was dressed in the prettiest deerskin blouse and skirt with ornaments around the hem that he had ever seen. It was much prettier than the ones the squaws wore. He thought that she was the prettiest girl that he had ever seen.

Why was he feeling that way? He had never felt like looking at a girl twice. Keep your thoughts to yourself, he thought; he must be on his way west and couldn't be thinking of any girl, especially an Indian girl that went up and down the stream each year. He could not consider staying there. But there she stood looking him in the eye, and she seemed as interested in him as he was in her.

Then he realized that the horse that he was riding had stopped and they were staring at each other. Then he realized that they had been staring at each other for a minute or two, so he kicked his horse into motion. As he passed her he had no intention of saying anything, but the word hello just kind of slipped out. Then he felt foolish because she just looked at him with those big brown eyes for a few more seconds and then looked away, saying nothing.

Then to make his embarrassment worse he noticed some of the squaws turning their heads and giggling; talking low in their language. They must have thought that it was hilarious when she ignored me, he thought.

Maybe she doesn't know how to speak English, he thought, but surely she could say hello. That bothered him because even though he had just seen her for the first time and she probably didn't know that he existed before, she shouldn't have ignored him like that. And why did she stand there and stare at him like that instead of going ahead with her work if she was going to ignore him if he spoke?

"I saw the prettiest girl that I have ever seen and she completely ignored me," he told Running Deer when they met after he had finished hauling meat to camp.

After Running Deer stopped laughing, he said, "I should have told you that young girls are not allowed to talk to a brave unless her father agrees that she can marry him. She is the chief's daughter called Early Flower. As I said before, the chief is my father's brother, so she is my cousin. She has not been promised to anyone yet, but you must not talk to her unless the chief decides that you are worthy of her."

"I thought she couldn't speak English."

"She can speak English almost as well as I can and she is so interested now that you have been teaching me that she wants me to teach her better English every chance I get. I'm surprised that you haven't noticed her before. You should feel elated because every brave here has been eyeing her but since you have been here she seems to have eyes only for you."

What could have been the reason he hadn't noticed her, he wondered? It could have been that he had been so busy that he hadn't taken time to see who was around him; he really hadn't had time to mingle with the tribe. Besides, Running Deer was the only one he knew that could speak English well and he didn't know enough of their language to carry on a conversation. But Running Deer had told him that before he had come he had been teaching some of the other braves as he was learning, but now that they were together most of the time, doing most of the hunting that he hadn't had time to teach them. He had tried to get the chief interested in speaking English, but he had refused to even try to learn.

"Why don't the braves help in getting the meat to camp," Jasper asked. "I was the only one helping."

"That is squaw's work. Some of the squaws thought it was funny when you helped by bringing the meat to camp and some of the braves wonder if they made a mistake in making you a brave. They can't understand how you can be such a good hunter and scout and still work like a squaw."

"My mother taught me to help people whenever and however I could, whether they were men or women. When you get more education and learn how other people live there will be no way that you will stay with the tribe and go along with their old fashioned traditions. You are too independent and you don't even talk or act like the other braves. When you get away you will find that people work together whether they are men or women. Maybe when the squaws and braves think about how much easier and faster it was getting the meat to camp, they will begin working together more."

"If I am different from the others it is because of your influence and I am grateful for your help, but my people have done things the same way since time began and you will never change any of them. The squaws have always skinned the meat and carried it to camp if it's not too far. If it's too far to carry it they take the old horses and lead them to where the meat is; then load all of the meat they can and then lead them back to camp."

"Not always, we skinned and dressed the wild hog before the women got there. I think that you're wrong; anyone can learn new ways."

"That was different. I wanted to impress the braves; show them that I could do the work of any brave so they would consider me a man."

"If you could do it under those circumstances, you could help out anytime."

Maybe that was the reason the squaws were laughing, he thought. They had never had any help with what was considered their work and they didn't understand. He thought that he might have done the braves no favor because the squaws may want the braves to do the same thereafter.

When the meat was in camp and his horse was taken care of, Jasper walked down to the water and was sitting on a log as he had done so many times on the plantation, thinking about all of the things that had happened since he ran away. He was paying little attention when someone said hello and he saw Early Flower getting water from the creek.

"Hello Early Flower," he said as he got up and offered to get the water for her. "I'm Jasper."

"I know," she said. "I have been asking Running Deer about you, but how did you know my name? I know that you haven't been paying any attention to me even though I have been parading myself around near you, sometimes right in front of you, when you were in camp."

"I asked Running Deer about you after we met while I was carrying meat to camp. I didn't understand when you ignored me when I said hello."

She explained that she wasn't allowed to accept his offer to get the water and then she said, "I have been watching you while you have been practicing with the bow and arrows and riding with Running Deer and the other braves. I shouldn't say this, but I like you. Are you going to stay with us and travel to our winter camp?"

"No. For reasons that I can't explain now, I can't go there this winter. Maybe someday it will be possible, but for now I'll keep going until I find a place where I can get an education."

"I would also like to have an education but my father says that it is not necessary, because the brave I marry will take care of me."

"Running Deer said that he was teaching you to speak better English, but you are doing fine with it already."

"I know that I'm not supposed to talk to braves but I have to speak our language with the older people. I must go now. My mother is waiting for the water and she will wonder why I am taking so long, but if you will let me, I will come and talk with you every chance I get."

"I like talking with you also. I would enjoy talking with you anytime you want, but Running Deer told me that your father is very protective of you and won't let you talk to braves, and he considers me one of his braves."

"He thinks of you as more than an ordinary brave and I feel the same way about you. I sometimes hear him talking about you. He is very fond of you and he would like for you to stay with us. He has never told me not to talk to you, but if he knew that I was, he would get very mad."

"Has Running Deer told you that I want to go west, maybe all the way to California, and get an education?"

"He told me and I am very disappointed that you won't stay with us."

"We really don't know each other. Why would you want me to stay?"

"When a young girl is old enough to marry, her father

chooses a husband for her. I am almost old enough, but my father has promised to wait until I learn more from the missionary before he chooses someone for me. The missionary said that we we're the only people anywhere that the father still chooses his daughter's husbands and I don't want him to choose for me. I want to choose my own husband."

"He will probably choose a good brave to be your husband."

"I don't want him to choose a husband for me," she said as she stepped forward and kissed him full on the mouth. "Do you see now why I want you to travel with us to our winter camp? The missionary showed us pictures and explained to us how to kiss. He said that's the way palefaces show affection."

Jasper was so embarrassed that he could only stand there dumbfounded, but his thoughts were running away. A girl! A young girl! A very pretty young girl and she kissed me! Kissed me right on the lips!

As he stood there trying to regain his composure she said "I must go now because I have been gone much too long already. I can't talk to you in camp but every chance I get I'll find you and talk to you."

Then she was gone and he was instantly lonely.

He couldn't understand his feelings for Early Flower. After all he really didn't know her. Some of the older girls on the plantation talked like they were interested in him; one of the oldest ones even put her arms around him once but she was a bit younger as were all of the others. Somehow he hadn't felt that way when he was with any of them. But none of them had kissed him. Maybe he would have felt just as dumbfounded if one of them had kissed him. Anyway, why was she talking and acting that way, he wondered? Surely she wasn't hinting that she wanted me as a husband, he thought. I'm too young to be thinking about such things. But why am I wishing that I had more time to be with her? If only she hadn't kissed me. Why did I get so excited? I didn't know that I would get excited if a pretty girl kissed me. Why am I suddenly thinking about staying with the tribe?

Jasper had been so busy since he had been with the tribe, and was having so much fun, he was thinking; why would I ever want to leave such excitement and such good companions? Yes, he admitted to himself, he was reluctant to leave the excitement of meeting and talking to Early Flower and having her kiss him, even for an education. Then he thought about his chances of being caught and sent back to the plantation.

CHAPTER 9

"I told you son, the man who told me about this place said that there were no Indians within a hundred miles of here. There's some to the north that attack hide hunters, but the only other tribe is too far south to bother us. They live clear down by the Gulf of Mexico and they would never travel this far north. The man also told me that there are no roads or even good trails through the woods to the south; there's nothing except thick forest and briars. We have this whole country to ourselves," the father of the other man said.

He was a short pudgy man with gray hair and a very un-ruly unkempt mustache and a worse looking beard. He had a very red face and the bulbous nose typical of the heavy drinker. He wore the blue bib overalls typical of a farmer and a plaid shirt. But it would seem that he was trying to impress someone because he was wearing one of the latest models of pistols in a new holster strapped around his waist. It was hung low on his hip; tied to his leg at the bottom as he had heard that the gun-fighters wore theirs. His pistol looked completely out of place in association with his attire; this would indicate a farmer or a plantation owner out looking over his plantation. He was carry-ing the latest model rifle, not in a saddle boot, but in his hands as if he might need it at any instant. They were riding horses; horses that looked like ordinary plow nags. They were riding ahead of a wagon; a shiny new one with ribs over the top but with no canvas top as the covered wagons had, as it was rolling across the open country southeast and across the creek from the tribe's summer camp.

"We have only the word of that one man and he has never been here. He had only the word of a man who had trapped farther west and his trapping had been done years ago," his son called Slim said.

"Even if there is a tribe nearby we'll have that wagon loaded with hides and out of here before any Indians know that we're in the country," the father said.

"I don't like it, Dad, if there's a tribe within ten miles of us they can hear these big rifles that you bought. Don't you remember the man saying that they were big fifties and that they would kill a buffalo within five hundred yards and that you would have a sore shoulder for a week? And don't for a minute think that Indians can't tell the difference between the sound of a rifle shot and a twig snapping in the woods. Besides, we're too far from town to get the meat back without it spoiling if we kill something. The reason that the Indians are killing people that are killing buffalo is that they're taking only the hides and leaving the meat to rot like we're planning to do. I don't like to see meat wasted."

"Don't worry about a little buffalo meat going to waste. Even if we were close to town, we couldn't take the meat. These buffalo are so big the wagon would only hold the meat from two or three. There's so many buffalo that the few that we kill won't matter. I told you that we would make a fortune with the hides that we will get, and with those slaves to skin them, we don't even have any expenses. While we're here we'll continue feeding them only buffalo meat, then it won't cost us anything," he said as he took another long drink from the large bottle that had been stuck in his inside coat pocket.

"You can't do that. I told you yesterday when you fed them that tough buffalo meat that you couldn't treat them like animals. Things are not like they were years ago, especially since all of the talk of freedom started. With all of the threats flying back and forth and the troops on both sides squaring off at each other, it seems that there will soon be a full-scale war. I have read about some slaves rebelling and killing their owners, not too far from our plantation. Besides, there is no need to feed them tough meat because we brought plenty of food to feed everyone until we have a load of hides."

"Food my foot! It will keep for later. Most of it is salted or smoked meat and it will keep until we're back to the plantation. While we're here they have no choice but to eat whatever we feed them. Besides I think all of the talk about freedom and war is nothing but talk. How can the United States Government set someone free that has been bought and paid for? When we bought that plantation we bought these slaves along with it. They are our property fair and square.

"Right now I can almost feel the money in my pocket. When we get into some real herds of buffalo we'll really clean up. I've been told that some of the herds number into the thousands."

"I still don't like any part of it. If you don't lay off that bottle you won't be able to see a buffalo if we stumble into one. We haven't seen but that one old buffalo and he was so old that he couldn't keep up with the herd that he must have been following. He's so tough that no one can chew the meat. I tried to eat it yesterday and if I didn't have that jerky in my sack I would be half starved."

"They will chew it when they get hungry enough. We have enough food besides what we brought for the slaves that Gabe can cook behind the wagon to last the three of us until we're home with the wagon load of hides."

"I tell you, Dad that we're going to have trouble with those slaves. You can't mistreat people that way anymore. They will know that we are not eating the same tough meat that they are. Suppose we run into some Indians with only those four slaves and us? They have been so badly treated that they would not think of helping us. We won't have a chance even against a small hunting party."

"We'll have a chance alright. If we run into Indians we'll just pretend that we're leaving and circle around, then when they think we're gone they will leave, and then we'll circle back and continue hunting. When they think we're leaving they won't attack us while we're going away. All they want is for people to stop killing buffalo and all they will see is that there are seven grown men and they will assume that we all have rifles and they will have bows and arrows. They'll be afraid to follow us."

"Since you never learned to read, you never keep up with what is happening. You don't really know anything about Indians. A lot of them now have guns and ammunition that they get in trade. And there's nothing wrong with their eyesight; they can fire them as well as anyone else."

"I do know a lot about Indians. Before we bought that plantation, don't you remember, we lived around a lot of Indians; some of them did odd jobs around the house and we had no trouble with them?"

"Those were Indians that were thoroughly whipped by the Army and were put on a reservation or that didn't want to fight and voluntarily went. These are Indians that want to keep their country; and it has been their country for millions of years, as far as we know. They have seen people not only plowing up their hunting grounds, but also destroying their game and their way of life. They call their country Indian Nations and they are ready and willing to fight for them."

"I tell you, we can handle them if they come after us. I've got enough rifles to give each slave one and they will be afraid not to use them, because I have told them that if Indians capture prisoners, they torture them for weeks before killing them and taking their scalps."

"I wouldn't give a slave a gun. As bad as you have been treating them and the way you have been frightening them, instead of helping us they will know that their best chance would be in getting away. They will turn tail and run and then you'll lose them completely. Then we couldn't operate the farm with only women and kids.

"If you would stay off that bottle and not stay drunk all day every day, you could think clearly and know that I'm right."

"I have told you before and I'll tell you again; the bottle has nothing to do with this or any other situation. You are always giving me a rough time about my drinking, just like your mother did before she died.

"I told you that those slaves would have no choice. None of them has ever held a gun and they won't be able to hit anything, but firing at them will run the Indians away. Then when the Indians are gone we will take the guns away from them before they have a chance to plan anything. Besides if we see any Indians it will be only a hunting party and we can handle them with no problem. With seven of us all with modern rifles; we won't let them get close enough to do any damage with their primitive weapons; It's against the law to sell them guns. Besides your brother is in the wagon with the slaves and he can see that they cause no trouble."

"You know that he wouldn't know what to do. He might get excited and do anything. Besides whether it's against the law or not, I have read about some of them having the most modern rifles."

"Why do you talk about your brother that way?"

"I see that there is no use to argue with you, but I think

that you are making a big mistake." Like father like son, he was thinking; neither of them have good judgment.

He remembered when their farm had been a profitable one, but when his mother had died, it had gone downhill financially until it wasn't even paying its way. It had been her that had been doing all of the planning, and he knew how himself, but he knew that his father wouldn't let him make any decisions. He had wanted to keep the slaves that his father had sold late in the fall the year before so he could buy two new wagons and all of the weapons.

"What will we do with two new wagons when we will only have four slave men and a bunch of women and kids left?" He had asked his father.

"We'll do like everyone else has been doing. In the spring we will go after all of the buffalo hides that we can get."

"You know nothing about hunting buffalo and you know that Gabe will be no help at all."

"Don't talk about your brother like that. He does a lot of things around here."

"Yeah! He goes out among the slaves and scares them half to death by carrying that gun and looking from one side to the other like a wild man."

"We can't leave him here. We need him to ride in the wagon and keep the slaves in line. They are so afraid of him that they will not dare do anything they're not told to do."

"If you would let me plan the work here, we could pull the farm out of its slump and buy some more slaves; then we wouldn't need to hunt buffalo. If things don't turn around soon so that we get some more money we will lose the whole plantation."

"I'll do the planning around here as long as I'm alive. You just want to take over the plantation."

There was as much difference as there was between night and day and then night again between the father and his two sons. The father wanted everything new and shiny and he would sell off anything, even their best assets to have things his way. He even looked and acted flighty when he saw something new. He would go around whatever it was, sizing it up and bickering with the owner about the price as if he were going to buy it, even if he had no money.

His son Gabe was short and pudgy like his father and even looked like him in the face. He always acted like a half-wit. They said that he didn't care whether school kept or not. He could learn nothing in school the two years that he went and his father finally gave up and kept him home.

Unlike either of the other two members of the family, the other son, who was arguing with his father — they always called him Slim — was just that. He had taken after his mother, both in stature and intellect. He was taller than either his father or his brother and unlike his brother, he could not only learn, but he learned fast. He had gone to school until his mother died and then he had no choice but to quit and help around the plantation. He had studied the way his mother planned things at the plantation and he knew that he could operate it at a profit if he were given a chance, because he had some ideas that would be a great improvement over the way his mother had planned the operation. Some things he had been taught in school which the others hadn't had the benefit of, and some he had worked out himself.

He decided that there was no use in arguing with his father and began greasing the wheel hubs, repairing the harness and loading one of the wagons to go buffalo hunting. He had no options on which horses to use because his father had sold all of the horses except the four workhorses. Two of them, although they were not fast, could be used for riding. His father thought they were the fastest two horses in the country. But they had mules, lots of mules. The slowest, meanest, most stubborn, most contrary mules known to man. He had sold some of the mules on approval but they had always come back home, but not voluntarily.

"Suppose we are shooting buffalo and the slaves decide to overcome Gabe and leave with the wagon?" Slim asked.

"They know that these are two of the fastest horses in the country. We would catch them before they went two miles. Besides, your brother may be a little slow, but they know he's trigger-happy. He shot at that slave, remember, when he was going into the woods with that mule. It didn't take that slave long to change his mind and come back with the mule.

"There's some buffalo now. I just saw one's back above that hill. Let's ride partway up the hill and then slip over the top on foot and surprise them."

"Dad, I think that I see smoke over there," Slim said as the slaves were skinning the buffalo they had killed. "It's hard to tell with the sun in my eyes, but it looks like little puffs of smoke coming from behind that hill."

"You must be getting skittish from worrying about Indians. I don't see anything. If you're so worried about getting caught by Indians, jump in there and give the slaves a hand skinning buffalo."

"I'm not that worried. I didn't want anything to do with this whole operation, remember. We won't make enough money on these hides to make any difference, but Dad, I know I see little puffs of smoke over that hill. They're little puffs of different sizes, rising at different intervals. I have read that Indians can talk to each other with smoke signals and I think that's what those are. I may be wrong but that's the way the writer described them."

"I can see something but they look like little clouds to me. I think that you're getting spooky about Indians."

"I wish those slaves would hurry so we could get out of here. I have had a bad feeling since we left the farm about this whole operation. We need to get out of here before whoever that is calls a whole tribe of Indians."

"You know that they never get in any hurry no matter what they are doing. But we're not leaving until we have that wagon loaded with hides."

"Dad, I think I just saw something over there near where I saw the smoke."

"Stop worrying and let's get those hides loaded and start trailing that herd. They haven't had time to get far. We should get a lot more hides today."

"Dad, I know that I saw something over there, it's a horse and one is over there, and over there, and over there."

"Those are Indians. Quick, give the slaves the extra guns. They think we're surrounded, but I can see one place to the east where we can get through. If they get there before we do, with all of the guns that we have we can fight our way through."

"Let's take a chance and run for it through that opening before we give them the guns."

"Give them the guns quick and tell them to follow behind us and start firing at Indians while we are leaving. That will keep them from getting closer to that opening and the wagon will give us some protection while we get away."

***

As Jasper and Running Deer were scouting across the creek to the southeast of their summer camp to see if another herd of buffalo was migrating north, they heard noises that sounded like gunshots.

"I think those were gunshots. They sounded like big rifles and someone may be hunting buffalo, but no one should be hunting near here," Running Deer said.

"They sure were big rifles. It was hard to tell exactly where the sound came from, but I would guess that they were directly ahead of us," Jasper answered. "Let's circle through those trees and ease up over that hill and see if we can find them."

They made a large circle and went through a stand of oak timber where there were countless leaves and underbrush, so they had to leave their horses and go on foot through the timber and up the small hill they were aiming for. They came into a clearing halfway up the hill, so they began crawling. When they crawled over the hill they could look directly down on the hide hunters.

"They have four down," Running Deer said when they were looking down at the hunters and skinners. "If you will ride as fast as you can for the braves I will send up a smoke signal warning them that there is danger ahead!"

"Be careful because they may see your smoke and come looking for you. Maybe you can send a signal from inside that clump of timber."

"That won't work because the trees will deflect the smoke and interfere with the signals. I must be in the open, preferably partway up this hill so the smoke signals will go higher before they dissipate."

"Then be careful and be ready to get away fast. You will have one advantage because the sun is directly in their eyes when they look up here. But they may still come after you if they think there is only one person here."

"There is little chance of that because they are too busy skinning buffalo. But if they do come after me I'll be back to camp by the time they can get up that hill. We're only a mile from camp. If you can make the braves understand the method that I explained to you, they will be surrounded by the time they are finished skinning and loading the hides from the four animals."

Since they were so close to camp the braves had heard the shots and had seen the smoke signals and were on their way. They met Jasper about halfway between the camp and Running Deer. Jasper decided that it would be best if he didn't try to talk to them because he knew too little of their language, so he motioned for them to gather around. Then he took a stick and drew a circle and then rubbed out a section where he remembered an opening to the east between the hills. He assumed that would correspond approximately to where the wagon had entered the little valley. Then he made little marks around the circle. Then he pointed to them individually and pointed to a mark for each of them. They understood instantly and they all left for their respective positions. He had laid out the surroundin g method of which Running Deer was so fond.

"Look at that wagon go!" Jasper said as the wagon went ahead of the two men on horseback toward the opening they had left for their escape. "They are firing at us but they are too far away to do any harm. No, they are firing at each other. There went one out of the wagon."

"They didn't stop to pick him up. The two on horseback didn't even stop to see if he's alive."

"We should wander over and see if he's wounded."

"That's just like you; always worried about someone. You saved my life, me being an Indian, and if I couldn't have spoken English, when I woke up I could have thought you had hit me on the head and done you harm. Now you want to walk up to a man lying on the ground that may only be wounded and shoot you." Running Deer said.

While they were discussing the man on the ground, the brave who was in charge came to them and said, "If you two will see that those men leave completely, we will take care of the meat and get it to camp."

When they passed the man who had fallen out of the wagon they saw that he had been shot and there was nothing that they could do for him; he was already dead, so they continued following the wagon.

"They are still shooting at each other," Running Deer said when it was getting dark. "We have followed them far enough to know that they are not coming back, so why don't we camp here and find out where that herd went on our way back tomorrow?"

They were making camp when the horse one of them had been riding came by them. They caught it and rode toward where the wagon had gone, leading the horse. They had gone only a short distance when they found one of the men, the one called Slim, whose horse had stepped in a hole and fallen on him, and he couldn't walk.

"What do you suggest that we do with you?" Jasper asked. "If we take you with us to the tribe they may not be very sympathetic with you after finding you killing buffalo for their hides. If we put you on your horse and start you on your way back to where you came from, you may not make it back."

"I know that we were doing wrong and I was not for it at all, but I am completely in your hands. My father will not stop chasing that wagon until he is killed; my brother is already dead. The slaves will be gone so the farm will be almost a total loss, but if you will tie me on my horse, I will make it back all right and I can take what is left of the farm and get it in production again."

"Do you have enough food and water to get back?" Jasper asked.

"I have the canteen and enough food tied behind my saddle to last until I reach the last settlement we passed. I will somehow make it," the man said.

"I think we should give him the chance, however slim it may be," Jasper said. "I don't think there is a chance that he will ever be back."

"I knew you would say that," Running Deer said as they were loading him on his horse.

CHAPTER 10

Jasper and Running Deer found that the herd of buffalo that the men had been killing for their hides, in the confusion they must have felt during the stampede, while running full speed from the depression in which they had been between the hills, had split up. Some went one way and some went another, then some changed direction and met the others and they had all gone south. The stampede had ended but they had continued south. They found no buffalo left in the immediate area; not even any stragglers were left that they could find within five miles.

The tribe was very disappointed. There had been no buffalo near their camp for weeks and they had been required to ration meat. Even though they had salvaged four buffalo, they needed much more meat from that herd. They knew that without it, unless they could find another source, they would have to ration themselves again soon because they were needing to go further away from camp to find deer and small animals and it was hard to find enough animals to supply meat for so many people.

Had the buffalo not gone south instead of north the hide hunters would have done them a favor because the herd would have stampeded toward their camp. By the time they would have crossed the creek the stampede would have been over and they would have slowly drifted by their camp as they normally did. Then the braves could have killed a few. Besides the four that they salvaged, which would last them for only a few days, they needed at least a dozen because they needed to begin drying meat for the coming winter. They had been so short of meat that they had used the jerky they had made earlier in the season.

They had little choice but to find meat from some source. The chief sent six braves with packhorses to follow the herd until it stopped and try to turn it north. If that failed they were to bring back all of the meat that their packhorses and horses could carry, but he kept Jasper and Running Deer in camp.

"I want you and Jasper to go north because you are the most efficient and know how far you can go. Take some packhorses with you and bring back all of the meat you can find. I will send a hunting party to the west and maybe between all of you, you can get enough meat to last until another herd of buffalo comes by," the chief told Running Deer.

Very early the next morning Jasper and Running Deer went north with two packhorses each. They were lucky enough to find a herd of deer the first afternoon and by evening they had four dressed and ready for loading. The next morning they had only to track them a short distance and they bagged another four. The following day they returned with all of the packhorses loaded and a deer on each of their horses.

The people were elated because since the hunting party that had been sent west had returned with only some small game, hardly enough to matter, the deer that Jasper and Running Deer had brought would last them for a few days.

Two days later the braves that had been sent south returned with their packhorses loaded with buffalo meat. They reported that the herd had circled around and were headed north again, and should reach their camp within a few days, but to be sure they had meat, they had killed another four.

After that Jasper and Running Deer would leisurely hunt for small game and deer; more like sport hunters instead of braves badly needing meat, as they had been the week before; not really rushing but merely drifting around the area, using their bows and arrows. That pleased Jasper because he had never had the chance to leisurely hunt. If he was allowed to go hunting with the slaves on the plantation, which he was rarely allowed to do, they had no guns and would use dogs to tree the game. Sometimes Jasper or another boy would be sent up the tree to shake out whatever had been treed, but sometimes they would use the saw or axes to cut down the tree so the dogs could catch the small game. They could only hunt at night, using torches for light, so most of the time Jasper never had a chance to see the game until the dogs had it killed. Jasper didn't really like to see so many trees cut because it made such a mess in the woods that it was hard for him to get through, but they served him well when it was time to build rafts. Especially when he built the raft on which he crossed the river when he ran away from the plantation. There had been plenty of small timber on the ground in the immediate area for his purpose.

"Jasper has become a real brave, hasn't he?" Early Flower asked Running Deer while they were walking near the creek after Jasper and he had returned from a day of hunting.

"He sure has. He puts every waking hour into learning something and he puts forth all of his energy into whatever he tackles. He will sometimes wear me out because while the other braves are lying around camp, he wants us to go hunting or practicing. He doesn't know it yet, but he can ride better, shoot better, track better and has better judgment when it comes to planning a hunt than any brave in camp, including me."

"Do you think that he will stay with us when we return to our winter camp?"

"I don't think he will. All he talks about is going to a place called Texas or a place called California and getting an education. He says that should be the most important goal for anyone while they are young."

"Where are those places that he wants to go?"

"He said that Texas is closer, but that California is more than two thousand miles to the west. He said that it is over five times as far as it is to our winter camp."

"I wish the missionary had taught us more about numbers and about other places, but I think he did well to teach us English and the few things we learned about numbers during the two seasons that he was there. He also had other things to do. The worst of which was trying to talk my father into letting all of the braves learn to speak English."

"He did a very good job. It's too bad that your father didn't let you start learning when I did. He wouldn't have let me go if he were my father instead of my uncle."

"Why does Jasper want to go so far? He could get an education when the missionary returns if he came with us. He should be back this fall."

"The kind of education he talks about, he couldn't get from the missionary. He wants to be a doctor or a lawyer."

"What is a lawyer?"

"He said it's a person who does papers for people. I don't understand all that he means, but he said that he goes to court with people when they have a problem with the law."

"Do you mean like the Indian agent the missionary was talking about?"

"They must be something like that."

"Do you think you could talk him into coming with us? He must really like you."

"And I like him, remember, we are blood brothers. But I wouldn't try talking him into doing something that he doesn't want to do. He wants to go west for an education more than anything else and the way he talks and as excited as he gets when he talks about going, I don't blame him."

"I like him too. Do you think that if I pleaded with him he would change his mind and stay?"

"When I would see the look in your eyes when he was around camp, I knew that you were interested in him, but I didn't know you were this serious."

"He didn't know that I existed until he was bringing a load of meat into camp. He never even looked at me before, but he knows that I exist now, because I hunted until I found him at the creek and I let him know how I feel. He now knows without a doubt how I feel about him."

"You know that your father would nearly skin you alive if he knew that you talked to him without permission. He would even be mad if he knew that you felt that way. You know that he will pick a good brave for you to marry when you are old enough."

"But I don't want him to pick a husband for me. I want to pick my own husband and I want him to be Jasper."

"You know that you're too young to make a decision like that. When you are older you may change your mind."

"I'll not change my mind. You'll see. If Jasper will come with us this fall and stay with the tribe, I'm sure that I can talk my father into letting me marry him."

"Just because you talked to him once, why do you think that he would marry you? He may think that you talked to him out of curiosity and may not know that you are interested in him. He asked about you once, but only to ask about why you didn't speak to him when he was bringing meat to camp."

"I not only talked to him, but do you remember the missionary telling us how the palefaces kiss each other? Well, I kissed him right on the mouth, but he only looked at me with a shocked look on his face."

"Don't tell anyone else about that because your father would be very mad and he may make Jasper leave. Besides, if you talked him into staying here and marrying you when he wants to leave, you could possibly both be miserable later, because he wants to go west for his education as soon as he can."

"Why is he so determined to go west? The missionary said that the best schools are up north where he is from. Did he ever tell you why he doesn't want to go north for his education? If he did he would be closer to where we are now, then maybe he could visit sometimes."

"He has never given me a hint as to why he wants to go west. He never even told me where he is from and I don't really care. If he wants me to know, he will tell me."

"Why don't you ask him? He may tell you."

"I would never do that. When he rescued me he said that he couldn't tell me anything about himself except that his name is Jasper. If you are as interested in him as you say, don't ask him because I can tell that he wants that to be his secret and I'm sure that he will resent someone prying into his past."

Jasper was taking care of the horses that they were letting him use, deep in thought about whether or not he should stay there with the tribe, when Running Deer suddenly appeared behind him.

"The chief wants us to go north for a day or two and find out where the buffalo are. We will need some meat within a few days," he said.

He had been thinking about things that he shouldn't, Jasper thought. He didn't even know that Running Deer was behind him. He decided that he was getting too careless and that he had to get his mind back on a way of getting started on his way farther west for his education. He had made up his mind; nothing or nobody would keep him from that, not even Early Flower.

Jasper was happy for the chance to do more scouting for game, although he didn't like the way they had killed the buffalo that were driven by the trees. He liked to stalk animals instead of driving them to where they would be slaughtered like cattle.

After a day of riding they saw a small herd far ahead of them, grazing and slowly moving toward the west.

"Maybe we could camp here and tomorrow morning we could make a wide circle to get ahead of them and head them south," Jasper said. "Then we could slowly push them toward our summer camp."

"That sounds like a good idea," Running Deer said. "We can try it but buffalo have minds of their own and are hard to get moving in any one direction; they may stampede and go in any direction. You said our summer camp. Does that mean that you will stay with the tribe?"

"That was just a slip of the tongue. I won't let anything keep me from getting an education."

"We'll be leaving for the winter camp in about two months. I sure hope you will change your mind."

"I can't tell you why, but lately I have been having thoughts of staying with the tribe."

"I already know why. Early Flower told me about the two of you meeting at the creek. I told her not to say anything to anyone else because her father may hear of it. And as I heard you once say; he would be fit to be tied; so mad he could chew nails."

When Jasper stopped laughing they began unloading their supplies so they could make camp before finishing their circling of the herd the next morning.

They were lucky that the herd, when they were in front of them, began turning toward the south, then began running, but not like a stampede. When the herd had calmed down and was only a half-day's ride from camp they circled them again and went back to camp. When they reported what they had done to the chief, he sent most of the braves out to make sure that the buffalo kept moving toward the trees where they had waited before.

Jasper had finished taking a bath and washing his clothes and was sitting on the same log that he usually sat on when Early Flower sat down beside him. He felt a little embarrassed with her sitting tight beside him, but he found himself enjoying her presence. He had never been that close to a girl before she had kissed him; except when the young girl on the plantation put her arms around him for an instant and that hadn't excited him in the least. Now he was excited because he didn't know what she had in mind.

"My father would never give me permission to meet and talk to you, and he would be mad if he saw me sitting like this, but I want to spend all of the time I can with you. I want to be with you all of the time."

"I'm glad you came because I wanted to be with you again before I leave."

"Before you leave? Then you are really going west all alone?"

"Running Deer said that if the chief approved, he would like to explore some of the country to the east and while I'm here I would like to see all of the country that I can, so I'll go with him. I'll be leaving as soon as we return."

"Running Deer told me not to ask you to stay here, and I won't ask you, but if I was your squaw I could go with you when you leave."

"Don't talk like that. We are both too young to make a decision like that now, and I don't even know where I'm going or what I'll find when I get there. After awhile you may change your mind and then you would be very unhappy. If you stay here you may find a nice brave for a husband. If you go with me I don't have any way of making a living and I can't go up and down the river all of the time. For reasons that I can't mention now, that would be unsafe."

"That's what Running Deer said. But I won't change my mind. I want to go with you if you won't stay here."

Jasper's emotions suddenly ran away with him and he turned and kissed her. She clung to him for a few minutes and suddenly said, "I must go now; someone may miss me, but I'll come and be with you every chance I get."

Jasper was thinking, why am I reluctant to leave Early Flower? She is too young now to know what she really wants. But I have become awfully fond of her in the last few days. Would she really be content to leave the tribe? If not, why would I even consider staying here? I could never stay with the tribe. I feel fairly safe here, but I would be worried every time we went south.

There was another thing to consider; he had been free of the Brisley's for only a few short weeks. But he was so happy to be able to make his own decisions and go and come as he pleased that he was constantly wondering how he could get his family away from the plantation. Then they could see what it was like to be free; but he could do nothing for them if he were going up and down the river.

For the present he had to get all of the other thoughts out of his mind and start thinking practical again. After all, his main concern had been in getting far enough from the plantation to be safe, and he hadn't as yet done that.

"Do you think Jasper will stay with us and go to our winter camp?" The chief asked Running Deer that same afternoon.

"I don't think he will. He wants to go west and find a place to get an education. He wants to have a way to make a living, he said, before he gets too old to go to school."

"The way he learns things, he will be able to do whatever he wants."

"That's all he talks about; being able to do what he wants."

"Did you know that Early Flower is very fond of him?"

"She told me. But how did you know? Did she tell you?"

"She didn't tell me until yesterday, but I knew it already. She said that she wants to marry him. She has been letting me know in other ways ever since he has been here. She would hint to me and make sure that I saw her looking at him when he was around camp."

"They are both so young now," Running Deer said.

"I know that they are both young, but she is afraid that if he leaves he won't come back here."

"Would you approve of them getting married even though he has nothing to offer for her? He has no horses; no robes; no skins; nothing. He has no blood ties to the tribe."

"You said that he is a blood brother to you; that's a blood tie. I have already decided to give him the horses that he is using. He is such a good hunter, if I demanded them, he could have buffalo hides and robes whenever he wanted them."

"You sound as if you like the idea of them marrying."

"I want Early Flower to be happy, even if it means breaking our traditions. And I could do a lot worse in what the palefaces call a son in law. I'm afraid that if he leaves he will not come back and she will be very sad."

"Then you need to try and convince him to stay. I have already hinted and done everything except ask him, because I would like for him to stay, but I won't ask him because I'm afraid he would be very unhappy here."

"I can't ask him because he may think I'm demanding that he stay and he may leave with hard feelings toward me. Since he likes to explore and travel; and both of you have been doing more than your share of the work and hunting, maybe if you and him went on a trip together and saw some of the other country around here, he would decide to stay. Since he has been here you two have done nothing except work and hunt for meat."

"We have discussed exploring the area to the east across the creek and I was going to ask your permission. I would like to see that area and a few more places around here that I haven't seen while he's here, but I'm sure that it would have nothing to do with whether he goes or stays. I don't think he would ever be happy here. Even though I want him to stay, I also want him to go for his education."

"He'll learn to like it when we get to our winter camp and he sees what a nice place it is. Then he'll marry Early Flower and make her happy."

Running Deer told Jasper that the chief had agreed that they could take some time to do some exploring. They decided that since they hadn't been very far across the creek to the east, they would go there as they had talked about earlier and see what that country was like. They may even find an area that the braves would like for hunting, since the game had been getting scarcer every year around their summer camp.

Jasper was reluctant to go because he knew that direction would take him closer to the cities of the east and closer to the plantation. If he should be recognized he would surely be taken back to Master George. His curiosity and his desire to please Running Deer were greater than his fears, so he agreed to go.

While they were preparing to go Jasper was down by the creek making himself presentable; he had finished bathing and had his pants on but his shirt was still hanging on a limb when he saw Early Flower coming with something under her arm that looked like rolled up buckskin.

"I made you something," she said. "Don't tell anyone where you got them because my father would be mad if he knew that I made them. By the time you get back they will look used so no one will notice. Running Deer will know but he would never tell anyone."

When she handed the roll to him he found it to be a new buckskin jacket and matching pants. They were made much better than the pair they had given him when he joined the tribe. He was grateful because his old ones were wearing out and he badly needed some.

Then she saw his back.

"Ooh," she said as she put her hands on his shoulders and began rubbing his back and shoulders. "Your back is all scarred where someone has used a whip on you. The missionary told us about slaves who were beaten by their owners. Now I know where you are from. I'll never tell anyone and it doesn't make any difference to me. I still want to be your squaw."

"Now you can see for yourself why I can't stay here and go up and down the river twice each year. Your winter camp would be too close to where I'm from. Besides, you may change your mind when your father chooses a brave for you. He may be a good husband and you may be happy."

"When an Indian girl marries the brave gives her father gifts and she is considered his property. She must do whatever he says. The missionary says that the palefaces do not treat their wives that way. I'm sure that you would never treat me like that. I have already told my father whom I want to marry and he has shown no objections."

Here I go again, Jasper thought; getting ideas that I can't afford to have; thinking about staying here and forgetting about going west. What would I have done without Running Deer and Early Flower along with the rest of the tribe? Even the chief has treated me better than I have ever been treated. Maybe I would be better off here. But what would I do when they put the tribe on a reservation? I could never stay under those conditions, so I would have to leave then anyway and I would be in no better position to make a living than I am now.

I'll go with Running Deer and explore some country and I will still have time to get over the mountains that the wrangler told me about before winter. I'll definitely leave as soon as we get back.

They were soon headed across the creek with a few supplies and their bows and arrows.

Jasper would have liked to have a rifle along in case they needed one, but the guns would be needed when the buffalo were near the camp, so even if he had been offered one he would not have taken it.

"How far have you or your tribe been this way?" Jasper asked as they were crossing the creek.

"No one that I know of has been more than a two-day ride in this direction."

"How far do you want to go this time?"

"I don't know what to expect so I wouldn't want to put a time or distance limit on the trip. I thought that we would go until we decided to turn back. The trappers have told me that there are some settlements not far to the east of here."

"Going until we decide to turn back sounds good to me," Jasper said. "But I don't want to go even near where some settlements are located."

"I don't either; I don't think there has been any trouble between the settlers and Indians in this area, but there is no need to take a chance. If you want to go another direction we can explore somewhere else."

"As soon as we get back to camp I intend to start west, but

I would like to see the rest of this area before I leave. Let's take our time and just loaf around for awhile and you can teach me more about stalking animals."

They had two good horses and provisions for a few days and they were sure that they could get what fresh meat they wanted, so the rest of the tribe was not expecting them back for some time. This would be the first time that Running Deer had been more than a three-day ride away from the tribe except with hunting parties. He knew that Jasper and he would be completely responsible for their own safety and would have to look out for each other if either of them had a problem, because the tribe would not come looking for them for quite some time.

Within a few miles after they crossed the creek they came to some rolling hills with fairly dense timber, mostly oak and pine mixed with some cedar and brush. There was a lot of small game as well as deer, and since they needed very few animals for their own use, they would practice tracking and stalking them. They would get as close as they could without scaring them away.

Jasper had never had time for that type of activity and he was amazed at how Running Deer seemed to know where the animals were before they could see them. They noticed that sometimes if they approached deer from behind brush and would shake a limb to make a little noise, the deer would sometimes come toward them to see what was there; especially a doe that had fawns. They could have killed many of them with arrows, but they didn't need the meat, so they made a game out of that activity while they were both getting some valuable experience.

"Have you enjoyed yourself while you have been with the tribe?" Running Deer asked.

"I have never had as much fun in my life. I just wonder how long that it will be before this area is all being farmed. I have heard that settlers are going all over looking for land that can be farmed. This would be good farm land and one of these springs you may come and find settlers all over the area."

"We'll run them off the land and take it back."

"There will be too many of them. When they are determined to farm you will never stop them."

"How do you know of all of those things? You never told me anything about yourself, and I never cared about where you came from, but since you have been talking about things that I have never heard of, I am curious."

"I still can't tell you anything about myself and I can't even tell you why, but I can tell you where I got a lot of information. When I was a little boy I met a man that seemed to enjoy telling me about all of the places he had been and all of the things that he had seen and experienced himself; maybe because I was such a good listener. He told me about settlers going west by the thousands looking for places to call home and how determined they are when they decide on a place they want to farm."

"Have you been to a lot of places yourself?"

"No, but that man would explain them so well that I almost felt like I had been there when he finished. He told me about driving a big herd of cattle from Texas to a place called Kansas. From the way he explained directions to me we may be in Kansas or Oklahoma now. He said that it would take weeks and it was sometimes so dry for a long time that they would lose some cattle from thirst."

"How could you remember all of those things when you were only a little boy?"

"I seldom got a chance to go to town, but when I did, I would go and talk to him. He was the only one who would talk to me, so I listened carefully to every word. Every time he would tell me of some place I would imagine me being there, and I thought that someday I would like to go to those places. I would also imagine doing the things that he would tell me about doing and I could visualize me doing them. Even now I sometimes dream about places that he told me about; places that I still want to go someday."

"I have never been to a town. The missionary told us about towns with stores where you can buy almost anything that you would want to eat and wear. He brought us some sugar when he came one winter. It was really good too, but we ate it from our hands. Then he told us that we should have put it in things that we cooked."

"We almost always had sugar, but we were never allowed to eat it out of our hands, unless we could sneak a handful. We were told that it was so expensive that we should keep it for cakes and pies."

"The missionary tells us about a lot of places, but not like the man you talked to. I would like to talk to someone like that. All I know about is our winter camp and our summer camp. I have been thinking about what you said about not staying with the tribe if I get an education, and I think you're right. I was going to try talking you into staying here and going to our winter camp, but now I think you should go west when we return. I was always excited when it was time to go north or south because I liked going up and down the river, but now I am beginning to wonder about the future of what we are doing."

"You could go to California with me. I don't know what to expect when I get there, but we could find out about the state together."

"I'm not as brave as you are about leaving."

"You're as brave as anyone that I have ever known. In my case it wasn't bravery that brought me here; I was scared stiff. To leave on your own for a place that you know nothing about takes more determination than bravery. If things get bad enough to seem unbearable you will do almost anything to get away from them."

"Things are not like that here. My uncle never bothers anyone. He just lets everyone do whatever they want, except when he sends braves out on hunting parties, but everyone works together without being told what to do."

"I have always been told what to do and could never do anything without permission," Jasper said.

"I think you just told me where you are from, but I won't say it, even to you. I wouldn't tell anyone if they were going to cut out my tongue."

"I have said a lot more than I intended. I had forgotten that you were smart enough to figure things out from a few words."

They spent a few days exploring further east, getting what small game they needed for their own use and just plain loafing around. Since Jasper had not been allowed to do any of that since he had been a small boy, he was really enjoying himself. They would sit or lie around for hours listening to the breeze blowing through the trees and to the small animals and birds feeding and scuttling about. There were squirrels, quail, rabbits and lots of small birds to watch and listen to. And they saw lots of wild turkeys. Jasper put an arrow through a young turkey and they had a change of diet; fire roasted partially burned turkey. They joked about it being the only way to cook a turkey; maybe not the only way but their only way.

They would sit and talk for hours at a time. Most of the time Jasper would talk about an education, while Running Deer would talk about life with the tribe; how they would travel back and forth year after year. Neither could talk about anything except their own little world, and Jasper didn't mention anything about the plantation. He was almost sure that Running Deer knew where he was from: that he was a runaway slave because of the slip of the tongue that he had made earlier. He didn't think that he would ever tell anyone but he didn't want to take any chances.

He also knew that Early Flower knew where he was from, but he was sure that she would never tell anyone. But he would have to watch himself in the future because if word got back to Master George while he was there or even after he found a way to go on to California, he would know exactly where to have someone to look for him.

He knew the wrath of Master George well enough to know that if he had any idea of where he was there would be someone on his trail immediately and he would never give up and stop searching for him.

While they were loafing around one day Running Deer said, "Early Flower said that the two of you were meeting regularly at the creek. Her father is very strict with her and she is not allowed to talk to young braves. Even though he knows that she is very fond of you and would like for you and her to marry, he would be very angry if he knew that you and her are meeting without his permission."

"We were mostly talking, but I really like her; so much that I have been having thoughts of staying here."

"She likes you too, probably more than you know. She would like for you to go down the river with us, but just be careful so that you don't give the chief the wrong idea."

"Even though I am reluctant to go west, I know that I would not be happy here and she probably would not be happy away from the tribe. She may think so now, but if she went with me when I don't know where I'm going or what to expect when I get there, things may not be like either of us expect and she may be very unhappy."

"I may be wrong, but I think that she would be happy with you no matter where you went."

Surely I can decide what will be best for both of us, Jasper thought. I am too young for the responsibility of a wife now, but I am still reluctant to leave Early Flower. Maybe it's because no one ever paid any attention to me before.

One morning Running Deer heard some horses coming toward them, and they decided that it would be best if they kept themselves hid until they found out if they had riders; and if so, who they were. There was a small level area with a clearing at the bottom of the hill, so they left their horses hidden in a small thicket and went on foot until they were in a position where they knew that the horses should pass. With their bows and arrows ready, they hid themselves to wait and watch.

CHAPTER 11

"Where do you think Jasper is now and what do you suppose he is doing?" his grandmother asked his mother.

"I have been reluctant to mention his name for a long time because it makes me so sad to think that he may be dead or in some kind of trouble," his mother said. "Every day I think that I may hear that he is alive and well."

"Oh, he is alive alright and he is doing well somewhere. I have all the confidence in the world in his abilities. He is a very strong young man and has a lot of self confidence and a lot of determination for his age so wherever he is you can be sure that he is in no trouble. He may even have a girlfriend or a wife by now."

"Jasper: no, not the Jasper that I raised; certainly not the Jasper that would be terrified of being caught and have to leave a wife or bring her to a place like this plantation. He said once that he would never marry a person that would have to work in the field everyday. He was never interested in any of the girls here. One of the girls here followed him around all of the time. I have seen her making eyes at him and flirting to the point of brushing against him when he was near and even putting her arms around him but he never seemed to notice or encourage her. Instead of having a girlfriend or wife, by now he is probably in Texas or even California, going to a school. All he ever talked about except getting an education were places that Wrangler had told him about."

"I think you're wrong about him not looking at a girl. I also heard him say that he didn't want a wife that was a slave and had to work in the fields every day; but he didn't say that he didn't want a wife, period. I just hope that when he made it across the river that he didn't get caught by some of the Indians there. But he wanted to be like an Indian so bad that if he found some, instead of them harming him, if he had half a chance, he would have made friends with them."

"What made you think that he went across the river? Did his father say something to make you think that he went that way?"

"No one had to say anything. I know that he went across the river. He loved the river so much that he would think of no other way to leave. Besides, as much effort as Mr. Brisley has put into finding him if he had gone in any other direction he would have been caught and brought back here by now."

"Don't even think about that area because if Master George even thought that he went across the river, he would have people scouring the whole countryside, looking for him and he would never stop searching. Besides, he had been told that he looked like an Indian so often, and played the part so much, I think you are right; he would be able to join them. He could surely do anything that Indian braves do. For all we know he may be an Indian brave now and as you think; he may have a young squaw."

His grandmother knew that his mother was saying those things as a way to bolster her faith that he was alive somewhere, but she didn't blame her in the least; she had been doing the same. She would like to change the subject but since they hadn't spoken of him for some time, Jasper was so strong on her mind that she wanted to discuss him.

"Since Mr. Brisley confides in you quite often, where does he think Jasper went? Has he ever mentioned that he may have tried going across the river and drowned?"

"He doesn't say much about him to me because he knows that it upsets me, but I'm sure he thinks he is alive and well wherever he went. After having the whole riverbank and all of the woods searched, he is sure in his own mind that he didn't try crossing the river. Since you know in your own mind that he went across the river, I can tell you that we are positive that he left that way. But the reason that they found no evidence was because his father went there immediately and erased every track and every bit of evidence that he accidentally left. Maybe he was in such a hurry that he didn't take enough time, but his father said that he left very little to indicate that he crossed the river.

"Mr. Brisley is getting desperate to find him. He had me to write some friends that he has known for years that live near Chicago asking them to look for Jasper, but I know that he has no confidence of finding him there. He went to school there and he said that there are so many cities in the north that it would be like looking for a needle in a haystack. Besides, he thinks that Jasper went by way of the woods and didn't head for a big city. That's why he had the woods here searched thoroughly. He is sure that he can survive alone in the woods."

"Do you think that Master George would whip Jasper if he did find him?" His grandmother asked. "He had been awfully mean to him before he left. I'm sure that he would still be here if he hadn't been so mean and whipped him with the horsewhip once."

"No. Mr. Brisley wouldn't let him whip Jasper if he did find him. In fact, Mr. Brisley told his father that if he was found that he wanted him brought directly to him and that he would guarantee that he would not be punished in any way. If he did whip him there would soon be no slaves left on the plantation except women and kids. The other slaves are as concerned about him as Mr. Brisley and they have vowed that they will start leaving immediately if Master George punishes him, especially since he has been so mean to the others since Jasper left. As you know, since the southern states have declared their independence from the Union and there has been some conflict, the slaves think it will be only a matter of a short time until they are freed. Listen to me! Talking about slaves as if I was not one! I am nothing but a slave myself, but I have been treated so much differently that I really don't feel like a slave. That is, except when Mr. Brisley tells me to do something that I would refuse to do if I was free to make decisions myself.

"Even if we were free right now, they would have to run me off to get rid of me until I found out Jasper's whereabouts."

"I feel the same way," his grandmother said. "When he was young, while you were taking care of Mr. Brisley and Master George made him work in the fields with me, he seemed more like my son than my grandson. And he talked so grown-up and independent then that I was afraid that he would try leaving long before he left."

"I was so afraid to think about him trying to leave and being caught that I would not admit it to myself, but I knew that he was conditioning himself and preparing to leave long before he did."

***

"We haven't seen anyone or any game for days," Drifter said to Jim as they were scouting and looking for game ahead of the wagon train. "It would seem that with all of this open country we should have seen something by now."

"There is an Indian tribe that has a village where they spend their summers a few days ahead of us," Jim said. "I hope they're in the same location this year, because they will know where to find game, maybe some buffalo. They should be there because it seemed to be a permanent village that they come to every summer."

"Do you mean that you know some Indians here in this wilderness? I have heard so many stories about the western Indians that I would think that they would be hostile toward us, trying to attack the train and take our scalps."

"Where they have their village doesn't seem like a wilderness at all; more like the beginning of the plains. As a general rule the western Indians are hostile, but to my knowledge those Indians are not hostile toward anyone. I consider them among my best friends. I only wish that Running Deer were here now. I'm sure he could find us some deer or buffalo before we have to butcher a cow."

"Who is Running Deer? He sounds like game himself."

"When I came by here last year I stumbled onto their village and was a little apprehensive and was circling the village when I ran into Running Deer down by the creek. He was so starved for company that he talked me into staying a few days and going hunting with him. I even traded them a few things that I could replace later, for furs. If they are at their camp you will meet him soon enough. You have a big surprise coming when we get there."

"I have an awful feeling that there is some kind of danger ahead," Drifter said. "I have this strange feeling that someone or something is watching us right now. They may have weapons trained on us right now."

"You and your feelings of danger; of course once when you had that feeling those wolves got into the cattle and killed a couple of cows before we could stop them and then the last time we ran into that bear. I hope your feelings this time don't signify some grave danger like they did the last couple of times."

When the two riders were close enough to be seen well

Running Deer recognized one of them as being a trapper, known to him only as Jim, who had stopped at their village for a few days and traded with them the past year. While he was there the two of them had become friends. He raised his hand in a sign of recognition and friendship and walked out of their hiding place. When Jim recognized him he dismounted and began walking toward them, leading his horse. During the last few weeks Drifter had come to trust Jim's judgment completely so he immediately dismounted and, leading his own horse began walking alongside him.

Jasper saw that one of them; the one called Jim, was tall, as tall as or taller than he was, and also somewhat slimmer than him, weighing no more than he did. He had brown hair and eyes and was wearing buckskin clothing that Jasper was later to learn, was typical of clothing normally worn by trappers and many other men that lived and traveled in the mountains.

The other man was somewhat shorter and weighed about the same as the tall one. He had lighter hair showing some gray and blue eyes. He wore the bib overalls and plaid shirt typically worn by farmers; he had the look of a farmer, except that he carried the longest rifle that Jasper had ever seen.

Jasper stepped out behind Running Deer and when they were close enough they exchanged greetings.

"Here's your danger," Jim said. "You are looking at Running Deer. This fellow is just called Drifter," Jim said introducing his companion.

"And this is Jasper. Jasper meet Jim and his friend Drifter," Running Deer said as they shook hands all around.

"Any friend of yours is a friend of mine," Jim said.

"He's not just a friend, he's my brother."

"So you are Indians from the tribe nearby. Jim didn't tell me that you could speak English," Drifter said.

"We sure are," Running Deer said.

"Now you can see what I meant when I said that you had a big surprise coming," Jim said to Drifter.

"According to all of the reports that we have been getting, the Indians to the north and also to the west are bloodthirsty and will kill every white person they see. I didn't expect to be greeted by anyone who was friendly," Drifter said.

"Where are the rest of your people?" Jim asked.

"They are at our camp past the creek where you found us last year. They will be happy to see you."

"Hey, you can speak better English. Last year we had trouble understanding each other."

"Jasper speaks much better English than I do and he has been teaching me. What are you doing here at this season when it's too hot to trap?"

"After I went by last year I decided to go farther east and visit my family, then I met some people who wanted me to guide their wagon train west, so I stayed until spring. They were having so much trouble with the Indians to the north that we decided to come this way and bypass them. It will be a rough trip because we will be going through some country that we don't believe has ever been crossed by wagon train," Jim said.

"I thought of you as only a trapper. Now I find that you are guiding a wagon train," Running Deer said. "Do you have any other traits that I don't know about?"

"You can never tell what a man has done or of what he is capable of doing by seeing him do one thing. When I got out of the Army after traveling across country I was looking for something to do and was offered a job as a guide. I have been the guide for two wagon trains over the Oregon Trail and we had to fight Indians twice on each trip. That's why, since this is a small train, these people wanted to try this route."

"I know what you mean when you say that a person may be able to do many things. Jasper has more education than I have and he says that a person can do whatever he wants if he tries hard enough. I don't know about the Oregon Trail but I have heard that many people are going west to look for gold and I have also heard that a lot of them don't find any," Running Deer said.

"You are pretty well informed for a person who goes up and down the river every year."

"The missionary comes to our winter camp and teaches us each winter; he tells us what he has learned while he has been gone during the summer."

"I was happy to see you for two reasons; I consider you a very good friend, and we are getting short of meat and I am sure that you can find us some. We have been hunting for days and we were hunting when we met you. Have you seen any deer or buffalo in this area?"

"We saw a herd of deer this morning. There were about a dozen of them and they were in the hills only a short distance from here," Jasper said.

"Would you two go with Drifter and me and help us get some meat for the people of the wagon train?"

"We will be happy to go. I'll get our horses."

When they reached the point where the deer had been seen Running Deer dismounted and began tracking them on foot. He trailed them for an hour or more and finally saw them in the distance.

Jasper had never hunted deer until he had met Running Deer. He had killed quite a few while he had been hunting with the tribe, but since they had been there they hadn't needed the meat, so when they spotted some they stalked them so Jasper would learn more about stalking game and then left them alone.

Jim and Drifter began stalking the deer, since they were the only ones with rifles.

"They are just as good at this as we are," Jasper said.

"Jim has been hunting and trapping in this country for years and he said that he always has a load of furs to take back east with him, so he has to be good."

"What do you know about wagon trains?" Jasper asked.

"I have never seen one. I know that they are crossing to the north of us every summer because the missionary has told us about them. He said that they go all the way across country. Some go to California where you want to go and some go to Oregon."

"I also want to someday go to Oregon. I want to go to every place that the man that I talked to years ago told me about and I probably won't be happy until I do."

When they heard four shots they brought the horses to where Jim and Drifter had bagged four deer.

They field dressed the deer in short order, leaving the skins on. When they were finished Jasper and Running Deer helped with loading them on the two packhorses. They mounted and were leaving to go ahead with their loafing around, when Jim stopped them.

"Would you two like to ride to the wagon train with us?" Jim asked.

Jasper had only heard of wagon trains from the slaves on the plantation, before he met Jim, but they had told such wild tales that Jasper doubted that any of them had ever seen one. How could they have seen one? None of them had ever been off the plantation except for an occasional Sunday at the little church near the plantation or when Mr. Brisley had taken someone with him to work in town.

But Mr. Brisley would sometimes tell some of them what

was in the papers and books that he had mailed to him. Then they would repeat what he had said, adding to it and talking as if they knew all about it. Surely that was where they got most of their stories. Then he wondered why Wrangler had never mentioned them. Maybe he had been in California and Oregon before the wagon trains began going. He was extremely glad that they had been invited to go with Jim so he could see a wagon train himself.

"I would like to go and see what one is like. I have never seen a wagon train," Jasper said.

"Neither have I," Running Deer said. "Lead off and we'll be with you."

"Where were you two going?" Jim asked as they were riding toward the train.

"We were going this way to see what it is like on this side of the creek and to see what it is like east of here,"

Jasper said.

"Maybe you shouldn't go any further in this direction because you are getting close to some settlements and they have had so much trouble with Indians in the past, you may not be very welcome."

Maybe Mr. Brisley and my mother were right, Jasper thought. Maybe I can pass as an Indian with anyone except an Indian. Jim has been with them a lot and he thinks that I am one, but I sure didn't fool the tribe for a minute. They knew that I wasn't an Indian from the start.

Since Jasper had never seen a wagon train before, when they went over a little hill and he saw the wagons for the first time, he was amazed. He stopped his horse and the others followed suit while Running Deer and he sat there and looked at the train as if they were stricken with awe. He thought it was a pretty sight. There were about twenty wagons and since it was late in the afternoon, they were in a large circle and the horses had their harnesses off and were grazing outside of the circle, with one person watching them. They were so tired and hungry from traveling all day that since they had stopped where there was some very lush grazing they were making good use of the time, just grazing and not wandering around.

The cattle were on the opposite side of the circle with two people watching them, keeping them in a small group, because cattle will wander all over the country if they are not watched every minute while they are grazing. Even if they have been going all day, they always take time for a bite now and then and they are never as hungry as the horses.

Jasper was reluctant to move as he watched the people going about their business. They finally started toward the train.

"Why do you put the wagons in a circle?" Jasper asked.

"That's our best protection from attacks that might occur during the night and from animals that may wander in at night."

"It looks like a very efficient means of protecting the people," Jasper mused. "I can see people inside the circle cooking and preparing everything for the evening meal. Some are checking the wagons and the children are gathering wood and playing. Some are checking harnesses and that must be the guard riding around the train and coming toward us."

As they were riding toward the train, the man on guard duty saw them and shouted a warning. Jasper saw all of the activity inside stop while most of them grabbed their guns and the ones that were cooking left their pots and pans and ran for cover under or in the wagons. He could see their guns pointed at them from their positions.

Half a dozen men ran to meet the horses, circling around them to help the man on the horse drive them toward the wagons. The other men ran to the wagons closest to Jim and the others and Jasper could see their rifles sticking out from between or under the wagons along with the others. When they were closer to the wagons Jim waved and when the guard recognized him he yelled at the people of the train, letting them know that everything was all right and then rode out to meet them.

"The sun was in my eyes and when I saw four people I thought we were being attacked," he said.

"I'm glad you were all so alert and ready to defend the train. This is Running Deer and Jasper from an Indian tribe ahead of us. They helped us get these deer and they will be traveling with is for a few days."

Before they had time to reach the train Jasper saw everything go back to normal. The cooks came out from cover and the horses were already being driven back to where they had been grazing. Jim must have trained them well, he thought.

Then Jasper thought about what Jim had said. He had already decided that there was nothing that would make him happier than to travel with the train back to the village, but how did Jim know. He said that they would be traveling with them, not that they may. Oh well, he got his wish without really wishing for it.

When they reached the wagon train Jim told the wagon master who they were and how they had helped in getting the deer. Then he told him that the tribe's summer camp was only a few days journey ahead.

"You are welcome to stay with us and I have already assumed that you will travel with the train back to your village. Since your camp is ahead of us, Jim would surely be happy for your help in guiding us there," the wagon master said.

"There is nothing that I would like better than for you two to help guide us there. I was about to ask," Jim said.

"I would like nothing better than to do that. I have always wanted to travel with a wagon train, we'll discuss it tonight," Jasper said.

"There is nothing to discuss," Running Deer said. "I would like to do the same, so we'll be up and ready when you are tomorrow."

"What is the trail like from here to the creek?" Jim asked. "I rode higher in the hills when I came by last year, where it was steeper and I haven't been through this lower country."

"The trail becomes non-existent after we leave this area. You will find places where it will be hard to get wagons through, but I think you can make it," Jasper said. "We were just loafing around, circling and checking the area. We were stalking game and we have been over most of this lower country. Even though it's quite a distance from camp, the chief may want to send hunting parties here when game is scarce near camp. The game here is plentiful and not easily spooked."

"We sure had no trouble getting those deer," Jim said.

While Jasper was laying awake thinking about going with the train to the summer camp he was just dying to talk to Running Deer and discuss their luck in running into Jim and Drifter. How they just happened to be at exactly the right place at the right time to meet them, but he thought that he was the only one awake. The more he tried to go to sleep the more his anxieties grew about learning first hand what it would be like traveling with the train. He already knew that what the slaves had said about the trains was inaccurate but he would soon find out how much so.

The moon was shining and they were sleeping near each other so he must have done something to let Running Deer know that he was awake. He broke the silence by saying, "do you have any idea how small the odds were that we would meet Jim along the trail. We had already explored that area and were leaving. If we had been just a few hundred yards further up that mountain they could have passed and we would never have known they were in the country."

"Yes I was just thinking about the same thing and I had wondered about wagon trains for a long time. How they could go so many miles across country when they are really sort of flimsy and cause a lot of trouble just hauling cotton and corn on the farms. They must have a lot of problems with them on a long trip like that."

"I had never seen a wagon and it will be a thrill to travel with them. But you just made another of your slips of the tongue. You should be very careful while you are with them because as an Indian you should know nothing about wagons and you just told me again where you are from."

"You are right! I must be more careful in the future."

"Jim knows that I am from the tribe because we hunted together last summer so while we are with the train I will help to inspect the wagons and act as if I know all about them. How will anyone know that we have no wagons at our winter camp?" Running Deer said.

Pretty smart, Jasper thought. I think Wrangler was right about being friends with Indians; with Running Deer I have no doubt that I have a friend for life.

The next morning while they were all hooking up their horses and getting ready to leave, Jasper and Running Deer, both excited about having decided to travel with the train back to their camp were ready and waiting for them to get prepared to leave. They were soon headed at a very slow pace toward the west.

"I would like to have you two to scout ahead with Drifter and me and show us the best route through the timber if you don't mind," Jim said.

It didn't take them long to agree; they would like nothing better. As soon as the wagons were lined out in single file and traveling steadily, Jim and Drifter moved ahead with Jasper and Running Deer with them. They stayed well ahead of the train so they wouldn't lead them into an impassible area. They would go ahead looking for the easiest way and one of them would sometimes stop and wait until the train was in sight, or they would double back to direct them through places that were especially bad.

When Jasper went to the left of the others to see if there was a good way through, he was surprised to see that Drifter rode with him. They rode for some time without either of them saying anything. Then Drifter broke the silence.

"The two of you seem to know what is ahead before we ever get there. We have had no trouble getting the wagons through, but we have gone places that I would have never tried. Some places looked impassable to me from a distance. We had been traveling in open more or less level country for days and it's nice to see timber again."

"Running Deer is the best there is at finding ways through timber and also at finding game. He seems to know where the game will go next while we're trailing them. When their tracks disappear he seems to know where to look to pick them up again. Guiding this train will be somewhat the same. If animals haven't gone through an area, there is no use for us to try."

"Don't sell yourself short. You are doing all right."

They came to a place where there seemed to be no way to get through, so they all split up and were each taking a different route, when Jasper met Jim again.

"What do you know about Drifter?" He asked. "I liked him immediately when we met."

"He told me that he had a farm when his wife got sick. By

the time she died he had borrowed so much money on the farm to pay doctors that he could not make enough money to repay the loans and eventually lost it. Now he is just drifting west. A young couple that he knows that are traveling with the train are kind of looking after him. He never talks about them and I don't know anything about their relationship. He said there was nothing for him back east and he was going with them to California and help them build a new life for themselves."

"I was sure that he wasn't just a drifter. I met a man once from Texas who said that some men wanted to be identified by a handle instead of a name, so I was assuming that Drifter was a handle."

"If you ever go west you will find a lot more people who use a handle than anywhere to the east. Jasper, for instance, could be a handle; you may or may not have another name. As for myself, I prefer to be called Jim, which is my real name. But if it's not necessary I never use my last name. Even so I am always curious about someone who uses only one name, thinking that they may have a past that they want to keep secret, but I never question their reasons."

"I appreciate your not asking questions. For the present I just want to be known as Jasper, which is also my real name. Is it a lot different to the west?"

"It's completely different. There is a lot less people, but every trip that I made I could tell that there were more people, especially near the West Coast."

"I don't know anything about wagon trains, but I can't believe that you are an ordinary guide. You talk like you know a lot of other things. I want to learn everything that I can, so I may ask a lot of questions and some of them may sound stupid."

"Just like I'm sure that you are not an ordinary Indian. But there are no stupid questions. If I can help in any way, just ask away and I'll do my best to give you an intelligent answer. You don't act like you would be happy just traveling up and down the river. Are you planning to do something except staying here and traveling back and forth like the rest of the tribe?"

"It makes me feel good that you asked. I have learned to read and write and can do some arithmetic, but my only goal now is to get a better education and maybe train as a doctor or lawyer. I need to find a school soon where I can continue my studies. What are the people like with the train? Are some of them educated? Are most of them farmers or are there business people among the group?"

"It seems strange that you should mention an education. There is one schoolteacher that has a husband who is a minister. He is going to Sacramento to build a church and she will teach school if she can get a job there. He has services along the trail when we are stopped long enough. I thought that he would have a flop the first time, but almost all of the people from the train came and the service was a great success.

"There are two men wanting to start stores. They each have a wagonload of goods with a driver following them. There are a few who want to farm, there are a couple of miners and there is one man who is going to San Francisco who has a job waiting for him in the legal profession. But they all seem to be going to stay because all of them have at least one cow and some of them have two or three."

"How do they all get along with each other?"

"Tempers sometimes get a little short as they would with any group of people who were traveling together after so many weeks along the trail. But they have so much work to do with them driving a team all day, then taking care of the stock and equipment; they are too busy to have very many disagreements. They are so tired at night, after the evening meal they are usually ready for bed."

Jasper had already learned that the talk he had heard about wagon trains going west from the people on the plantation was completely wrong, as he had already surmised, because they couldn't go anywhere to learn anything about them; that train was nothing like they had described. But even though they had been wrong with their stories, they had gotten him interested in seeing a wagon train, but he had never dreamed that he would be traveling with one, even for a few days. He was amazed at how slow they went and how few miles they actually traveled each day. He could go at least three times as many miles each day riding a horse without waiting for the wagons.

But maybe it was better that they were slow because they were able to stay in front and scout for the train. They were going at least three times as far while they were in the timber going back and forth looking for the best routes. If the wagons had been as fast as they were they would have to scout one day, and a long day at that, for a place to travel the next.

He remembered going to town with Mr. Brisley when he had been very young. It seemed like an eternity to him because the wagon was so slow and he was always so anxious to get there, but compared to the wagon train that had been traveling day after day for weeks and would have to stop occasionally to let the horses rest, they had probably been going pretty fast. Besides, those wagons were probably so overloaded that they couldn't go very fast. Then he thought about Mr. Brisley; if he hadn't gotten ill and put his son George in charge, he probably wouldn't have left. When he had time to think about it, he had been good to Jasper and he suddenly realized that he really missed him very much. He sure didn't miss Master George, but after them growing up together and him spending so many years with George he couldn't help but have some feelings of compassion for him.

He also felt sorry for George because since his father's

illness he had been placed in a position for which he was not qualified. From the beginning the position in which he had been placed was so far above his capabilities that Jasper, even though he was young, knew that it must be very trying for him.

They had been traveling about four days when they came into more open country. Jasper decided that they were nearing the halfway point on their way back to their summer camp, when they met three men heading east. Since it was time for the wagon train to camp for the night, all four scouts had returned to the train. They had circled the wagons and were getting ready for supper when Jasper saw one of the men come in to talk to the wagon master. He was curious so he came to where he could hear what was said.

"Would it be all right if we camped with the wagon train tonight? We have traveled many miles today and a little company would be nice," the man said.

"That would be fine with us. In fact we are having a potluck supper tonight. Maybe you would like to try our roast venison and sweet potatoes. That's the closest thing we have to a home cooked meal. Our man Smith who is building a fire now is good with these potlucks. He will set up some poles on each side of the fire, and fasten them together to form an upside down V at each side of the fire; in short terms, a tripod on each side. Then he will place a pole that he carries with him on top and fasten some deer quarters on it; then crank it over and over and then turn it the other way for awhile and then burn the meat."

The man chuckled and said, "We would love to."

Jasper had never seen men that looked like those three. They were rough looking and even though Jim wore a pistol on his hip, he looked clean cut and shaved and bore no resemblance to those men. All three of them had pistols in holsters on their hips and one of them wore two. When Jasper was near them he could see that the insides of each of their holsters looked slick and smooth like harness looks after it has been freshly oiled. Each of them had a rifle fastened to their saddles in open topped boots that also looked like they had been oiled inside. They all had what he thought was a mean look about them, but he thought the one with two pistols looked especially mean.

He was tall and thin with a heavy beard. Jasper thought his eyes, which were large and almost black, could look right through a man and his heavy eyebrows and lashes helped to make him look mean. He wore a wide brimmed hat tied under his chin with a piece of rawhide and a bandana tied around his neck. He wore buckskin pants and a blue shirt that looked as if they hadn't been washed in a long time. Jasper wondered why he didn't wash his clothes in the creek when they crossed it.

He rode one of the tallest bay horses that Jasper had ever seen with a somewhat worn but very nice saddle. He sat

in the saddle as if he had grown up in it, and it was just an extension of him on the horse, seeming to be completely relaxed, with his hands with their long slim fingers always hanging near his pistols, as if he would need to use them at any time. And he looked as if he could use them.

Jasper couldn't see any brand on his horse and he wondered at him having such a big horse, that some people would call beautiful, with no identification marks of any kind on it in case it was stolen. It looked like a horse that anyone would be proud to own; a horse that some people would kill for and not bat an eye.

One of the others was a bit shorter and of medium build, but other than that, he looked similar to the one with two guns. He looked almost as mean as the tall one, also having dark hair and eyes, but he had large hands with short stubby fingers. Jasper knew nothing about pistols, but when he saw the short fingers, he wondered if he could use a pistol as well as the one with slender fingers. He was dressed in denim pants and a flannel shirt that also looked like they hadn't been washed in a long time. He also rode a good looking horse of a color more like a roan, but it didn't compare with the big bay.

The other man was shorter yet, and Jasper thought that he could see less contempt in his eyes. He was the only one that smiled and Jasper thought that the whole front of his face smiled with him. He was much better looking than the others and was not so dirty. He also had a clean-shaven face and with his blue eyes and light hair, he looked more congenial than the others did. He also wore buckskin pants and a flannel shirt, but they appeared to have been washed recently. But even though he was more conscious of his appearance, and his apparent friendliness, Jasper thought that with his hand over his pistol at all times, he could also be mean.

Jasper knew from his experience with horseflesh that all of their horses could run faster than the average and they looked as if they could go for many miles without tiring. He knew that it would take a very good horse to keep up with any of them for an extended period of time. Some horses, some of the Indian ponies included, were fast at the beginning but would tire and begin slowing, but Jasper knew that all of those horses were built for endurance.

They must be three of the gunfighters that Wrangler was talking about, Jasper thought. He vowed that he would be cautious around them.

Jasper had never seen a saddlebag, only a sack tied behind the saddle like Jim and Drifter had, so he wondered how they could carry enough supplies in the little leather bags that they had their bedrolls tied onto. Maybe they had some of their supplies rolled up in their bedrolls, he thought.

"Have you ever seen men who looked that mean?" Jasper asked Jim.

"I have seen many of them. When you get out west you will also see lots of them. They may just be bedraggled from traveling so far, but it seems unlikely to me. They look more like what is called hard-cases. Some of them hang around mining camps waiting to find a prospector who has found a rich vein and has a lot of gold with him. Prospectors seem to have one thing in common; they brag when they find gold and there's always someone wanting something for nothing, so they will take it from them. Some of the prospectors are killed in the process.

"That tall one not only acts as if he is ready with those guns, but he could probably outdraw most men. Those pistols he has are the very latest models that only the Army should have. He may have stolen them or he may be a deserter."

Jasper didn't know what a deserter was and he was embarrassed to ask Jim. He would like to ask Jim if there was any fighting between the north and south, but he was afraid to mention it because Jim may get suspicious of him. He didn't want anyone to know that he knew anything about the obviously impending conflict, so he only asked, "If they are robbers, do you think they may cause trouble or try robbing someone while they are with the train?"

"It's unlikely because most people in wagon trains have very little money and they wouldn't know if people had money and in which wagon it would be."

He said, "when you get out west," Jasper thought. "How did he know that I wanted to go west? I only mentioned an education."

Jasper was a little uneasy about the three riders, although he was also interested, because he had been wondering what it would be like to wear a pistol. Since he had learned to shoot a rifle so easy and so fast, there shouldn't be any reason that he wouldn't be equally good with a pistol. But what would a man want two pistols for, he wondered? Could he aim both of them at once? Could he get both of them out of their holsters at the same time or would one hand be faster than the other one would? Someday I would like to see if I could handle two pistols at the same time. Why am I thinking about two guns? I wouldn't have money for ammunition if I had one gun.

Jasper had always admired Mr. Brisley because he had always worn a pistol. But he had never seen it out of his holster. Why would he need to take it out because no one else on the plantation had one and it would be foolish to provoke him to the point of drawing it? He must not have trusted Master George with a pistol because of his temper. He never carried one with him, unless, as he had thought a few times, the bulge under his coat indicated a concealed one. If he had worn one that Jasper could see he would have been even more reluctant to stay and may have left sooner.

They had no problem telling who was in charge. The man with two guns dominated the other two to the point of having them to wait outside of the wagon ring until he had gotten permission to stay and then come in only long enough to eat. They went outside again to take care of the horses while he stayed inside and talked to some of the people, but Jasper could see that he was uncomfortable and would like to leave.

When the other two had their three horses unsaddled and ready for the night, Jasper wondered why they didn't turn them out to graze with the others.

"Where are you headed?" One person asked.

"We're just passing through, heading east; going no place in particular."

"Have you come far?"

"It has been too far to suit me; where are you going with the train?"

"We are going to California."

"This seems a strange way to travel with a wagon train; seems to be the long way around."

He didn't even wait for an answer. With those few words, he said goodnight to the people and went outside where the other two men were.

Jasper wondered why the man wasn't very talkative, and why, when they asked him where they were from and where they were going, he just evaded the questions and changed the subject.

He also wondered why, when it was bedtime, the man with two guns hesitated just outside of the wagon ring until most of the people were inside of their wagons. He still didn't leave there until Running Deer and he were making their beds, then they went a short distance from the wagon ring, tied their horses to some trees and made their camp in the trees away from the wagons.

CHAPTER 12

"I don't want anyone going to sleep," the man with two guns said. "When it's completely dark, while the moon is behind those trees, I want you to saddle the horses quietly while the sentry they placed is on the other side of the train so that he doesn't notice you."

"What do you have in mind?" One of the others asked. "We should be safe here until morning. I don't think any of those people will bother us. We have been traveling so many hours each day that I would like to get a good night's sleep."

"When everyone is asleep I will sneak in under that wagon and get that runaway slave. You two have everything loaded and we will immediately leave with him."

"What runaway slave? I didn't see one."

"The one with that Indian brave; the one that acted so curious and watched us all while we were eating and making camp; the last one to go to his bed."

"Those are two Indians that are scouting for the wagon train. Didn't you see them coming east ahead of us while we were approaching the wagons? You will have the whole tribe after us if we kidnap him."

"I can assure you that he's a runaway. For many years I lived and traded with Indians. I have also lived in the south where most of the slaves live. I know a runaway when I see one and he is definitely a runaway. Didn't you see his hair, or lack of it? He has shaved or cut off all of the little curls so they won't identify him as a slave. Didn't you notice him rubbing down and caring for his horse? He has been trained to take care of horses like I try to get you two to do while we're traveling long hours in the heat."

"That doesn't mean anything. Lots of people take care of horses like that."

"Yes, but not Indians. Most of them have no respect for a horse. They will ride him hard all day and then jump off and they may remove the rope bridle before turning him loose with the others; they sometimes don't do that much."

"I say that we should wait until morning and leave like we planned. Then no one will suspect that we are anything except three travelers trying to get back to the East Coast. If we take him they will know that we are not ordinary travelers and they will be after us immediately."

"What do you mean, like we planned? Have you forgotten that I make all of the decisions here? We agreed on that before we left the West Coast."

"I think you are making a bad mistake this time. I, for one, think you should reconsider your decision."

"I made that decision when we arrived here. That's why I waited until they were making their beds before I left. That's why I had you to make our camp here under the trees. That's why the horses are tied under those trees so they can't readily be seen after dark. If you follow my instructions they can't see you saddle them."

"There's enough moonlight now for them to see us if we leave; we'll be in the open for a hundred yards."

"When the sentry starts around the other side, I can have the runaway up and ready to ride out before he gets back around. It will be close, but we can go through those trees and be away from here without anyone noticing."

"We can't get his horse from the remuda so someone will have to ride double. We'll be traveling so slow that they will catch us before we get very far."

"That big horse of mine can carry double at a fast walk all night if need be. There is no need to travel fast: who would come after us for a runaway slave? No one will even give him a second thought. They will only think that he decided to run in another direction."

"If you are wrong and they come after us, they can catch us easily with one riding double."

"As I said, we won't need to travel fast. We will have at least a nine-hour head start, and tomorrow when my horse tires, we can change him to one of your horses and with the fresher horse, we can travel faster. Besides I know how to cover our trail so no one will have a chance of trailing us. Maybe you have forgotten that I have been doing this sort of thing for years."

"I have always worked with cattle or on farms and have never been mixed up in something like we have done until you talked me into going to California with you. I still have bad feelings about what we did and I was happy that we were getting far away from there as fast as we could. Now you want to take a man that I am convinced is an Indian along and I still think it's a bad idea, but I have to admit, the plan of escape is a good one."

"That's why I'm in charge."

Jasper awoke with a start when he felt a hand over his mouth and something pressing hard against his head.

"Get up and don't make any noise," the man whispered to him. "This is a gun against your head. Leave your knife and tomahawk here and bring your clothes with you. If you make a sound you won't see the sun rise."

Jasper had little choice so he picked up his buckskin clothing and pulled the top skin that he had been using for a bed lately up over the bottom one as if he was making his bed for the day. Then he dropped his weapons on the skins, his bow and quiver on one end and his knife and tomahawk away from them.

The man didn't seem to notice what he was doing; he was concentrating on keeping his gun to Jasper's head. But he knew that Running Deer would notice instantly because when he crawled out of his bed even before he went to relieve himself, he normally did as Running Deer had instructed him; he strapped on his knife and tomahawk. Then he went with the man to where their horses were tied.

While he was getting dressed, he could see that they were saddled and ready to go. The tall man with two guns had Jasper to get up in front of him and then they all very slowly went through the trees where their horses' hooves would make no sound against the pine needles. They went in an easterly direction, soon swinging back to ride over the trail that the wagons and stock had made.

Pretty smart, Jasper thought. It would be hard to follow a trail with so many old tracks from cattle and horses rambling in all directions while they were being slowly driven behind the train. But he knew that Running Deer would have no trouble tracking them. The man was so sure of himself that he hadn't even bothered to tie Jasper's hands.

He thought of suddenly shoving the man off the rear of the horse, but he noticed that he was just as relaxed and as content as if he were in the saddle and he would be hard to dislodge; his long arm was around Jasper holding the reins so that he could control the horse.

"I still think we are making a big mistake by bringing him along," one of the men said, the one that had protested earlier; the other tall one that Jasper thought would be fast with a gun. But his voice was losing its sternness and he seemed to be reluctant to argue. Jasper knew that the man with two guns had them subdued to the point that at least that one was afraid of his two guns. Maybe he had seen those guns in use, he thought.

"You should let me go," Jasper said. "When the people of the train come for me you won't have a chance."

"You know that no one would come for a runaway. The trail we left would be almost impossible to follow, but if they do come and they have someone smart enough to trail us, we will be in town, have the money for you, and be on our way before they get organized and work out our trail."

"They will be on their way as soon as it's daylight. Running Deer will know exactly where to find you."

Jasper knew that at least one of them doubted the wisdom of bringing him along and he hoped the third man would have doubts about bringing him. Maybe if he could get the three of them to arguing with each other, the other two would talk the man with two guns into letting him go. But it was doubtful because one of them would not say a word, the one with the short stubby fingers, and Jasper assumed that he was more afraid of the man's two guns than the other one.

"If they do come after us you will be the first one dead, then there will be no reason for them to risk being killed to catch us."

Jasper was thinking, maybe I should have kept my mouth shut. He seems to have a foolproof plan and the others, although at least one of them is reluctant to do so; are going along with it. Since one of them had voiced his objections, he had thought that two of them may get rattled and make a strong argument for letting him go.

When daylight had fully come and the sun was rising they stopped in a little clearing for breakfast and were discussing him while one of them; the one that had argued with him earlier, was cooking breakfast.

"Why do you insist on cooking breakfast while we're holding him and taking a chance of them finding us?" The man doing the cooking asked. "We should eat something cold and make tracks before someone misses him and they come looking for him."

"You should know by now that I always insist on a hot breakfast and supper," the man with two guns answered. "They will just now be getting up and they may not miss him until time for the train to leave. If they notice his bedroll they will think that he is taking a long time to relieve himself. If they care enough to come looking for him, the way we covered our trail, they will never be able to track us."

"You must not know much about Indians. The one that was with him could probably track a squirrel over a flat rock."

"He could never untangle the trail we left. I could hear the rocks under this horse's hooves for a half-mile after we changed directions. Then we changed directions again. Besides we will be in town and see how much money he is worth before they could catch us."

"Why did you want to bring him along anyway? We got plenty of gold from that old timer to last the three of us for a long time. We are taking a big chance in bringing him along for a mere pittance compared to the gold that we already have."

"I told you that there is always a big reward offered for a runaway slave; especially a young strong one. We can get a lot of money for him."

"If you are wrong and he is an Indian, we have someone on our hands that we will have no need of. We can't be sure if he is worth anything to us until we get into town and see if there is a reward poster for him. If there is no reward, what do we do then? We can't turn him loose or he will tell the rest of the tribe, and we will not be safe anywhere in this country. How will we find out about rewards and get the money? We are known in the next town."

"The brand on that horse you're riding won't be recognized there and you're not as well known there as we are, so it will be up to you to check the reward posters and make the contacts. Since he was with that Indian that must be from a tribe close to here he must be from this area."

"I say that we should turn him loose now. We haven't harmed him and he won't make a big fuss about being brought this far. He will go back to his tribe and we may never run into them again. You are not getting me to take a chance like that for a few dollars when it was your idea in the first place. One of you will have to go into town and check the reward posters. Then what do we do with him if there is no reward offered?"

"I can't take the chance of going into that town. I lived there for a few years before I got into trouble. Half the town knows me," the other man said.

My plan seems to be working, Jasper thought. That's it; get at each other's throat. Maybe they will fight among themselves. If they do there is a chance, no matter how slim, that I will be turned loose or be able to sneak away from them.

"What difference does one Indian or one runaway make? If he's not wanted, he will be worth nothing to us. We'll just dispose of him in our own way. We'll do him like we did that old timer that refused to give up his gold."

"I still say that we should turn him loose now while he has not been harmed."

"Why are you arguing with me? You agreed that I would make the decisions when we went to look for someone with gold."

"You have all of the gold. I say that we should split it now, turn him loose and go our separate ways in case someone is on our trail."

"You know our agreement; if someone comes after us, you

two will cover me while I get away with the gold and we'll meet where we planned, then we'll split it there."

"Where you planned; you made that agreement after we had the gold."

"You have the option of pulling iron and taking all of the gold; then you can split it as you wish."

"What chance would I have against you? I would have to be awfully stupid or awfully mad to try it."

While they were arguing Jasper was thinking about all of the chances he had taken by running away and all of the hardships that he had gone through, only to be returned to the plantation; or worse yet, to be killed. He was pretty sure that Master George would not have posted reward notices that far north. In that case it would mean certain death for him.

During breakfast, they were getting louder, and Jasper wasn't used to how outlaws would respond to a heated argument like that, so he was surprised when the man with two guns suddenly drew one of them and shot the man he was arguing with. He then calmly took the rifle from the dead man's saddle, told Jasper to mount up and tied his hands to the saddle horn. He unbuckled the dead man's gun belt and hung it on his own saddle horn. He untied Jasper's reins, tied one rein to the other and tied it to his saddle so that Jasper would be directly behind him. He told the other man to roll up the utensils in a blanket, tie them to the saddle behind Jasper and follow Jasper. Only then did he turn his horse and calmly start him walking toward the east. He kept his tired horse to a walk as if he were in no hurry to put more distance between him and whoever may be pursuing them.

"Now you have no choice; even if you are known. It's up to you to ride into town and see if there is a reward," he told the other man.

"If I go into that town they'll know me all right. After I pulled that job there and was recognized, they will hang me to the nearest tree."

"It looks like that is a chance you will have to take. We're not going to let a reward pass us by."

How cruel could a man be, Jasper wondered? He was calmer than most people would be if they shot a deer or buffalo, as calm in fact, as if nothing at all had happened. He knew from that example what would happen if he was unable to get free and there was no reward posted because he would never tell them what plantation he was from. At least as long as he was alive and free from Master George, he would have some chance of escaping and staying alive. No matter how slim that chance was he would take it rather than to be returned to the plantation and forever being under bondage as a slave. And no matter how slim his chances would be; if he had a chance he decided then that he would try escaping.

After the shooting Jasper had seen the fear in the other person's eyes as he looked around him as if he was looking for a place to escape. But they were in an open area and the man with two guns would have no trouble shooting him before he could reach the heavy timber for protection. And Jasper doubted that he would have any qualms about shooting him in the back, because he had taken advantage of the other man by starting to draw his gun before the man he shot could have expected him to draw; his gun hadn't even cleared leather before he had been shot.

Jasper hoped the other man wouldn't try shooting the man with two guns in the back because he was between them.

Now I have really gotten myself in a bind, he thought. If I ever get away I'll be careful of everyone while I'm traveling. Why didn't I notice things that they were doing more closely? If they didn't have some meanness on their minds, why would they have gone out to that thicket to camp and have tied their horses to those trees instead of letting them graze?

As he was being led along through the woods he was thinking that he was not much unlike the old cow that he had always led into the barn at milking time. All he could do was to sit in the saddle and be led wherever the man wanted to go. He was just as helpless as the old cow.

He tried very hard to work his hands forward in an attempt to reach the bridle of his horse, but the man had tied a very good knot and he found it impossible. Then he thought that it might have been a bad move because the horse seemed to be a little lazy or didn't like to be led and there was almost always some pressure on the rein. If he released the rein the man would feel the release of pressure on his saddle. Besides if he did get loose and kicked the horse, he would more than likely run ahead past the other horse and he would be vulnerable because he would have no way of controlling the horse he was riding.

He knew that if he gave the man an excuse to shoot him he would merely be shot and dumped on the ground for the animals and birds to take care of and none of his family would ever know what had happened to him.

He had nothing to do but sit there, so he started daydreaming about events and people in his past. He thought about what may be happening at the plantation. He had been worried about how he could help his family, but now he needed help himself, partly because of his ignorance of the way crooks worked and partly because he had never had reason to be cautious of people because most of the people he knew were those that he had lived and worked with every day for most of his life.

He thought about the big house where Mr. Brisley lived. It really was a big house. It was a large two-story structure made entirely of sawn lumber, not logs, and whitewashed until it literally shined in the sunlight, with tall columns and a wide porch across the front. It had narrow tall windows in front that came almost to the porch floor, which gave it the appearance of being even larger and taller than it was. On the porch was a swing where his mother and he sometimes sat, while she would comfort him when Mr. Brisley would go to town, taking only George with him. He could almost see his mother sitting there right then. When she had breakfast done and Mr. Brisley taken care of, she would sometimes go and sit on the swing and read a book to him or teach him his letters and numbers for awhile before she had to cook dinner. He wondered if she was worried about what had happened to him. If he couldn't get away before they got to town and found out there was no reward poster, she would never know.

There was a white picket fence across the front to keep out the cows that would sometimes get out of the pasture. Flowers; there were oh, so many flowers. Why not, he thought, all Mr. Brisley had to do was to tell some of the slaves to come and take care of the flowers and it would be done. How he would like to have a house like that some day. If he had a plantation with a house like that he would not let his mother work like she had always done, but let her sit on the porch and admire the flowers. Then she wouldn't have to live in the house with dirt floors that they had lived in since he could remember. From there she could see all of the other buildings.

The other buildings! If it were his plantation he would build new houses for the slaves, with wood floors and wood siding that would not let the wind and rain in like the log ones did when the mud would wash from between the logs. There I go again, he thought. I should be thinking about when the slaves are freed, not what I would do if I owned some.

The closest building was the barn with the hayloft above, with stanchions for cows on one side and stalls for horses on the other. On each side was a corral where cattle or horses could be held when necessary. Next to the barn was the blacksmith shop, where there was everything that was needed to repair all of the equipment. Then there was the corncrib, where they kept the corn that they would feed to the hogs and horses during the winter. Then the row of one, two and a couple of three room houses where he and the other slaves had lived.

When a family would outgrow their house they would simply add another room. It would be behind the original rooms, in a straight line, one room behind the other. They were built from plain unpainted logs, with the roof overhanging both sides so they could hang their tools and the wash tub in which, after they had heated water in pots and pans on the wood stove and poured it into the tub, they would all bathe. Since they all had dirt floors, when it would rain an awful lot, water would soak under the walls and they would have wet floors near the walls inside of the house.

Would his family get into trouble because of him leaving? Would Master George punish his mother, thinking that she could tell him where he had gone? He knew that Master George could be very mean to the slaves if they did something that he didn't like, but he didn't think that Mr. Brisley would let him mistreat his mother. After all, she would more than likely be taking care of him full time because of his illness that had been getting progressively worse year after year before Jasper had run away.

Jasper didn't like to think that he had run away and abandoned his family; only that he had left to improve his conditions and that he would someday return and take them away unless they were someday freed.

Then he thought about Master George and how unreason-able he had become. If he could ever learn to shoot a pistol like the man with two guns, should he manage to get a pistol and go back and challenge him before he killed some of his family? Maybe his little brother, who was not his little brother any more, but almost a grown man, that had been allowed to work with his father; would Master George be taking his vengeance out on him instead of Jasper. But even if he was faster and out-drew him, would he have the nerve to shoot a man? It had made himself somewhat sick at his stomach to watch the man, even if he were a crook, lay there with his blood running from him. And what would be gained by shooting George? He would probably be caught and hanged and it would still do his family no good. Besides, he liked Mr. Brisley very much and wouldn't want to do something that would hurt him.

Besides, under the mean front that Master George showed the slaves, even to the point of whipping them for no appar-ent reason, Jasper knew that he was scared of his shadow. It was doubtful if he would draw against someone that also had a gun.

Maybe someday he could accumulate enough money to buy his family from Mr. Brisley. Or better yet someday the slaves would be freed, even though Jasper had doubts. Only then could he take a chance on going back to that country.

I had better stop this daydreaming, he thought. I should be alert and ready at all times in case I should have a chance to get away.

They traveled the rest of that day, not even stopping at noon, and Jasper was getting pretty hungry, since they hadn't let him have any breakfast. Shortly before dark he was in a half trance, listening to the sound of the horse's hoofs on the hard ground behind, until they came to a meadow where he could hear only the few sounds of saddle leather behind. When they left the meadow Jasper noticed that there was no noise behind. He looked back and watched as the man went into the woods in the other direction as fast as his horse could run.

Now, he thought, with only one of them, I should have a better chance of getting away. I didn't leave the plantation to die at the hands of a crook. I'll get away somehow.

He knew without a doubt that Running Deer would be on their trail right then, but the question he asked himself; would he find them in time? If he didn't it surely wouldn't be because he didn't try.

The man with two guns stopped his horse near a small thicket, looked around and saw that the other man was gone.

"Now it looks like the only thing to do is to shoot you," the man said as if he was musing aloud and that shooting Jasper might be like killing a rabbit. "I'm not about to go into that town myself and take a chance that they will recognize me. Besides, having all of the gold myself, I will have enough to last me for many years."

To Jasper he said, "I'm not much of a cook, so if you will cook me some supper, I may let you live until after you cook breakfast; then you're a dead runaway slave. I have taken a shine to that buckskin suit someone made for you but the pants would never fit me. But the shirt was made loose and a little too long; it should fit me like a glove. Take it off and put my shirt on before you cook supper."

He untied Jasper's hands and had him to take off his shirt and lay it on a log, then move away. Then he lay one of his pistols on the log and put on Jaspers shirt. Even though the shirt was a little short and a little tight Jasper knew that he had lost his shirt.

"Now get busy cooking; I want it done before dark." When

he had finished eating, the man tied Jasper's hands together but left a little slack so that he could eat some of the food that was left. Jasper wasn't really interested in food but he knew that he should keep his strength in case he had a chance to escape, so he ate the food. When the man tied him to a tree he forgot to tie his hands tighter and he had tied them around the sleeves of the man's shirt that were too long for Jasper.

The man got up and mumbled as if talking to himself "better check the back-trail." He wandered out of the thicket following the tracks they had made coming there. The second he was gone Jasper began working his hands out of the ropes. The hands readily came loose but he could barely reach the knot on the rope tied around the tree and the knot was tight.

After what seemed hours Jasper finally had the ropes loose and off him. I am free again he thought as he immediately jumped up and, going around the tree, headed for the open area behind the tree, Heading for some timber that he could see ahead. He had gone only a few yards when a gunshot sounded ahead of him and he felt pain in his left side. The man had circled and was coming out of the timber a short distance ahead of him. Jasper went down on his face because he didn't want to risk another shot which would probably kill him.

As Jasper was lying there thinking that if he stayed flat on the ground, maybe the man would think that he was dead and leave him, but the man said "get up and stop playing Possum because I know where I shot you. You've been hit in the left side and the worst you may have are some broken ribs. I didn't want to kill you and have the animals fighting over you during the night."

What a hard hearted man, Jasper was thinking as he was being tied to the tree again without even checking his side. But he knew that he was lucky that the man was such an expert with a handgun because if the bullet had gone two inches to the left he would more than likely be dead.

CHAPTER 13

It was just breaking day when Running Deer awoke the morning after Jasper had been abducted. He saw that he and the three men were gone, but his bedroll was still as it had been when he went to bed.

Then he saw the knife and the other weapons neatly laid on the bedroll. He knew that, as he had impressed on Jasper during the first days of his training to become a brave, as soon as he put his clothes on his knife and tomahawk would be in place on his belt, so he knew that something was wrong. He immediately caught Jasper's horse and tied his bedroll on it, then loaded his own bedroll. He didn't wait to get any food to take along because he still had some jerky in his bedroll. He was preparing to leave when Drifter came out of the young couple's wagon, and seeing him ready to leave with Jasper's things, he knew that something was wrong.

"What has happened to Jasper? Those men are also gone. They must have taken him with them for some reason. I'll get my horse and go with you."

"It would be better if I go alone. I can travel quieter because these ponies with no shoes will not make as much noise as a horse with steel shoes."

"I suppose you're right but I'm sure that we could get some men together that would be willing to go after them. The people of the train like Jasper."

"They probably think that will happen, so they will be trying to hide their trail by going in different directions in places where it will be difficult to track them. The more people we have the less chance there will be of following their trail, because some would try to rush ahead and hinder the pursuit by obliterating the tracks."

"You're right again, but we could follow at a distance until you locate them, then we could surround them and they would have to surrender."

"If you did that they may shoot him to keep him from trying to help us or keep us away by threatening to shoot him."

"You're right again. I have no doubt that you will come back with him, but I feel so useless not being able to help."

"I think I know how you feel, but I also think this will be the best way."

"I know you're right, but I have become fond of him during the last few days and I don't want them to harm him. Since you are brothers why would they take one of you and not the other? Of course they could want to force him to act like a slave and take care of their horses or do something else for them."

He's getting awfully close to the truth, Running Deer thought. I had better defray his thoughts. "They may be looking for someone and Indians are known to be good trackers. If that's the case, they have the right man; he's much better at tracking than I am. I feel responsible because I know that he came on this trip only to please me," Running Deer said.

As Running Deer was trailing the men, he was thinking about what they had talked about a few days before. Jasper had told him enough for him to know that he was a runaway slave and he assumed that those three men had thought that also and were returning him to his former master, hoping to get money for him. He had to prevent that at any cost, because he knew from what the missionary had told them; life would be almost unbearable for a person if he were returned to a plantation after he had escaped.

He had lost the trail and was circling some brushy areas with so many rocks that there were no tracks, trying to locate the trail again when he heard what sounded like a gunshot, which was a long ways to the east. He continued his circling until he found the trail. Pretty smart if that was one of them that fired the shot, he thought, because while they were going across those rocks they changed directions. They made a turn to the south and went into that thick brush before heading east instead of southeast.

He had been riding his pony until he was almost to his limit, so he stopped long enough to change to Jasper's horse from his, and with the fresher pony under him he could make better time. He could follow them then with relative ease because the men must have thought they were far enough ahead that they were safe and were making no attempt to cover their trail. He knew it was near noon when he came to a place where someone had apparently cooked breakfast and one of the men had been shot. That must have been the shot I heard, he thought. He could see that he had been dead only a short time because only the millions of flies had found him. There is one that I don't have to worry about. Maybe the other two will shoot each other, but that is too much to hope for.

Late in the afternoon after pushing the horses almost to their limit, he had stopped to let them rest a few minutes, when he heard a horse coming his way at a full gallop. He rode into some bushes and waited for the rider to pass. He saw that it was another one of the riders who had taken Jasper. He was going as if he had somehow been terribly frightened and thought that whatever it was would be right behind him. But Running Deer was happy to see him because then there was only one to worry about.

He soon came to a meadow where the ground was softer

and he could see that the horses had not been stepping out as fast as they had been earlier in the day. He could see the tracks clearly and he saw where the other man had turned back; apparently walking his horse until he was out of sight. He knew that since they had been riding hard all day without stopping to eat or rest their horses they would soon, out of necessity, be camping for the night.

He didn't want to ruin his chance of surprising the man with two guns by making noise or having the other horses to alert the man. He tied their horses at the edge of the meadow and started ahead on foot: that's when he heard another shot. He continued going ahead on foot as he would have done if he were stalking game. He had no idea of how far ahead they were because he was not familiar with the sounds of a pistol and he assumed the shot was from one of the tall man's pistols, but he had decided that he would walk for miles if necessary to keep from alerting the man.

Then he, after a couple of miles, smelled rather than saw the fire, so he knew that he was getting close. He could see that they were following a game trail and knew that they would keep to the trail until the man found where he wanted to camp, so he sat down to wait for the right time to approach the camp.

As Jasper sat there with his back tied to the tree he was thinking that even though he hadn't eaten since the day before, he had not really been interested in food because of the tension he was under, but he was glad that he had eaten some to keep from getting weak from hunger, because he was then getting hungry and feeling weak. He could feel the blood running down his left side below the wound. Maybe he would bleed to death before Running Deer found him, but even though it hurt him when he tried to get loose, he continued to try. Maybe a miracle would happen and his fingers would loosen the knots as they did before and he would have a chance to get his body free.

Get free! That's what he thought he was doing when he left the plantation weeks before, but he was more a prisoner then than he had ever been. At least his hands and feet had not been bound most of the time and he could walk around.

"If you have any idea again of getting away," the man had said while he tied Jasper the last time, "these are the latest and most accurate weapons the Army has. I took them away from two Union soldiers just before I left for California. I am a very light sleeper and if you make the slightest noise I will wake up and immediately shoot you and this time I won't just make a sore place." The man had then thrown his bedroll on the ground nearby and went to bed and almost instantly he heard snoring, so he began working frantically with the knots.

Then Jasper knew that he was in a much worse predicament. He was determined to free himself, but after many fruitless hours, even though he was cold and uncomfortable, it hurt him so bad and he was so tired that sleep finally overtook him. Suddenly he realized that someone was cutting the ropes that held his hands. It was just breaking day and he wondered why the man would cut his ropes, but when he looked around, he saw Running Deer. "Quiet, don't wake that man," he whispered.

"No need to worry about him. He won't hurt anyone else. He has gone to the happy hunting ground or wherever palefaces go when they die. I followed you here yesterday before dark, and was waiting for a chance to get you free. I left the horses a mile or two back on the trail so they wouldn't wake the man and walked the rest of the way. He awakened once and looked at you, but he was in a position where I couldn't get to him and by the time he went to sleep again it was so dark here in this thicket that I didn't want to take the chance of bungling the job. I waited until just before daylight when he was getting up," Running Deer said as he was wiping his knife, which still had blood on it, and putting it away.

"I knew that you would come. I thought that I had one chance of getting away and even though it seemed risky I took it anyway because he said that he would kill me this morning. I was only hoping that you would make it in time."

"What's wrong with your side? I see blood on your shirt," Running Deer said. "I can see that you have been shot. Let me cut the shirt away and I will soak the cloth away that is stuck to you."

"He shot me when I tried to escape but I don't think it's very bad. Nothing is broken because I felt before he tied me again," Jasper said.

When Running Deer went to work on him it reminded Jasper of watching him while he was skinning a deer. He was as calm as if he took care of wounds every day. He cut away the cloth and checking the saddlebags of the first man that was killed, he found some clean cloth. He poured water from one canteen, wetting a piece of cloth and soaked the cloth loose from the wound. Then he bound it with a long strip of cloth, pulling it tight enough to keep it from bleeding.

By working together they managed to get Jasper's shirt off the dead man and he put it back on. By then it was completely daylight and they looked through both the men's saddlebags. They found some small sacks and when Jasper examined them he found that they contained gold, a lot of gold. It was in the form of nuggets with very few small flakes.

"There's lots of gold here," Jasper said. "We should have as much right to it as anyone, so I'll split it as equally as possible."

"We have no use for gold," Running Deer said. "There is no store within many miles of either of our camps and everything we need, we get along the river or at our winter or summer camp. Our ammunition, we get from trading with trappers that pass this way. You take it and use it for your education. I know that you will do well and if I ever leave the tribe I may look you up and ask for assistance."

"You could keep it until people begin settling around your camps and then there would be stores that you could buy things from."

"Someone would eventually find out that we had it and would either kill some of us for it or would steal it from us. The missionary said that when people start moving in they would kill Indians for anything valuable. I think it would be much more valuable for your education."

Since Running Deer wasn't interested in the gold, Jasper thought that since there was so much of it, he may have enough for his education. He didn't know how much gold was worth, but if it was valuable enough for people to kill for, it must be worth a lot of money.

Jasper hadn't wanted to go toward the cities of the north and he didn't know the way to Texas, so he decided to definitely go west for his education now that he had the financing available. He would go toward the mountains and get as many miles between him and the plantation as possible before he stopped. He didn't want to take the chance of someone else trying to take him back to Master George, so he would head west and maybe, just maybe, he would go all the way to California.

"You are faster and better with guns than I am, so you take the two pistols and one of the rifles and I will take the other pistol and rifle," Running Deer said. "Then we won't have to use the guns that the chief got by trading furs for them."

Jasper took off the man's pistols and strapped them on himself, then tied them to his legs as the other man had done, took out what little ammunition there was and split it with Running Deer. He didn't know enough about guns to know what a coincidence it was that the ammunition would fit either of their guns. He put his in the saddlebag of the horse with no brand. He put one of the rifles in the saddle boot and gave the other one to Running Deer. He checked the bedroll and found it to be much better than the rags that he had been using, and the hides were awfully bulky to tie behind the saddle, so he tied the bedroll behind the saddle. When he was back to the other horses he would tie the hides on one of them. He decided that all he had to do was wash the bedroll and he would have a good one for the trip west.

Running Deer had Jasper to hold the rifle and stand while he gave him the eagle eye, then he said, "I thought you looked like an Indian before but now you look like the gunslingers the missionary showed us pictures of; except for the buckskin clothing. I'll just call you an Indian gunslinger."

Jasper checked the man's boots and found them to be better than any that he had ever seen; much better for traveling than the old moccasins that he was wearing, so he decided to try them on. When he put on a boot it was a perfect fit and he was amazed that it felt so well after wearing moccasins for so long, but it seemed to have a lump near the top on both sides. He checked and found that the man had them made with little leather pouches inside on both sides of each of them near the top and all of the pouches were full of gold nuggets.

"So," he said. "He was cheating the other two by hiding some of the gold in his boots. I'll just leave it there in case I ever have an emergency and need some money that I can get to quick.

"I'll turn the other horse loose because he has a brand on him. We are near some settlements so he will probably go to one of them."

"There's no need to turn him loose because brands mean nothing to the tribe. No one gets a chance to check our horses anyway. Anyway I will be the only brave in the tribe with a fancy saddle," he said, laughing. The other braves will laugh at me, but let them laugh. I have earned the right to use this saddle. Then if I ever leave I can leave in style like the palefaces."

They mounted up and started toward camp, Jasper riding the tall bay horse and Running Deer riding on the first saddle that he had ever straddled and sporting the first saddlebags that he had ever seen. They soon came to the two ponies that Running Deer had brought. They rearranged their loads, Running Deer tying his bedroll consisting of animal hides with the hair still on them behind his saddle, and leading the two extra horses, they headed west.

"You should know," Running Deer said, "that Drifter was so worried when he learned that you had been taken that he wanted to come with me. When I explained that his horse with shoes would make more noise, he wanted to get some people together and come after you. You have a friend there who will be loyal forever."

"I appreciate his concern and I respect his friendship, but I could never have better friends than any of your tribe. But I think the way you handled the situation was best, because they probably wouldn't have gotten there in time. From the way that man acted and talked, he would definitely have killed me after breakfast, or sooner if he knew or even suspected that people were on his trail."

Jasper was so excited about having his own pistols and rifle that he unloaded the pistols and started practicing drawing them from his holsters, first the right, then the left, then both of them at the same time. Even though it hurt his side when he drew his left pistol, he didn't let that slow him down in the least. He remembered how fast the man with those two guns had drawn and fired one of them. He had a small advantage because he started his draw first, and he had shot the other man before his gun was halfway out of his holster. But he knew that he didn't need the advantage he had taken because he was so much faster that the other man wouldn't have had a chance if he had an equal break.

Would he ever be able to draw and shoot like that? He knew that he would have an awful lot of practicing to do before he was nearly that fast. Suppose he was ever that fast, would there ever be a time when he would have to draw and shoot another person? He certainly hoped not because his mother had taught him never to harm other people.

She didn't know it but he had harmed a few kids on the plantation. He had to; they would challenge him and he knew that if he didn't whip them they would really give him a bad time. He would only fight or wrestle with them until they yelled calf rope because he really didn't want to hurt anyone badly, especially a slave that he must work alongside; maybe as he had been told, for the rest of his life if they weren't freed.

He thought about his mother: a very gentle and kind woman who had a calm and patient nature. She had never even spanked him hard. Maybe because she had seen slaves beaten and had seen them beat their own children and she had too much compassion to whip him. He knew that he had given her reasons to whip him many times by doing things that she had told him not to do. But when he thought about it, except for going into the woods and going to the river alone when he had been told not to, he had not been very disrespectful of her wishes; or Mr. Brisley's either since he had been very young.

But even though he thought that she knew that he would be leaving, he knew that she really didn't want him to leave. If only he had a way to get her a message! But he couldn't take the chance there would be by trying.

She respected other people and their property. She had

taught him from childhood not to take other people's property. He had already taken another man's property, but he reasoned, the other man was dead and the gold that he had taken was taken from a man that he was reasonably sure, from their admission, was killed by the robbers. He would also have killed him if Running Deer hadn't followed them, so he had as much claim to the guns and gold as anyone had.

Then he wondered what would happen to his family if they should be freed. They had never known anything except working for the Brisley's and since Master George had gotten so mean they could probably not work for him as free workers, so what would happen to them? Suppose they were freed and had to leave the plantation while he was in California, would he ever see them again? The only people who could read and write among the family, and for that matter, all of the slaves, was his mother and his younger brother, and neither of them would have any idea of where to contact him.

Jasper decided that his best option was to go all the way to California, try to get an education and someday return. He had been so busy that he hadn't thought of his birthday, which had passed, but he remembered that he was then eighteen, and since he couldn't go to school before, he had to get started with his education soon.

He thought about how he would get to California. Instead of taking a chance and going alone over the high mountains that he had heard about, maybe he could make arrangements with the wagon master and go on with them. Perhaps he could work with Jim or some of the people with wagons in the train. He was pretty good at repairing wagon wheels and he could make most of the parts that would be needed in case of a breakdown, including hewing out wooden spokes for wheels and replacing those that would surely break along the trail; not many people could do that.

Suddenly Running Deer awakened him from his trance like thinking.

"Hey, wake up man and let's eat something," he said as he handed Jasper some jerky.

Jasper knew that he had to get out of the habit of getting into such deep thoughts like a daydreaming kid because he could be ambushed without knowing anyone was near. But he realized that he had always daydreamed; that's where he had gotten a lot of his ideas, but now he should stay alert and protect himself and the gold, if he was to keep it for his education.

On their fourth day they came to the creek, and after crossing it, they learned from a brave that the wagon train was three miles past the Indian village, letting the stock graze and rest up for the long journey ahead. Jasper went to the train with the intention of talking to the wagon master to ask about going with them, but Jim saw him when he was approaching and came to meet him.

"If you would consider traveling west with us, we could use another scout and I would love to have you," he said.

"I was coming to ask the wagon master."

"No need to bother because I somehow knew that when you got free from those men that you would be going with us, so I have already discussed it with him. He would be as happy to have you along as I would."

"Then it's settled. Let me know when you are ready to leave and I'll be ready when you are."

"I think that we should rest here for a day and let the horses and cattle graze where there is plenty of grass. We'll leave the day after tomorrow."

"Are you going with us?" Drifter asked when Jasper was ready to leave for the Indian camp.

"Yes, probably all the way to California," Jasper said.

"I had a feeling that you would and after seeing how you handle yourself, I know that you would be good to be with in a pinch. Do you mind if I trail along with you? Jim said that he had no doubts that you would go with us and that he would keep you busy blazing trail ahead of the train."

"That's fine with me if Jim doesn't need you with him."

"We knew that you didn't leave with those men voluntarily and we were worried that Running Deer wouldn't find you in time. I won't even ask you how you managed to get those pistols and gear away from them, but are you as good with those pistols as Running Deer says you are with a bow and arrows and also a rifle."

"I have only fired these a few times and I don't have enough ammunition to practice. If I wasted the ammunition and needed it, I couldn't do any good with them, but just between you and I; I am practicing drawing and aiming them any time I am alone and out of sight of people, and I plan to keep doing so."

"I may not be very good with a pistol but when I was younger I could shoot a squirrel's eye out with a rifle," Drifter said.

Jasper had no doubts whatever that he could shoot a rifle and he thought, someday I may need the help of another rifle.

Jasper excused himself, saying that he was going back to the creek to wash his bedroll and take a bath, then say goodbye to Running Deer and the rest of the tribe.

"I'll go back with you and wash your bedroll while you're busy with other things," Drifter said.

While Jasper was at the camp the chief called the braves together again, as he had done after they had arrived there, and they had what Jasper called a party; a party that Running Deer said was in Jasper's honor. They beat drums and danced around the fire, and the women gave them drinks from gourds. That time, they gave Jasper a gourd and when he tasted it he found it to be some kind of alcoholic drink. He only drank a few sips to be sociable because he had tasted it once with the kids on the plantation and he didn't think that he would ever like drinking alcohol.

Once again it reminded him of when the slaves would get together sometimes on Saturday afternoon, play drums and maybe an old banjo, until late at night. He remembered that when they got permission from Mr. Brisley and the neighbor, the people from the next plantation would come and they would really have a good time. When the whiskey or home brew would show up, some of them would get drunk and occasionally there would be a fight. Jasper didn't want to see that happen among the braves of the tribe, but there was no need to worry; the chief knew just when to stop the flow of alcohol, although some of the braves were disappointed.

Mr. Brisley also knew when to stop the merrymaking and drinking, but when Master George was put in charge, with him and the neighbor being so mean to the slaves, they stopped them from getting together at any time. The Brisley plantation slaves resented it so much that some of them started sneaking away to another plantation at night and having their parties. That made Master George furious when he learned of it, but he was so reluctant to go near the slaves' houses at night, he was powerless to stop them. Even though he would whip some of them occasionally, they would still go. There was a lot of discontent and talk of running away among the slaves, but to Jasper's knowledge he was the only one that had left without being caught and brought back to be punished by Master George.

He knew, of course, that he was still not free from Master George and the plantation. The worry was always present that he could be recognized and returned. If those men that kidnapped him had not fought among themselves he could very well be on his way back then.

When Jasper was ready to leave the chief brought the horse that he had been riding with Running Deer and gave it to him. He was reluctant to take it because he thought that the tribe had done enough for him by letting him stay with them, but Running Deer assured him that it would hurt the chief's feelings if he didn't accept it. He was grateful because he thought that he would be a good packhorse for the trip to California.

Jasper thanked the chief for letting him spend the last few weeks with them and for all they had done for him and said goodbye to everyone that he had met in the tribe. While he was talking to Running Deer he saw Early Flower looking longingly at him as if she wanted to talk to him.

"Early Flower really likes you and wants to marry you right now. My uncle thinks of you as one of his braves and he thinks that you would be a good husband for her," Running Deer said.

"I like her also and no one could ever know how hard the decision has been for me to leave. I would like to spend more time with her so we could learn more about each other. But since your chief won't permit it and I have no way of making a living, for reasons that I can't explain now, I can't consider a life with anyone at the present time. But I'll be back someday, and then I'll see if she is still interested in me. I couldn't ask her to wait because it may be many years before I return."

"She wants you to stay here or take her with you wherever you go."

Why was he still reluctant to go? He could stay a few days until he had a chance to talk to Early Flower and explain to her the reasons for his leaving, then catch up to the train. Then it would be even harder to leave her. If he left, he thought, it would be a long time before he could finish his education and establish himself so he could come back for her.

Maybe he should stay until he was sure of what to do. Jim and Drifter surely wouldn't be too disappointed if he stayed there. They would want him to do what he thought would be best for both of them.

He could use the gold to help the tribe. He knew how to operate a store and could teach some of them, so maybe he could open a store there when settlers started coming in greater numbers.

If he stayed he may never get another chance to go with a wagon train and he may not have enough nerve to tackle the trip alone. In that case he would never get an education.

Jasper went down to the creek to wash himself; he had no chance while he had been a prisoner of the man with two guns to even clean himself up and he was needing a bath bad. He had taken a bath and washed his clothes and was letting them dry while he was wearing the cloth Running Deer had given him when Early Flower came down on his right side, moved around in front and kissed him soundly.

Then she saw that he had a strip of clean cloth ready to tie around himself and then she backed off and looked at him; then she saw his left side. Then, contrary to the normal Indian's lack of emotion she turned pale in the face and said with emotion showing:

"You've been hurt! It looks like you were shot. That's a bad tear so you're coming to our house until you are better."

"It's only a crease and it will be fine in a few days; besides your father would never stand for me being there.

"Don't worry about that; he and my mother left after the pow-wow to visit the tribe to the north. They won't return for at least a week. We can get better acquainted while your side heals and by then maybe you won't be so anxious to go west."

"No matter what happened, if I even rode by your house while the chief was gone it would ruin your reputation."

"You are right," she said as she kissed him again and even though at that moment he had no intentions of staying there, for the first time, he passionately returned her kiss.

Why did I do something like that, he wondered? I have to leave in two days and I am still trying to make up my mind and still longing to stay here with Early Flower.

So what! How important is an education! He had enough education to operate a store and that should make a living for him and Early Flower. He had become awfully fond of her and he was sure that she wouldn't be happy somewhere else.

As he stood there mulling everything over in his mind he convinced himself that he was in love with Early Flower and that it would be best if he stayed there and lived with the tribe.